# SNAKE EYE

# SNAKE EYE

William C. Dietz

ibooks

NEW YORK

An original publication of J. Boylston & Company, Publishers.

**ibooks**

1230 Park Avenue
New York, New York 10128
Tel: 212-427-7139 • Fax: 212-860-8852
bricktower@aol.com • www.BrickTowerPress.com

**Library of Congress Cataloging-in-Publication Data**

Dietz, William C.
SNAKE EYE
ISBN: 1-59687-357-4
ISBN: 978-1-59687-357-5
Library of Congress Control Number: 2008924515

Fiction/Suspense, Adult/General

Copyright © 2008 William C. Dietz
First Edition
10 9 8 7 6 5 4 3 2 1

For my dearest Marjorie. The best is yet to come!

## Acknowledgments

First and foremost, special thanks goes to Nancy Savage, special agent, FBI, who was there from the beginning, and stayed the course. Then, I want to thank all of the wonderful people and subject matter experts who gave so freely of their time and knowledge. Errors, if any, are mine. Daniel Abrahamson, CPO, LPO, and lecturer, University of Washington; Michael Bove, master chief, USCG; Richard Curtis, literary agent extraordinaire; Tom Howard, American Airlines, captain ret.; Ed Kaetzel, commander, USCG ret.; Jeffrey Pollinger, PA 3, USCG; Dr. Bill Pratt; Chris Souza, Pyro Spectaculars Show Producer; Aaron Wilson, assistant special agent in charge, ICE; and Sarah Wilson, Derelict Vessel Removal Program Manager, Washington State Department of Natural Resources.

Thank you, one and all!

# Chapter One

The view looked south, toward Seattle's Bell Town, and the staggered tops of the high-rise buildings beyond. What Jack Dexter thought of as "habitat" for the people he spied on each evening. Women mostly, since he was heterosexual, but a few men as well. Lonely souls who lived lives as isolated as his. Neon lights blurred and streaked as the spotting scope panned the skyline.

Dexter kept it dark within his sixth-story apartment because to watch with the lights on was to attract the attention of other watchers—and there were at least two in the surrounding buildings. One was the old lady he thought of as "Glass Eye". She preferred to peer out from between her floral curtains, and spent a good deal of time staring at "Hoser," who liked to watch in the nude and frequently sported an erection.

The Nikon came to a stop as Dexter's practiced eye recognized the texture of Amy's apartment building and zeroed in on her unit. Her real name wasn't Amy, but that was the name that he had bestowed on her, and "Amy" was nicer than "the woman with the unusually long nipples," which was the way he sometimes thought of her.

Of course there were other things that Dexter liked about Amy, including her punctuality, and the fact that she was a creature of habit. No sooner had the Nikon come to rest on her unit than the lights came on. Dexter could see straight through her living room into the tiny entry beyond, and took pleasure in the ritualistic way that Amy placed her purse on the table just inside the front door and dropped her briefcase onto the floor before removing her coat.

Judging from the dark blue pin-striped business suit, Dexter figured she had met with her boss or an important customer earlier that day.

The first thing Amy did was kick off her shoes, pick up a remote, and aim it at the TV. With that part of the routine out of the way the young woman shrugged her jacket off and laid it over the back of a chair. Then it was time to remove her blouse. Some tops came off over Amy's head, others had buttons, and Dexter enjoyed both. Next, the business woman stepped out of her skirt, and went to place both the skirt and the jacket on a hanger. Dexter was neat, too, and even went so far as to arrange his clothes by color, purpose, and season. A habit left over from the Navy.

After she slipped her pantyhose down her long slim legs came the part that Dexter liked best. Amy was down to just her bra and panties. Not consciously sexy stuff, like from Victoria's Secret, but *real* underwear. The sort husbands see every day. Functional lingerie that isn't supposed to be looked at, but was all the more sexy because of that, or so it seemed to Dexter. There were times when the pieces didn't match, which was charming, and a sure sign that Amy needed to do some laundry. Then came the moment when Amy reached back to undo her bra and her breasts hung free. They were just large enough to sag slightly, which Dexter liked because it meant they were real, and he had no interest in the huge saline-engorged orbs that porn stars sported.

But more important than Amy's breasts were her nipples. Dexter would never get to measure them, but guessed they were at least half an inch long when erect, which they now were. There were evenings when she turned away so quickly that he couldn't see them, but this wasn't one of them, and Dexter felt himself begin to grow hard as Amy approached the window.

That was the moment when he wondered, as he always did, why Amy always took her clothes off *before* she closed the curtains? Did she *know* he was out there? Waiting for her just as a husband might? Welcoming her home? If so, that would mean the ritual was consensual. A possibility that evoked mixed emotions because the voyeur preferred to watch *without* permission. He could ask her of course, but that would transform him into a stalker and that was a line he didn't want to cross. "Goodnight, Amy," Dexter said out loud, and watched the curtains close.

Missy was angry, something she conveyed by slouching down into the car seat and refusing to speak. It was a punitive measure that wouldn't make much of an impression on a full-time mother but was surprisingly effective where part-time mom and full-time FBI agent Christina Rossi was concerned. The traffic light changed to amber. Rossi applied the brakes and tried to restart the conversation. "I'm sorry hon, I really am, but I don't have a choice. Qwan has some sort of bug—and someone has to sit in the car with Kissler. Not my idea of a good time but that's the way it goes."

"But you *promised*," Missy said, resentfully. "What will I tell my friends?"

"Tell them your mom is sorry…and hopes they can come later."

"But there are *lots* of parties," Missy objected. "If I wait too long they won't be able to come."

When light changed, Rossi paused for a moment to make sure no one would run the red and drove through the intersection. The neighborhood in which her ex-husband and his new wife lived was a step up from her home in Wallingford. And why not? Ed had been promoted since the divorce, computer software architects made six-figure salaries, and Vanessa had inherited some money from her parents. Rossi sighed. "I don't know what to say sweetie…. People count on me. I have to work tonight."

"But what about *me*?" Missy demanded as the car pulled up in front of a brightly lit contemporary style home. "Why can't *I* count on you?"

It was a perfect exit line, calculated to hurt, and delivered at exactly the right moment. The passenger side door swung open allowing cold air to rush in and remain there long after Missy was gone. Rossi knew the interchange had been fueled by pre-teen angst, and knew Missy could be manipulative, but it hurt nonetheless. The agent waited for her daughter to put her key in the lock, saw a rectangle of buttery light appear, and caught a glimpse of Vanessa's perfect profile as the door closed. There would be tears. Vanessa would handle the problems created by Rossi's last-minute cancellation with the aplomb of a social secretary, and Ed would shake his head in perpetual disgust.

Everything had gone well for the first few years of her marriage to Ed, but later on, when their finances began to improve, the software engineer started to look at Rossi's job like he would a competitor, something that stole time away from both him *and* their daughter. A perspective eventually upheld by the courts. When Rossi returned from a long undercover assignment, Ed had filed for divorce and wanted custody of their daughter—a battle he ultimately won.

Tears trickled down the agent's cheeks as she pulled away, and aimed the Maxima toward home and a refrigerator full of little girl treats. Her shift would start in a little less than two hours, just enough time to take a shower, get dressed, and do something about the redness in her eyes. An eighteen-year -old Santa waved from the parking lot next to a pizza joint, and a sign wished her a "Merry Christmas," as the rain continued to fall.

Even though the streets were lit, and lights remained on in some of the surrounding buildings, most of the University of Washington campus was dark. Evergreen trees threw heavy shadows onto the ground, dimly lit walkways threaded their way between boxy halls made out of brick, and tendrils of steam twisted up out of gratings. Most of the people who passed the darkened doorway were in a hurry to get back to their dorms, meet friends for dinner, or head home for the holidays.

And, as Americo Lopa watched from the shadows, he felt nothing but contempt for the people who passed by him. Because rather than question the crap they were taught, the *sheeple* bought the capitalistic bullshit that the university handed down to them, and couldn't wait to begin their lives of privilege, lives in which they and their fellow elites would consume eighty percent of the world's quickly dwindling resources while lots of other people starved. And Lopa knew they would continue to do so until someone found a way to stop them.

Not just one person, but *thousands* of people, all operating in small self-directed cells, bound together by a set of common beliefs and striking at targets of opportunity. And there wasn't a goddamned thing that the FBI assholes sitting in the Crown Victoria up the street could do about it! The thought made the eco-terrorist grin. The Motorola Talkabout 200 fit in the palm of his hand. He thumbed the transmit button. "We're good to go. Execute." There was a double-click by way of reply and the sanction was underway.

The late-model sedan was parked in the turn-out opposite Rigg Hall on the University of Washington campus. Both of the agents who were seated in it would have preferred to be home with their families.

"But experiments never go home." That's what Professor Posada liked to say, and if the Earth Liberation Army (ELA) had a list of targets, the biological geneticist was somewhere towards the top of it. Because thanks to his work, third-world farmers were laying waste to primordial forests so they could grow more crops and trade them for the products that the big conglomerates wanted to sell them. Not only that, but it was a well-known fact that deforestation leads to global warming, which was getting worse with each passing year. So, if the terrorists could intimidate *Posada*, they could instill fear in his peers as well. And that would slow the process down.

Proof that Posada had been targeted could be seen in the graffiti that had been spray painted onto the hood of his car, the threatening voicemail that greeted the geneticist when he went to pick up his messages, and the spooky letters that appeared on his doorstep—all items that the FBI's ECODOOM team considered to be prime indicators of a potential attack. And that was why Special Agent Mike Enger and Special Agent Paul Nealy were sitting in an unmarked car waiting for their shift to end.

Nealy, who was seated behind the wheel, restarted the engine, set the fan to high, and pushed his feet in under a vent as the rain turned to snow. The flakes fell slowly, as if reluctant to end their brief lives on the gradually warming windshield. The wiper blades made a *squeaking* sound as they swept the moisture away. Nealy fiddled with the multi-function control, reset the interval, and leaned back in his seat. "So, Rossi is taking Qwan's shift."

"Yeah, that's what I heard."

"Kissler's lucky…. I wouldn't mind pulling a shift with Rossi. How long has she been divorced anyway? I'll bet she's pretty damned horny by now."

"Nobody is horny enough to go to bed with *you*," Enger replied. "Besides, Rossi isn't…."

Whatever Enger was going to say was lost as a young man rapped on the passenger-side window. He had approached the car from behind and Enger chastised himself for having missed it. The student, because that's what he appeared to be, wore a knit cap, a bulky REI parka, and a backpack. He smiled engagingly.

The agent touched a button in the armrest, waited for the window to whine down, and looked up into Larry Shaw's face. "Yes? Can I help you?"

"Yes, you sure as hell can," Shaw answered, bringing his father's .38 Special up over the edge of window. "You can fucking die." The first bullet missed Nealy by an inch, the second struck him in the temple, and the third took him in the mouth.

Enger was reaching for *his* weapon by then, but he was seated, and the 10mm Glock was trapped under his jacket. He thought about his wife as the gun barrel swung his way, wished there had been an opportunity to say goodbye, and saw a spark of light. Shaw watched the FBI agent jerk as the bullet slammed into his torso. He pulled the trigger again and felt a sudden rush. Was it the act itself? Or the cocaine? It hardly mattered.

Shaw's body hid the muzzle flashes and the sedan's interior muffled most of the sound. He straightened, took a look around, and turned back to the car as if speaking with the occupants. Pedestrians, those close enough to hear, saw the pantomime, and kept on walking. Having heard no hue and cry Shaw spit on Enger's corpse, stuck the weapon into his pocket, and turned away.

Meanwhile, inside Rigg Hall, a grad student named Helmut Kossel heard the doorbell ring and went to the door. A girl's face was framed by the tiny window. She had blue eyes and pretty features. Kossel touched a white button and spoke into the metal grill. "Yes?"

Marci McDonnel locked eyes with the sandy-haired grad student, knew he was heterosexual from the way he looked back at her, and amped the charm. "Sorry to bother you, but I left my lab notes in room 110, and I need them for a final."

Kossel was doubtful but the girl was pretty and appeared harmless. "Okay, but make it fast, because I'm not supposed to let anyone in after 5:00 P.M." Kossel turned the knob, pushed the door open, and felt a blast of cold air as the girl entered. She was dressed in an oversized coat and looked bigger than Kossel had imagined she would. Her right arm hung straight down along her side but came up as she turned, and the grad student saw the gun in her hand. The door made a thud as it closed and the pistol sounded like a cannon as it went off within the enclosed space. The .22 caliber slugs didn't pack much wallop, but at close range they were quite effective, and Kossel went down.

McDonnel opened the door for Greg Aspee. He wore a knit cap pulled down over his ears and an oversized navy pea coat, and carried a 1.5 liter container of gasoline in each hand. He looked down, met Kossel's eyes for a fraction of a second, and stepped over his body. Blood stained the front of the grad student's shirt and Aspee felt lightheaded.

McDonnel looked for Shaw, saw him coming down the path, and waved him inside. He was high, *very* high, and wrapped her in a clumsy embrace. The plastic bottles hidden beneath their clothing made it impossible to get very close. The blonde pushed Shaw away. "Did you take care of it?"

"Hell, yes…. You should'a seen the inside of that car! There was blood everywhere."

"That's good," McDonnel told him, "*real* good. Now, did you reload your gun like I told you to?"

Shaw looked embarrassed, pulled the weapon out of his pocket, and released the cylinder latch. "Sorry, Marci, I forgot."

"No problem, honey," the young woman said soothingly as she broke the old High Standard .22 open and carelessly spilled three empties plus six unspent rounds out onto the floor. "Let's reload and go find Posada. Then, after we kill him, we'll go see my sister."

Shaw nodded, fumbled more shells into his weapon, and flipped the cylinder closed just like he'd seen detectives do in the movies. He nodded to Kossel, and said, "Hey, man" as he stepped over the graduate student and walked down the hall.

The bullets had entered Kossler's abdomen within inches of each other but his entire belly had begun to hurt. The darkness was starting to gather by then, and it took everything the grad student had to remove the cell phone from his shirt pocket and thumb 911. Finally, after what seemed like an hour but was actually a couple of seconds a woman answered. Kossler managed to say, "U-dub campus…Rigg Hall…they shot me," before he lost consciousness.

Posada had his eye glued to a microscope as the terrorists entered his lab. He assumed the footsteps belonged to Kossel and spoke without looking up. "Hey, Helmut, take a look at this...." Both McDonnel and Shaw brought their weapons up and opened fire. Posada jerked spasmodically, glassware shattered, and a .22 slug made a neat little hole in the flat-panel display on the far side of the room. The researcher slumped to the floor.

"All right," McDonnel said grimly, "wet the place down."

Aspee stood with gas cans in hand staring down at Posada's bloody corpse. A look of revulsion appeared on his face. His cheeks started to bulge and he threw up. The three of them had shared a special celebratory dinner four hours earlier and his share splattered all over the floor. McDonnel made a face. "That was gross, Greg. Okay, Larry, it's up to us. Grab a can and let's get going."

The terrorists slopped gasoline over the countertops, and poured the liquid into file cabinets and onto the lab's computer equipment. "All right," McDonnel said, as sirens sounded in the distance. "Time to get out of here. Greg, are you ready?"

Aspee looked pale but determined. He nodded stiffly, lit a kitchen match, and tossed it into the middle of the room. There was a loud "whump!" followed by a wave of heat. The threesome backed out of the room.

The building's sprinkler system came on, but it didn't really matter, since the group had already accomplished what they came for. The first stage of the operation was complete. The second was about to start.

Rossi knew something was wrong the moment she saw Nealy's sedan. Half a dozen students had gathered around it, the passenger side door was open, and a body was sprawled out onto the pavement. The agent grabbed the mike off her dash, identified herself, and told the dispatcher to send an aid unit plus back-up.

Then Rossi pulled over, jumped out of her car, and ran toward the scene. She could hear sirens and knew help was coming, but took out her weapon just in case. The agent held her badge up for people to see, and yelled "FBI! Move away from the car!"

It was a dramatic moment—and one that Americo Lopa managed to capture on tape from the edge of the steadily growing crowd. He wore his ball cap backwards so it wouldn't interfere with the viewfinder, and the lower part of his face was obscured by a scarf. Other than that he was dressed student-style, in a parka, jeans, and boots.

Though manufactured for the high-end consumer market, the GR-SXM93OU JVC vid cam put out broadcast-quality images, even in low-light conditions. And that was important because the stuff that the cops would eventually harvest from the surrounding security cameras would be too static and vague to claim people's attention for very long. And Lopa, who ran what he thought of as the Red Cell from the back of his van, wanted to ensure that the sanction received a lot of coverage. That was important because while there seemed to be a nearly inexhaustible supply of Muslim martyrs, people willing to die for the sake of the environment were in short supply.

Most of the bystanders moved back out of the way as Rossi arrived, but one, a resident from the university's hospital, stood waiting. A stethoscope dangled from her neck. There was blood on her hands. Her eyes locked with Rossi's. "Did they belong to you?"

The agent nodded mutely.

"I'm sorry. Both of them are dead."

"You're sure?"

"Yes, I'm afraid so."

Rossi nodded for a second time. "Stay with them, Doctor. Don't let anyone touch the vehicle or the bodies. Not Medic One…not anyone. This is a crime scene." The resident nodded.

The agent's hand shook as she pulled the Nextel phone off her belt, told the dispatcher that two agents were down, and that the killer or killers might still be in the area. That was when someone yelled, "Rigg Hall is on fire!" Rossi ran toward the brick building and Lopa panned. Meanwhile, having been alerted by 911, a member of the University of Washington's police force arrived on the scene even as a fire engine bulled in from the north.

In spite of the fact that the sprinkler system had kept the flames down, flammable materials were stored in the lab and it wasn't long before the fire found them. McDonnel heard a loud "whoosh" as additional oxygen was sucked into the room through the open fire door, and knew it was time for the second part of the operation to get underway. "Okay," McDonnel said, "this is it. Greg, come here."

The young man did as he was told. McDonnel told Aspee that she loved him, kissed him in spite of the vomit on his breath, and pulled back in order to look at him. He was crying. "Don't worry, honey," she said. "It won't be that bad. Don't forget what you're supposed to do."

Aspee shook his head. "I won't."

"Good. Larry? Are you ready?"

Shaw grinned, took McDonnel in his arms, and stuck his tongue into her mouth. He would have gone further except that she laughed and pushed him away. "Alright," she said, her eyes shiny with emotion, "let's go. I'll see you in Paradise." It sounded believable the way she said it, as if people went to Paradise every day and you could go there on a bus.

Aspee trudged in the direction of the door, saw Shaw push it open, and stumbled out into the cold. There were things he was supposed to say, slogans he was supposed to shout, but he couldn't remember the words. Aspee heard a woman's voice shout, "FBI! Stop or I'll shoot!" and ran for the nearest bystander.

Rossi fired, felt the Glock buck in her hand, and saw the man go down. But then the subject was up again. The bastard was wearing body armor! The FBI agent considered a head shot, but the crowd was on the move by then and a number of people were running through the area immediately behind the suspect by that time. If Rossi were to miss, or if a bullet were to pass through the suspect's head and keep on going, a bystander could die.

Aspee's side hurt where the 10mm round had hit him, and although he could feel something wet running down his leg, there was no way to know whether it was urine, blood, or gasoline. The lady in front of him stood as if rooted in place, a look of terror on her face, as the terrorist closed in on her. She made a strange squeaking sound as Aspee wrapped his arms around her torso. Then, because the middle-aged office worker smelled just like his mother, he tightened the embrace.

The push-button lamp switch, which had been duct-taped to the inside surface of Aspee's right wrist, made a *click* as he pressed the button. Electricity from a pair of batteries surged through a short length of wire, and a spark was introduced into one of six bottles of gasoline strapped to the terrorist's body. There was a gentle "whump," as Aspee burst into flames and the woman began to burn, too. Their voices formed a gruesome harmony as they screamed in unison and danced within a cocoon of flames. McDonnel had promised Aspee that it wouldn't hurt, that the cocaine would suppress the pain, but she'd been wrong.

Lopa, still located a safe distance away, knew what would happen next and pulled wide to capture the action. Though disappointed by Aspee's failure to shout at least some of the agreed-upon slogans, everything else was going well and the cell leader was pleased.

Rossi pointed toward the spot where the two fiery bodies were locked together and shouted, "Smother those flames!" just as Shaw and McDonnel emerged from Rigg Hall and ran towards the crowd. Most of the bystanders turned and ran but one student tripped and fell. McDonnel screamed something incoherent as she prepared to throw herself on top of the helpless male.

Rossi yelled, "FBI! Stop or I'll shoot!" but it made no difference. Having learned from the first episode Rossi aimed for the terrorist's head but missed. Then, careful to lead her target, the agent fired again. McDonnel went down. There was no way to know whether the young woman triggered the fire bombs prior to being shot, or whether the explosion was the result of an involuntary movement of her thumb, but it didn't make much difference. Her dead body exploded into flames, fell just short of her intended victim, and lit the surrounding area with an obscene glow.

Shaw was only twelve feet away from a campus cop by then. The police officer shouted for him to stop for the third time, fired his 9mm, and saw the young man stumble. But then the terrorist was up firing a pistol as he staggered forward. *I should have gone for the bastard's head*, the cop thought to himself, and was just about to squeeze off another round when Rossi fired her Glock. The bullet removed the top of Shaw's skull, sprayed the area behind with gore, and hit Rigg Hall. The terrorist toppled over backwards, landed with an audible "thump," and was left to stare sightlessly up into the night sky.

Lopa lowered the camera and frowned. Rather than unfold the way it was supposed to, the sanction had been compromised by the female FBI agent, and that made him angry. *Very* angry. So angry that it might be necessary to cap the bitch. But that was for later. He had work to do.

Unsure of how many more opponents she might face, and which direction they might attack from, the agent tilted the Glock up and turned a complete circle. She saw bystanders, television cameras, and firefighters all waiting to see what would happen next. The first terrorist, the one that she hadn't fired on, lay wrapped in someone's steaming raincoat. A medic tended to him while the other worked to revive his victim.

Then, having completed her turn, Rossi realized that the fire department had water on the building, the police were pushing the crowd back behind yellow crime tape, and Kissler had arrived for work. He stood with his pistol pointed at the ground and a look of amazement on his moon-shaped face. "Jesus, Rossi, what the hell happened?"

Rossi shook her head, wrinkled her nose in response to the odor of burned flesh, and felt a snowflake touch her nose. "Something bad, Kevin. Something really bad."

About a hundred feet away, toward the rear of the crowd, Lopa touched the camera's power button. In spite of some initial misgivings, the sanction had gone fairly well and the day's work was done. His van was parked on the west side of the U-district not far from the I-HOP. The terrorist stowed the camcorder in his pack, slipped his arms through the straps, and sauntered away. He had news to deliver.

The morning sky was Seattle gray, a steady drizzle fell, and most people were on their way to work as Jack Dexter stepped out onto the street. Baghdad, Mosul, and Fallujah were thousands of miles away, his forebrain knew that, but his hind brain, the so-called reptilian brain, was alert to the possibility someone could fire at him from a passing vehicle, blow him to smithereens by triggering an IED (improvised explosive device), or kill him with a randomly fired mortar shell. That's why the ex-SEAL had to force himself out of what he still thought of as cover.

*The leg*, by which Dexter meant his left leg, was a little sore after the run the day before, but that was not only typical but hardly worth thinking about compared to the pain he had experienced when the so-called resistance fighters had ambushed his convoy. He and his team had been in the process of escorting four VIPs from the Defense Department out of the green zone to an Iraqi government building located near Haifa street when their vehicles came under attack.

An IED had been used to destroy the lead Humvee, while the second vehicle, the one Dexter had been riding in, was struck by a rocket-propelled grenade (RPG.) He knew he was hit but didn't realize how badly because there wasn't enough time to think about it. The bad guys rushed in hoping to take hostages that could be sold to Al Qaida—but Dexter and his men had other plans. They sprayed their attackers with CAR-15, MP5, and M203 fire even as the rest of the convoy bull-dozed its way out of the trap and a crowd of Iraqi civilians began to throw rocks at the infidel occupiers.

Unable to break through the defensive fire, and having suffered more than fifty percent casualties by that time, the black-clad fighters were already in the process of pulling back when a Cobra helicopter arrived on scene and sprayed both sides of the street with 20mm cannon fire. Sixteen terrorists were killed, plus twelve civilians, one of whom was a woman holding her baby. The baby, amazingly enough, survived.

That was when Dexter felt the pain, and looked down at where his leg should have been, but saw nothing but mangled flesh. He passed out, woke up in Germany, and was put back to sleep. The amputation of what was left of his leg took the better part of three hours. From there, the lieutenant was sent to Walter Reed, where he had been fitted for a prosthesis and put through a grueling regimen of rehab before being discharged from the Navy. Now, more than two years later, Dexter was used to the pain and the inconvenience of wearing an artificial limb. What he hadn't been able to accept was the disfigurement itself. Eventually he would adjust, that's what the shrinks told him, but what the hell did *they* know? Every single one of them had both legs—and could take their clothes off without embarrassment.

Even though Jack Dexter hadn't consumed much coffee when he

was younger, he had acquired the habit during his Naval service and still enjoyed it now. That was why he began each day at Starbucks. It sat on a corner in the space previously occupied by a tiny grocery store, one more indication of the way in which the neighborhood had been gentrified.

Dexter held the door for an elderly woman who he recognized as a regular, grabbed a *Post Intelligencer* off the inside rack, and scanned the front page as he waited in line. It seemed that a bomb had exploded in Manila, there had been some sort of shoot-out at the University of Washington, and Boeing had won a big contract from China. "Are you having the usual today?"

Dexter looked up to discover that the people in front of him had been served. The woman behind the counter was in her late twenties and had blonde hair and a nice figure—something Dexter already knew, had known for six months now, but done nothing about. He had considered making a pass at her but knew that doing so could trigger a series of predictable events. Success would lead to a date, which could lead to a second date, which could lead to sex. Or the *expectation* of sex, which would force the ex-SEAL to undress and show her the leg. Maybe it would turn her off, or maybe it wouldn't, but how to know? It was a helluva lot easier to simply have sex by himself. "Yes, please," Dexter replied warmly, and smiled to seal the bargain.

Annie smiled in return and turned to fill a paper cup with drip coffee. A drip, plus a blueberry scone, was what the man with no name ate each morning. He was single, she felt certain of it, but never attempted to make a move on her. Because he didn't find her attractive? No, that didn't make sense because she had seen him look at her. So what was the problem? He was tall, had short, sandy hair, penetrating hazel eyes, and even features. He wore nice but non-descript clothes, sported a complicated-looking watch, and walked with an almost-imperceptible limp. Maybe, in spite of all the signs to the contrary, he was gay. Annie made use of a pair of metal tongs to select what looked like the nicest blueberry scone and placed it in a brown paper bag. "Will there be anything else?"

Dexter gave her a five, waited for his change, and dropped a dollar into the clear plastic tip box. Then, oblivious to the way that the barista's eyes followed him, the businessman took his paper and his breakfast over to what he thought of as table number two. It was back in a corner, where the ex-SEAL could put his back to a wall, but too close to the side door. Table one was perfect, but had already been claimed by a rumpled man equipped with a cell phone, PDA, and a laptop.

Dexter brushed some crumbs off the table, dropped into the chair, and laid out his breakfast. Having swallowed his first bite of scone, the businessman chased it with some black coffee and turned to the classifieds. His ad was under the heading "Downtown." It read: "View of Elliott Bay! This newly remodeled luxury apartment is located in a quiet twelve-unit complex with on-site parking, a high-tech security system, and 24/7 management. Enjoy three cozy bedrooms, two and a half baths, and a spacious living room with a sweeping view of the bay. $2,500 per month."

The ad was followed by a phone number, *his* phone number since the complex belonged to him and had ever since his father's fatal heart attack more than two years earlier. The news that his son had been wounded in Iraq, plus his generally poor health, had been too much for the old man. But Dexter didn't like to think about his father's death, or the war in Iraq, and turned to the funnies instead. He chuckled over his favorites, washed the last bite of scone down with some coffee, and eyed the blonde as she carried a bag of trash out through the side door. She was pretty, no doubt about that, and he wondered what she would look like naked.

The mixture of rain and snow continued to fall with the same determination that it had earlier, but Dexter was used to that and enjoyed the cool two-block walk to the only home he had ever known. The apartment house had been forty years old back when his parents bought the building and moved in. There had been twice as many units back in those days, and as time passed, the people who lived there became family—especially after Mrs. Dexter passed away and the residents took turns looking out for the little boy that everyone called Dex, and the father who drank too much.

Rents remained low, a lot of the maintenance was deferred, and the structure began to fall apart—so much so that by the time Dexter returned from the war the complex was in need of a complete renovation.

The ex-naval officer felt a distinct sense of pride as he turned a corner and the freshly painted building came into view.

It stood six stories tall, and had a flat roof and big windows. What had been a maze of smallish one- and two-bedroom apartments had been combined into large two- and three-bedroom units designed to appeal to the carriage trade, people who enjoyed the ambience of living downtown but for reasons that never made sense to Dexter, preferred to rent rather than buy. He was grateful, however, and now that the renovation was complete, the ex-naval officer planned to sit back and relax. And, depending on who took unit 6A, he might be in for some entertainment as well. Dexter smiled, waited for a light, and stepped out onto the street.

There had been a time when the forty-year-old, two-bedroom frame house had seemed too small for a man, woman, and child, but not anymore. Now it felt big and empty. The place where Rossi went to have a Lean Cuisine, watch some television, and grab some sleep. She had considered selling it and using the proceeds to buy a condo, but there was Missy to consider, including the need for a yard to play in.

The FBI agent went to the front window, pushed a blinds slat up and out of the way, and peered out onto the street. She could see two news vans and knew that others lurked nearby. The attack on Rigg Hall and the resulting homicides would have been news under any circumstances. But the fact that the ELA had taped the entire incident and sent copies to the local television stations had raised the ante. The footage of the first terrorist wrapped in a fiery embrace, and of Rossi shooting his companions, had been played countless times during the last twenty-four hours. And not just locally, but nationally, until she was sick of looking at it.

Should the networks have run the extremely graphic footage or shouldn't they? Pundits were still debating the issue. Not that it mattered much since the networks *had* run the footage, *had* granted the terrorists the significance they wanted so badly, and *had* trashed Rossi's life. In addition to the reporters camped outside, various media outlets had literally filled the FBI agent's voicemail with requests for interviews. Additionally, one of her ISP's employees had leaked her email address and her inbox was filled to overflowing with hundreds of messages. Some supportive—some filled with hate.

Meanwhile, she was on administrative leave while the Bureau assembled a shooting review team and prepared to judge one of their own. Not that there was much to talk about, not in Rossi's opinion, since nobody seemed to dispute the fact that the eco-terrorists had murdered two FBI agents, attempted to kill a grad student, and shot Professor Posada in cold blood.

Still, one member of the Seattle City Council, an individual with a longstanding dislike for the Seattle Police Department (SPD), had actually gone so far as to question the agent's decision to fire on the second and third suspects, saying "Why shoot for the head? Couldn't this Rossi person just kneecap them?"

That in spite of the fact that Aspee's female victim died of a heart attack shortly after he wrapped his arms around her, while *he,* ironically enough, managed to survive the flames and was on life support at Harborview hospital. There was a sudden flurry of activity out front as an unmarked Crown Victoria pulled up in front of the house. Its flashers came on and the media types converged on it.

Rossi turned away from the window, grabbed her briefcase off a side table, and walked back through the bright yellow kitchen. The refrigerator was plastered with photos of Missy, the drying rack was full of dishes, and the phone rang in steady bursts. Rossi opened the back door, checked to ensure that the lock was set, and made use of her right foot to keep Snowball from slipping outside. The cat issued a plaintive meow as the door swung closed.

Some of the video vampires had been camped in the alley, but the stir caused by the sedan had been sufficient to pull them around front, and none were in sight. Rossi crossed her tiny backyard, opened the gate, and realized that she had forgotten to put the garbage out the day before. The truck wouldn't come for another week, which meant that she would have to live with the results of her own forgetfulness.

The maroon sedan, the twin of the one out front except for the color, sped up the alley, paused just long enough for Rossi to jump in, and accelerated away. Supervisory Special Agent (SSA) John Theel glanced in his rearview mirror. He was a big man, about six foot three, with wide shoulders and a taste for well-cut suits. He had salt and pepper hair, mocha colored skin, and intelligent eyes. He grinned. "Pretty slick, huh?"

"Very. Who played decoy?"

"Kissler. Hold on while I turn him loose."

Theel activated the two-way radio feature on his Nextel cell phone, said, "We're in the clear," and received Kissler's acknowledgment.

"So," Theel said, pointing to one of two paper cups resting in the center console. "One latte…extra hot. Did I get it right?"

"Yes," Rossi lied, "thank you. That was very thoughtful. So, what's on the agenda?"

"First we have a cup of coffee while I bring you up to date…then we head down town. The ASAC will do the best she can to deal with the brass from Washington D.C. while you meet with the inspectors."

Theel had turned onto Stoneway by then. He followed it south to Lake Union, pulled into a parking lot, and killed the engine. They could see the back end of a marina, rows of expensive yachts, and the gray wind-ruffled waters of the lake beyond. Further away, beyond the south shore, the Seattle skyline shot upwards, with the Space Needle off to the right. Most of the wet snow that had fallen the previous day had melted.

Rossi took a sip of her drink. It warmed her hands but did nothing to counter the cold emptiness in the bottom of her stomach. She had nothing to hide, not in her opinion, but that didn't make the process any less frightening. "Fair enough…. I'll do my best. So, what's the buzz? Was it a good shoot?"

Theel stared out through the windshield. Rivulets of moisture zigzagged down across the safety glass. "The board will make that determination and they haven't finished their investigation yet."

"Don't bullshit me, John. I'm not asking what the *board* thinks—I'm asking what the folks in the office think."

Theel looked her way. The agent's face was so pale that her lipstick looked unnaturally bright. Judging from the deep circles under her eyes she hadn't slept very well and was struggling to look normal. He knew the question had many levels. Rossi wanted to know if she was in trouble, but more than that, she wanted to know how the rest of the team felt about Enger and Nealy. "They were grown ups, Christina, experienced agents who were in the wrong place at the wrong time. Not only that but you arrived on the scene ten minutes early. The fact that you did saved at least two lives. Everybody knows that...and everybody supports you."

"Even Val?" Rossi asked bitterly, referring to Enger's wife, "and Holly?"

"*Especially* them," Theel replied evenly. "They didn't like the risks, but they knew about them and chose to marry the kind of men who were willing to take them. And, while it might not be politically correct, they're grateful for what you did.

"No, they blame the ASAC. They know you warned Haxton and that she refused to request more resources, so they figure the ambush was *her* fault. The only problem is that they're wrong. Even if the ASAC had alerted the entire planet, odds are that Enger and Nealy would still be dead. They knew the kind of people they were after, or should have, and chose to sit on their weapons. It sounds harsh, hell, it *is* harsh, but they could have been more vigilant. Anyway, no matter how you cut it, there's nothing more you could have done."

There was silence as Rossi took it in. "Thanks, boss. That helps."

"No problem," Theel said, glancing at his watch. "I hate to do this, but there's a couple things we need to talk about before they run you through the red, white, and blue wringer."

Rossi nodded. "Shoot."

"You prepared a signed statement?"

"Yeah, the chief inspector has it. You'll find a copy in your email."

"Good. Everybody's seen the tape about a million times and we have statements from at least a dozen witnesses, not to mention one very grateful campus cop, but it's important to make sure that your account squares with theirs. Speaking of which, did you hire a lawyer?"

Rossi frowned. "Why? Do I need one?"

Theel sighed. "Don't get defensive, Christina. It's SOP. You know that."

"Sorry, I'm feeling a bit paranoid right now. Yeah, I talked to the counsel for the Agent's Association, and she hooked me up with an attorney here in Seattle. Some guy named Paul Gregory. He reviewed my statement and said it was fine. He's supposed to meet me at the office."

Theel started the car, looked back over his shoulder, and backed out of the spot. "Excellent. Gregory has a good rep. He was a cop once... and he bleeds blue."

"So, fill me in," Rossi demanded. "What have we got on these people?"

"You're on administrative leave."

"Oh, yeah? Then why I am in this car? On my way to the office? On a Saturday?"

Theel laughed. "Okay, but you didn't hear it from me. You knew about McDonnel, hell, you predicted that the psycho bitch was up to something. And, having sifted through the stuff in her apartment, it looks like she became interested in Buddhism, did a whole lot of reading, and stumbled across some material on self-immolation.

"It turns out that until recently all Sinitic monks and nuns were burned as part of their ordination ceremonies, and some of them, like the monks who lit themselves on fire to protest the Vietnam War, practiced 'shao shen,' a term that originally referred to cremation but was subsequently extended to include the willing incineration of living flesh as part of a sacrifice or protest."

"So, McDonnel was on a heavy-duty religious trip."

"Maybe," Theel replied cautiously, pulling up onto Aurora Way south, "but in spite of the religious overtones and the so-called experts the networks came up with, I don't think so. No, I think the self-immolation thing was intended to generate some attention-grabbing video and dress the whole thing up to look like an act of self-sacrifice rather than the cold-blooded murder that it actually was."

The rain was falling steadily by then and Rossi watched the wipers smear it back and forth. "What about the video? Who shot it? They had to know about the attack in advance."

"Yes, they did," Theel agreed grimly. "We're looking at the footage shot by the local TV stations and the university's surveillance cams. The lab has it along with the folks in Counter Terrorism."

Rossi nodded. "Good. I want the bastard. Or bastards as the case may be."

Theel glanced her way. "We'll get them. How's Missy?"

Rossi sighed. The ELA videographer was efficient if nothing else. All three of the local TV stations had copies of his raw footage within an hour of the murders—and all three broke into their regular programming to run it. While she was still at the university, working to secure the crime scene and coordinate the initial response, Missy had been at her father's place watching television. The special news bulletin popped up right in the middle of *A Charlie Brown Christmas*. Within a matter of seconds, the little girl was looking at pictures of a person on fire and a woman firing her pistol. Then, as the agent turned to scan the crowd for more perps, Missy saw a tight shot of her mother's face.

Vanessa said Missy had been hysterical at first, certain that her mother had been hurt in some way and desperate to talk to her. Later, after the two of them spoke on the phone, the little girl finally started to calm down. She hadn't been allowed to watch TV since. "It was hard," Rossi replied bleakly. "Really, really, hard."

Theel nodded, and conned the car through downtown traffic and into an underground parking garage. The building swallowed the sedan—and the Bureau swallowed Rossi.

# Chapter Two

Though nothing like the storm raging out in the Pacific, thirty-knot winds pushed six-foot waves east through the Strait of Juan de Fuca, which would have been a problem for a small boat but were barely noticeable on the bridge of the 53,000-ton ship *South Wind*. It was warm inside the tightly enclosed bridge, *too* warm by Captain Hans Kroger's standards, but the rest of the multi-national crew liked it that way. The fact that the air was thick with stale cigarette smoke, the smell of strong tea, and the helmsman's rank body odor made the situation that much worse. Vertical wipers thumped from side-to-side, banks of instruments glowed green, and the soft mutter of radio traffic could be heard in the background as the Coast Guard's Puget Sound Vessel Traffic Service Center (VTS) kept in contact with two dozen ships. It had been six months since Kroger had been to Seattle and the merchant marine officer was looking forward to making port. There were bars to visit, plus a woman who had proven to be cooperative in the past, and what more could any sailor want?

A blast of cold air invaded the long, narrow space as the hatch that provided access to the starboard bridge extension slid open. First Officer Akio Suzuki closed the door, shook himself in the same way that a dog would, and sent rain water flying in every direction. The yellow storm suit was so bulky it caused him to waddle. The Japanese officer had a broad forehead, almond-shaped eyes, and was perpetually in need of a shave. "Captain."

Kroger nodded gravely. "Number One."

Neither one of the men spoke the other's native language, which was why all of their conversations took place in English. "It's time to cut our speed to five knots."

It was an unusual request, since there was no ostensible reason to reduce the ship's speed, but Kroger understood nonetheless. Though not especially fond of each other, the two men had one thing in common, and that was their mutual desire for large quantities of money—the kind of cash available to merchant officers who were willing to tolerate the presence of a few extra bodies on their ship and reduce revolutions at the proper moment. Kroger ran blunt fingertips through his short, bristly beard. It was heavily shot through with gray, a reminder of how many years had passed since his graduation from Breman's Polytechnic University. "Is the pick-up crew ready?"

"Yes."

"Then reduce speed we must," the German said evenly. "The VTS people will notice the change and ask what we're up to…. I will inform them that we're running ahead of schedule—and need to slow down in order to meet the pilot on time. Let me know when the passengers clear the stern."

Suzuki thought about the sick, frightened men huddled on the ship's fantail and wondered if they qualified as passengers. They certainly had paid enough money to justify the title—or would once they completed up to ten years of indentured service. But that was in the future. At the moment they were cargo that the crew needed to jettison before the pilot came aboard off Ediz Hook. The Americans had become more security conscious since 9/11 and that made everything more difficult. The officer nodded. "I will notify you by radio."

Suzuki was still making his way off the bridge when the communication came in over VHF FM Channel 5A. "Freighter *South Wind,* my radar shows you have slowed to five knots. Do you have a problem? Over."

Kroger keyed the mike. "Seattle Traffic, this is the *South Wind.* I am slowing my speed to five knots to make my ETA for the Port Angeles pilot station. Over."

There was a pause followed by a whisper of static. "Freighter *South Wind*—I have no reported opposing traffic. In the future adjust your speed to avoid loitering near the precautionary area. Over."

Kroger smiled thinly. "Seattle Traffic, this is the *South Wind.* Roger…. I will increase speed within ten minutes. *South Wind* out."

Meanwhile, back on the stern, ten men stood in a tight little group.

They wore brightly colored Viking SOLAS PS5002 Immersion Suits, all of which had been purchased secondhand to save money, and were at least one size too large for the men from Fujian Province. Strobe lights, one per suit, flashed in quick succession.

But, surplus or not, *any* protection would be welcome, since every one of the illegal immigrants knew that he was about to jump into some very cold water. Still, Lok Lee was a strong swimmer, and if anyone could survive, *he* could. That's what the young man was thinking when Suzuki appeared and Hector Battoon sent the first illegal out onto a specially rigged plank. He was Filipino and spoke halting Mandarin. "You must walk out to the very end before you jump off!" the crewman shouted. "Otherwise you could be sucked into the props! Move quickly so you land in the water together…. That will make it easier for the boat to pick you up."

Then, conscious of the need to get them going before they had too much time to dwell on the danger, Lee and the rest were herded into place. Huang went first, quickly followed by Wong and Ma. Then it was Lee's turn. A strange world of wind, waves, and lights swirled around the young man as he made his way out onto the plank, took a deep breath, and fell into the void.

It was a long drop and the youngster felt the impact as his feet hit the surface quickly followed by a cold slap as the water made contact with his face. He sank, but not for long, as both the air in his lungs and the suit acted to lift him up. Lee broke the surface as a small boat roared past. The freighter was smaller by then and receding fast. "Hey!" he shouted, "I'm over *here!*"

But the man in charge of the fourteen-foot Zodiac Futura Mark 3 and his assistant couldn't hear anything over the roar of their engine as they reduced speed in order to pull other illegals into the open boat. That was when Lee noticed that his strobe light had stopped functioning and yelled even louder. But no one heard. The currents pulled him away and the cold began to invade his rail-thin body. Lee remembered his sweetheart, the one he had promised to send for, and called her name. But she was back in Fujian Province, on her way to the local village, to buy medicine for her mother.

Mi Sung felt a sudden chill as the sun slipped behind a cloud. She pulled the shawl that Lee had given her up around her shoulders and wondered what he was doing.

Huang had entered the water first, bobbed to the surface, and been rescued in a matter of seconds. It took two attempts to pull himself up into the Zodiac, but once onboard, Huang discovered that he enjoyed the exhilarating ride. Ten minutes later all but one of the illegal's companions had been brought aboard to huddle around him. Huang told the snakeheads that Lee was missing, and they spent ten minutes looking for him, but saw no sign of his strobe light. Finally, convinced that the missing illegal had drowned, they accelerated away.

The young men held on for dear life as the boat turned toward the east and powered through the waves. The ensuing trip lasted for the better part of twenty minutes and ended when the semi-rigid boat coasted into the lee of the sixty-foot *Zhou Wind*. Once the Zodiac appeared on the scene, a series of terse orders was given, and a team of SCUBA-equipped divers splashed into the water alongside.

Huang saw the fishing boat loom up ahead and felt the wind virtually disappear as the driver steered the Zodiac into position next to it. "Grab a weight belt," the assistant snakehead shouted as he pointed towards the bottom of the boat. "And put it on."

Once the passengers were ready, the second order came. "You must jump!" the helmsman instructed. "Divers are waiting in the water."

And divers *were* waiting in the water, although Huang couldn't imagine why as both he and Ma tumbled into the sea just a few feet away from a group of bobbing head lamps. All sorts of things began to happen then as dry-suited divers closed with the illegals—and demonstrated how to breathe via the second-stage regulators connected to their tanks. Then, having barely had time to become accustomed to the breathing devices, the first two men were escorted down through the murky water to the fantastic world below. Lights glowed, but there was barely enough time to catch a glimpse of the sunken ship's superstructure before Huang and Ma were pushed into a dimly lit lock. Once inside, the out door was sealed, water was pumped out, and it wasn't long before they could breathe without benefit of the SCUBA equipment.

Once the water fell below the level of the coaming a hatch opened. A Maori was there to meet them. He had frightening *Moko* tattoos on his face, a wicked-looking taser, and a no-nonsense attitude. He ordered the men out of their survival suits, then marched them through hot showers and out into a bare-bones locker room. Piles of clothing and other items waited on wooden benches. "Grab a set of overalls and a shaving kit," the snakehead said brusquely. "Hot food is waiting."

"Oh, and one other thing," the Maori said, as he paused in front of a hatch. "Welcome to America."

Dexter stepped into the walk-in closet, flipped a switch, and waited for the can-style recessed lights to come on. His neatly hung clothes made a subtle swishing sound as he pushed them out of the way. The door, which consisted of half-inch maple veneer plywood, whispered as it slid to one side. A sudden rush of cool air invaded the closet. It smelled of plasterboard, carpet, and sealant.

He felt a momentary sense of pride as he stepped into the hidden room and paused to admire his handiwork. When sober, and in the mood to work, Dexter's father had been good with his hands. And Dexter had not only learned at the old man's side, but inherited all of his tools, which he kept in the shop just off the parking garage. But some, those that Dexter required to finish the job, lay waiting at his feet.

The viewing room, as the businessman liked to think of it, was six feet long and three feet deep. A large portion of the wall opposite the secret door resembled a window, but actually consisted of a see-through mirror, similar to those used in police stations. It looked out into 6A's master bedroom—a significant modification that had never been discussed with Dexter's architect, the general contractor, or the city's building inspectors, all of whom had plans that showed 6A's bedroom as being three feet deeper than it actually was. It was sick, Dexter knew, but harmless. After all, the businessman told himself, *what they don't know won't hurt them.*

The room was something of a gamble of course, since there was no way to be sure that the people who rented the apartment would be *worth* watching, but that was part of the fun. If not the first renters, then the second, or the third. Eventually, if he waited long enough, Dexter knew his investment would pay off.

But first there was work to do. Rather than mess around with complicated electronics, Dexter had rigged the overhead ducts to conduct sound, but the system worked in reverse, too. That meant he would need to be quiet when he used the viewing room or his neighbors would hear him. And that was why it was so important to finish the space *before* someone took the apartment. All Dexter had to do was install the trim around the window, paint the walls, and lay some leftover carpet. He'd be done within two hours, knock off, and head for the gym. The businessman whistled while he worked.

In spite of the fact that Greg Aspee was alive, he very much wished that he wasn't—first because of the pain caused by the second- and third-degree burns that covered nearly seventy percent of his body, second because he felt guilty about what he and the others had done, and third because Marci had abandoned him.

That's the way it felt anyway, even though the would-be terrorist knew she was dead, just like *he* was supposed to be dead, except that he wasn't. Because unlike Larry, who always knew what to do, he was what his father always referred to as "…a worthless piece of shit." Now, laying on his back in Harborview's Burn Unit, Aspee had been reduced to little more than a carefully tended *thing*, a project people were forced to work on, but didn't really want to, having seen the *thing* kill an innocent woman on TV.

Further distancing the *thing* from the people around him was the fact that everyone who entered Aspee's room was required to wear a cap, mask, and surgical gown in order to reduce the possibility of infection and thereby keep the *thing* alive long enough to kill it, because Washington State had the death penalty and there were plenty of people who believed that it should be a prime candidate. Or maybe the Feds would get to try it first. It hardly mattered to Aspee.

Some of the people came to renew the *thing's* IV, or to apply dressings, or to dispense medications. Other people came to ask the *thing* questions. They wanted to know why the triad lived together, why they wanted to die, and what they hoped to accomplish by murdering innocent people. Some of the visitors threatened the *thing* with the death penalty, or tried to organize the *thing's* defense, or claimed that the *thing* could go to heaven if only it would repent.

Still other people were noticeable by their absence. His father, who had told one of the television reporters that his son was "one sick puppy," his mother, who couldn't afford the trip up from Florida, and Marci, who had gone to Paradise without him. The only friends the *thing* could rely on were the medications that lessened his pain—plus the occasional release granted it by sleep.

The *thing's* left foot started to itch. A hand started to reach, metal rattled, and the chain brought the motion to a sudden halt. The *thing* swore and wished it were dead.

The elevator stopped at the garage level, produced a loud bong, and prepared to rise. The doors slid open. Kissler gestured for Rossi to precede him and waited for her to do so. Both said "Hello" to one of the Bureau's support personnel before passing between a pair of parked cars and out into a pull-through. It was raining outside and wet tire tracks led toward the rear of the garage. Kissler found himself lagging behind and hurried to catch up. The female agent's heels made a soft clacking sound as they hit the concrete. "Hey, Rossi, hold on…. My car's over there."

"And mine's over here," the agent replied evenly. "Feel free to follow me if you wish."

"I thought we were going to lunch."

"And we will—right after we visit Harborview."

"Harborview?" Kissler asked, his normally smooth forehead furrowed with worry. "I'm not sure that's a good idea. You're on administrative leave."

"*Was* on administrative leave," Rossi corrected him. "I came off this morning. Remember? Anyway, if you don't want to come you don't have to, but I have some questions for Aspee."

"But what about his lawyer?" Kissler asked desperately as they passed between a couple of cars and he was forced to follow her again. "Shouldn't he be there?"

Rossi stopped suddenly and turned. "Yes, *she* should be there, if Aspee wants her to be. But first I have to ask him don't I? And, given the fact that he already agreed to see other law enforcement officers sans attorney, he may do so again."

Kissler was about to reply when Rossi took a full step forward and entered his personal space. Their noses were only six inches apart and her eyes were locked with his. "Listen, Kevin, Haxton told you to keep an eye on me didn't she? Not just my ass, which seems to hold a special fascination for you, but my actions as well. She told you to make sure I stay out of trouble, or words to that effect, and *you*, being a spineless wimp, agreed. Right or wrong?"

"Wrrrong," Kissler stuttered. "It wasn't like that! She said I should take care of you, let her know if you had any problems, and...."

"Don't embarrass yourself," Rossi interrupted. "Come, stay, do whatever you want." And with that she turned toward her car. Kissler considered his options, chose the one that was best for his career, and hurried to catch up.

Although Americo Lopa wasn't adverse to committing murder in order to further the cause, he preferred to let others handle the wet work for him, thereby maintaining a certain amount of emotional distance from the "corrective" aspect of the movement. Besides, forensic science had improved a great deal over the last twenty years, which meant that a single hair, fingerprint, or cell phone call could result in an arrest.

However, balanced against the risks connected with homicide were the risks associated with leaving Aspee alive. There weren't many people who could describe the terrorist but Aspee was one of them and that made him a threat.

Of course there was the distinct possibility that Aspee had already told the authorities everything he knew in return for a deal. But, given the fact that no description had been released to the public, Lopa didn't think so. That's why the terrorist had gone to all the trouble of making himself over to look like a female janitor. Security was tight, and there were plenty of cameras, but he had the solution: An ID, stolen from an orderly who had been foolish enough to leave the card, her cell phone, and a copy of *Parasite Rex* on a table while she went to refill her coffee cup.

Lopa had appropriated all three items the day before, wiped them clean, and tossed the two he didn't need into a trash receptacle. The orderly would report the missing card, but not till Monday, and it wouldn't make any difference by then.

The ID, complete with a shot of his new female persona, wasn't perfect but it was plenty good enough to fool anyone who failed to examine it closely. Lopa smiled at a doctor, pushed the janitorial cart onto the elevator, saw that the floor he wanted had already been selected, and nodded to the elderly couple who stood on the other side of the car. They smiled in return. The male visitor thought he detected an odor that didn't fit the situation, but hospitals are rife with strange odors, so he didn't pursue the matter. Later that evening, when he sat down to watch the news, he would realize what the mysterious substance was: Gasoline.

Rossi steered the car out of the garage, turned left onto Spring, and headed up toward Capital Hill. She wanted to turn right after that but couldn't due to construction—the story of her life, her *recent* life at any rate, since her fifteen minutes of fame had done nothing to smooth things with Ed. There had been an unexpected side benefit, however which derived from the fact that some of her sudden celebrity had rubbed off onto Missy. The previously canceled sleepover had been rescheduled, even more girls wanted to come, and preteen life was momentarily good. *If* she could find time to clean the house, *if* she could come up with decorations, and *if* she could handle all the other details that Vanessa was so good at.

"So," Kissler said out of nowhere, "what was it like?"

Rossi forced herself to change mental gears. "What was *what* like?"

"The shooting review."

Rossi glanced at her temporary partner. "It wasn't as bad as I thought it would be. There was one guy who thought I should have knee-capped the terrorists rather than go for head shots, but the rest were pretty reasonable. The video made me look like Dirty Harry—but it also served to verify my version of what took place. That's why I'm back on the street."

"Oh," Kissler said thoughtfully, "I thought they were tougher than that."

"Sorry," Rossi replied, as she took a left hand turn, and headed up hill. "Maybe they'll apply the thumb screws next time."

Kissler wanted to tell Rossi that he truly admired what she'd done that night, that he had cashed in some hard-earned suck points in order to be partnered with her, and that she had a great ass. But he couldn't figure out a way to say any of those things without getting himself into trouble. With that in mind he chose to remain silent, which, based on recent experience, seemed like a wise decision indeed.

Lopa stepped off the elevator, paused to get his bearings, and pushed the cart down the corridor. A uniformed member of the Seattle Police Department had been assigned to guard Aspee's room. The hospital had provided him with a chair, some old magazines, and a small table to put them on. His radio burped gibberish as a patrol unit responded to a car prowl near Pioneer Square. He had gray hair, a bit of a paunch, and the relaxed demeanor of a man who was no longer bucking for sergeant. He heard the cart coming, looked up, and smiled. He liked people and wanted them to like him. "Hi, how ya do'in?"

Lopa had practiced both the voice and the slightly stilted version of English that his mother spoke. "Hello. I am fine thank you. I was told to clean this room."

The policeman wore a name tag. It read "Prosser." He looked surprised. "Really? Benny was here about an hour ago."

Lopa shrugged. "Somebody spilled something."

Prosser eyed the badge that hung from Lopa's neck, made a note on the pad that he kept at his side, and smiled encouragingly. "Okay, go ahead."

Lopa nodded and was reaching for the doorknob when the policeman said, "Wait a minute. You need to suit up."

Lopa swore silently, wondered how he could have been so stupid as to forget, and turned to a large cart loaded with hats, masks, and gowns. The error might have been fatal had he been trying to impersonate a nurse, but janitorial staff weren't expected to know such things, so the cop was cutting him some slack.

Five minutes later Lopa entered the room. He wore a hat, mask, gown, and latex gloves. Aspee would have slept around the clock had his body been capable of doing so, but there was a limit to how long he could remain unconscious, and the staff never left him alone for long. That's why the terrorist was in a half-conscious reverie when the door swung open and then clicked closed. He heard the squeak of an unoiled wheel, followed by the gentle rustle of a gown, and a whispered male voice. "Greg? How's it going?"

There was something familiar about the voice—but Aspee couldn't place it. "About the same as yesterday.... Dr. Schultz? Is that you?"

"No," Lopa replied, "it's Marcos."

Aspee tried to see but couldn't. "Marcos? No shit? They let you in?"

"Sort of," Lopa replied cautiously, "under a different name."

"I didn't tell them anything," Aspee said eagerly, "nothing at all. And I won't either."

"That's good," Lopa replied somberly, "*very* good."

"I need a favor though," Aspee said desperately, "and I need it real bad."

"Yeah?" Lopa said as he bent over and removed a one-gallon plastic bottle from the cart's bottom shelf. "What's that?"

Aspee tried to roll onto an elbow and winced as the newly crusted burns broke open. He started to weep. His chains rattled. "I want you to kill me."

"Hey, that's great!" the other terrorist replied cheerfully as he opened the bottle. "Because that's what I plan to do."

Aspee smelled the characteristic odor of gasoline, realized what it meant, and tried to scream. But Lopa jammed a cleaning rag into the terrorist's mouth before he could do so. A piece of pre-cut duct tape served to hold the gag in place.

Aspee was fumbling for the call button by that time, but Lopa made a clucking noise and pulled the device away. "Sorry, Greg. I wish I could handle this with a bullet or something, but the whole point is to send the establishment a wake-up call. The fact that you were determined to sacrifice yourself, and that the ELA is so powerful that it can reach inside the hospital to help you, sends a powerful message. Just like the suicide bombers in the Middle East. Now those guys have balls! Or *had* balls, before they blew themselves up.

"It's all about fear Greg," Lopa continued conversationally. "Fear that will slow their research, fear that will keep the sheeple awake at night, and fear that will influence who they vote for. Now lie back and take it easy…the whole thing will soon be over."

The gasoline felt cold, *very* cold, as Lopa slopped it over Aspee's nearly naked body. The pain came next as the harsh substance flooded the burn patient's open wounds and set them on fire. Aspee was thrashing by that time, jerking at his chains, and screaming into the gag.

Lopa ignored Aspee as he opened another jug of gasoline and doused not only the patient, but the bed. That was the most dangerous moment because a single spark could trigger an explosion that would kill them both. But there was no spark, which meant Lopa could toss the empty bottle into a corner, and open the door a crack. The falsetto came more naturally now. "Officer Prosser? I need your help."

The police officer caught a whiff of gasoline, frowned, and dropped the month-old copy of *Time* magazine. The cop was pretty mobile for a guy with a pot belly and was on his feet in no time. Prosser had the door open and had just started to speak when Lopa grabbed hold of the police officer's shirt and pulled him into the room. Prosser went for his side arm at that point, but the terrorist was ready, and brought a piece of pipe down on the top of the cop's head.

The policeman was already falling when Lopa struck him twice more, laid the length of pipe on the floor, and checked the $20.00 Timex Ladies Gold watch that was strapped to his wrist. A full ten minutes would pass before the trigger was scheduled to arrive, plenty of time for the fumes to accumulate while he left the building. Lopa walked over to the bed. "Hey, Greg, say hello to Marci for me."

Aspee thrashed back and forth and made gagging noises.

The terrorist laughed and left the room.

Aspee heard the door close and pulled at his chains. They rattled so he did it again. Maybe someone would hear…maybe someone would arrive to save him. But somehow, deep in Aspee's heart, he knew that they wouldn't. The seconds ticked away.

Mary Marie Brenner paused, placed the cake on a deep windowsill, and checked her watch. As with all surprise parties timing was important. Her contact had stressed that—and she didn't want to screw up. In spite of the fact that she had participated in the WTO demonstrations, and even spent a night in jail, the inner core of the group to which Brenner belonged had never fully accepted her. Perhaps that was because her father was vice president of marketing for one of the very companies that her friends held responsible for the economic and cultural colonization of the third world. Or maybe it was her tendency to come on a little too strong. Whatever the reason, she had yet to bond with the other members of the group and desperately wanted to do so. Now, with the invitation to play a key role in a counter-culture celebration of Aspee's birthday, it seemed that she had finally been accepted.

Brenner removed the book of matches from her pocket, lit each of the twenty-four candles, and continued down the hall. A man and a woman were approaching her but they looked like visitors. Brenner saw an empty chair, a cart loaded with gowns, and the isolation sign. But where was the crowd? The other members of the group? The people from the media? Perhaps it was a large room and the guests were inside. Brenner imagined how impressive her entrance would be and was singing, "Happy birthday to you, happy birthday to you," as she approached the door.

Rossi saw the empty chair, wondered where the cop was, and began to walk faster. In the meantime Brenner balanced the cake on one hand—and opened the door with the other. "FBI!" Rossi announced. "Hold it right there!"

But it was too late. The gasoline fumes found the flames. The resulting explosion blew Brenner out into the hall and Aspee's room was transformed into a raging inferno.

Operating more on the basis of instinct rather than a plan, Brenner fought her way to her feet, heard a man shout, "FBI! Stop or I'll shoot!" and started to run.

Kissler raised his Glock. Rossi yelled "No!" but a red flower blossomed between Brenner's shoulder blades.

The 10mm slug threw the protester forward. She landed face down and slid across the highly polished floor. A fire alarm went off, sprinklers came on, and a visitor screamed. Rossi took one look at the fire raging in Aspee's room, knew there was no way that the terrorist could have survived, and ran down the hall. A quick check confirmed what she already knew—the suspect was dead.

Kissler approached from behind. His face was pale and his weapon was pointed at the floor. "Is she dead?"

Rossi stood. "I'm afraid so."

Kissler looked worried. "You saw what happened, right?"

"I saw you shoot a woman with a birthday cake—if that's what you mean."

"But *you* ordered her to stop!"

"True," Rossi replied wearily, "but I don't shoot everyone that I order to stop."

"What's going to happen now?"

"You remember the shooting review board you asked about?" Rossi inquired. "Well, you're about to get one of your very own."

In spite of the fact that it had once been *called* Chinatown, and did boast some Chinese restaurants, Seattle's International District had become more Asian than Chinese over the previous fifty years, and had never been on a par with similar neighborhoods in San Francisco or New York. It wasn't all that large for one thing, nor very colorful, although the old brick buildings did have a sort of brooding quality, as if they had secrets to hide—which some certainly did.

Still, even allowing for that, the International District clung to its traditional ways—some of which were good, like efforts to start new businesses, and some which were bad, like the criminal class that preyed on would-be entrepreneurs. Men like Kango, Hippo, and Weed. Their job was to ensure that bad things happened to bad people—which was to say anyone who got in the way of Sam Chow's business interests.

Except that things were complicated sometimes, like when Mr. Chow became upset with his son and sent his heavies to bring the young man in. A no-win situation if there ever was one, especially given the fact that the old man was sick and Joe Chow was going to inherit the family business. But that was the sort of thing Kango was good at—just one of the reasons why the others were happy to follow his lead.

The black Lincoln Navigator was spotlessly clean and boasted tinted windows. The suspension gave slightly as Hippo hoisted his three hundred–plus pounds up into the front passenger seat. He had a half-eaten HoHo in one hand and a Diet Pepsi in the other. "So?" Kango demanded. "What did you find out?"

Hippo swallowed the last of the HoHo, washed the mess down with a Diet Pepsi chaser, and wiped his fat fingers on his meaty thighs. He had a shaved head, moon face, and slit eyes. "He's home alright," Hippo proclaimed. "The guy who owns the convenience store saw him arrive about 5:00 A.M."

Kango was fifty-seven years old and still wore a fifties style ducktail haircut. His hair was so black that everyone assumed it was dyed. He wore shades on cloudy days, rarely smiled, and had personally popped seven men. "Is anyone with him?"

Hippo belched. "Yeah," the big man replied. "A woman. The same bitch he's been using for the last couple of months."

Weed flicked a Bic lighter on and off. It was an annoying habit, but part of a laudable attempt to stop smoking so Kango let it go. Weed had acne scars, nicotine-stained teeth, and a rail-thin body. "How 'bout his bodyguards?" the thin man wanted to know. "How many will we have to deal with?"

"There's two of them," Hippo answered. "One at the bottom of the stairs—and one outside of little Chow's front door."

"Okay," Kango said thoughtfully. "Good work. Here's the plan. They don't know Weed, so he goes in first. Then, while he talks to the first guard, the rest of us enter. He'll have a radio so grab it. And remember, don't hurt the bastard, because when big Chow croaks we'll be working for Joe. Once the first guard is out of the way Weed will head up upstairs and we run the same drill again. Questions? No? Then let's get this over with."

Doors opened and slammed in quick succession as the snakeheads sauntered up the street. Curtains in the surrounding second- and third-story apartments started to close, people scurried in off the streets, and the entire population of Chinatown became deaf, dumb, and blind, because while the police weren't far away, no one trusted them, and there were plenty of things to be afraid of, like tips to Immigration and Customs Enforcement (ICE), beatings, and mysterious fires.

The curtains were drawn so that Joe Chow could sleep, and that meant it was murky inside the messy second-floor apartment where Lena Ling lived in virtual slavery. She had long black hair, a small heart-shaped face, and a very shapely body. And that was just as her grandmother had said that it would be—a blessing and a curse. A blessing, because her body had been her ticket out of China, and a curse because of the way in which it was being used. The present user, clad only in boxer shorts, said something unintelligible and rolled onto his side.

Ling lit one cigarette off the butt of another, drew the comforting smoke deep into her lungs, and let it dribble out through her nostrils. She treasured such moments since they were the only times when she could be herself instead of a well-dressed accessory, or what Joe Chow often referred to as his "fuck toy."

And, not having a life of her own, Ling liked to borrow her sister's. Because, thanks to the bargain that Lena had agreed to back in Hong Kong, her sister May Ling was a student at the University of Southern California—something made possible by the younger girl's facility with the English language, a well-executed identity theft, and a number of well-placed bribes. May would graduate in four years, which was when Lena would be free. Until then, the older girl liked to imagine what it would be like to live in the California sun, go to classes with the sons and daughters of movie stars, and prepare for a life of wealth and privilege. And that's where she was, walking across an imaginary campus, when Hippo hit the front door with his shoulder, and it shattered, pieces of wood flew in every direction and Ling screamed.

Like his father Joe Chow had enemies, lots of them, which was why he slept with a .9mm Browning High Power. But the pistol had migrated during the night and Chow was still in the process of searching for it when Kango placed a hand on his back and pressed downwards. "There's no need for a gun, Joe…. Your father sent us. He wants to speak with you."

Chow swore into the rumpled sheets and rolled out of bed. He was tall, about six-two, muscular, and heavily tattooed. A highly stylized python occupied most of his hairless chest. It had a widely flared hood, a long, thin tongue, and ruby-red eyes. The snakehead could have lived rent-free in one of his father's properties, but had chosen to have his own place instead, and didn't like the way in which his hard-won independence was being violated. "Couldn't the old bastard call? And why break the door down? You could knock for Christ's sake."

Kango spread his hands. "I'm sorry Joe, I really am, but you know the old man. He left a message, waited for you to call, and when nothing happened he ordered us to pay you a visit. A *noisy* visit. It ain't nothing personal. You know that."

Chow had known Kango his entire life. That, plus the conciliatory tone and the reference to his father's foibles served to cool his temper. A jumble of clothing, fast food containers, and other detritus covered the floor. He went fishing for some pants, came up with a pair of reasonably clean pair, and started to pull them on. "You were lucky I didn't find that gun.... Where would my father find another old fart like you? Especially one who looks like a Chinese Elvis Presley?"

Kango smiled. The insults, which were intended to restore some of the face that Joe had lost, were a cheap price to pay for his future well-being.

Little Chow was ready five minutes later. He eyed Lena Ling. She was still on the bed, still smoking a cigarette, and still half-dressed. "I'll be gone for a while," he said emotionlessly. "Get up and clean this apartment. If you get hungry you can lick the sheets. They have some of my cum on them."

That elicited a hearty guffaw from Weed who was staring at the scantily clad girl with open lust. Kango saw the danger, ordered Weed and Hippo out of the apartment, and followed Chow down into the street where the SUV idled by the curb. Doors slammed, the motor purred, and the entire neighborhood let out a sigh of relief as the snakeheads left the area—but not unobserved because even as they left, an ICE agent continued to snap photographs from an apartment on the other side of the street.

Ling peered through what remained of her front door, saw that one of Joe's bodyguards had been left to keep an eye on her, and turned away. Maybe, if she was fast enough, there would be enough time to tidy up the apartment *and* take a bath before her owner returned. But, even if there was, the young woman knew it wouldn't make any difference. Scrub though she might, Lena Ling would never be clean again.

The penthouse occupied the entire top floor of the twenty-story Chow building. It was located on First Avenue, just a few blocks south of Seattle's Public Market, and offered a sweeping view of Elliott Bay. It was vista that Sam Chow never tired of, partly because of the ships that came and went, and because of how beautiful the sunsets were, and partly because the gunmetal gray water held special meaning for him.

It had been chilly on that June night in 1947 when he had slipped over the side of the old *Singapore Star*, and swam through the inky black brine to a floating landing stage. Once there he had been forced to wait in the cold water for what felt like an hour before the night watchman left to take a pee.

And it had been then, while a fat Caucasian emptied his bladder, that the United States of America received its newest citizen. Not an *official* citizen, that ceremony wouldn't occur until many years later, but a citizen nonetheless. It was the realization of a dream conceived after the Japanese captured Hong Kong during World War II, slaughtered Chow's parents, and left a young boy to fend for himself, not as the son of privilege that he had originally been, but as a coolie, working on the docks. It was there that the teenager came to understand ships, and after many months of careful planning, hid himself deep in a fetid hold. For that was his single-minded ambition, to travel to America, and become very rich. How didn't matter.

There was a gentle *bong* as the white-jacketed Vietnamese boy who served as Chow's majordomo tapped a large, richly decorated gong, and thereby summoned the old man back to the present. "Your son here. You like refreshments?"

Chow touched a control and a motor whirred. His wheelchair turned a tight circle. It, like everything else in the penthouse, was the best that money could buy. The old man released the green oxygen mask and let it dangle. "No. Send him in."

The boy bowed in a show of old-world respect and withdrew.

Though relatively small, the reception area was nicely decorated. Stylized dragons dominated the red, black, and gold foil wallpaper and the silk-covered couch, which fronted a spectacular aquarium. Except, rather than the fish that most people would expect to see, this enclosure was home to a five-foot long Black Headed Python. It was currently rather torpid, having recently consumed a rat, and was draped over an artfully placed limb—all of which was lost on Joe Chow, who felt mixed emotions as he waited to be shown into his father's home. Resentment that stemmed from the way he had been treated, impatience, because he didn't like to wait, and fear, because Samuel Chow was a ruthless man.

Never, not so long as Joe Chow lived, would he forget the day fifteen years before when he had been forced to watch while Sam Chow slit one of his competitor's throats. "You must cut deep," the old man explained, "or risk running into the bastard out on the street!"

The doors swung open, the majordomo bowed, and Joe did what he could to project an aura of confidence that he didn't feel as he entered what he thought of as the museum. The room was a study in carefully chosen colors, strategically placed furniture, and valuable art. A piece of Neolithic pottery rested on a sleek, black stand, a vessel from the Shang Dynasty stood on a well-lit shelf, and a two-foot tall Ming burial horse stood with one foot eternally lifted. And there were paintings, too, including important works by the likes of Chen Chun, Chang Da-chien, and Tang Yin. All perfectly illuminated, staged, and juxtaposed.

But what *really* dominated the room were dozens of snakes. Wood snakes, brass snakes, and bronze snakes that slithered across the walls, sat coiled on tabletops, and twisted their way up chair legs, because Sam Chow had been born in 1929, which along with 1917, 1941, 1953, 1965, 1977, 1989, and 2001 was the year of the snake, a portent the old man took very seriously indeed.

The snakes were cool, but the rest of the furnishings were junk insofar as Joe was concerned, and he would sell them one day. He bowed long enough to convey his respect and straightened again. In spite of the fact that his father's face looked gaunt and his color was bad, the old man still looked formidable. Thanks to the multiple layers of clothing that he wore, and the bulk of the chair he sat in, he looked larger than he actually was. "So," Chow senior said disapprovingly, "they found you."

"I was asleep," Joe replied resentfully. "What's so important that it couldn't wait for a few hours?"

"*Everything* is important," Sam Chow responded sternly. "Rapidity is the essence of war."

The younger man sighed. He had been raised on such quotes. "Sun Tzu."

"Yes," the old man hissed, "and Sun Tzu was right. Things happen quickly these days and the quicker we respond the more likely victory is! Have you seen this morning's paper? No, of course you haven't…. You were asleep. Go ahead. The article is on page two."

Joe saw that a copy of the *Post Intelligencer* had been placed on the coffee table in front of the couch. He sat down, opened the paper, and scanned the second page. The sub-head, "Body Found," quickly caught his eye. A quick read revealed that the body of an Asian male had washed up near Port Angeles. There were no signs of trauma, so in spite of the fact that the John Doe had been dressed in a marine survival suit, hypothermia was the presumed cause of death. An unfortunate occurrence, but not unheard of, especially given the number of ships and fishing boats that traveled through the Strait. What struck local authorities as strange was the fact that no one had been reported missing. The Coast Guard had been notified, and efforts were underway to contact ships that had passed through the area forty-eight hours prior to the discovery, but no one had come forward with useful information.

Joe felt something cold trickle into the pit of his stomach but knew better than to let any of the uncertainty he felt register on his face. He tossed the paper aside, leaned back onto the couch, and braced his Air Jordans against the antique map table. "So?" he said disdainfully, confident that his father's technicians would have found listening devices if there were any. "They have nothing! The survival suits are untraceable, I made sure of that, and the rest of the cargo is safe."

Sam Chow started to speak, felt a distinct shortness of breath, and was forced to take three long pulls from the oxygen mask before he could continue. His tone was conciliatory but firm. "Let's say you're correct, and I truly hope that you are. The man who washed ashore was worth fifty thousand dollars…. That's how much money our clients would have paid for his services.

"Yes, we're bound to lose some inventory during shipping, but the Triads hope to move humans *with* their drugs, and we must operate more efficiently than they do. Hard work, entrepreneurship, and increased productivity. That's what makes America great. Are we agreed?"

Joe heard the change in tone, and knew his father was right about the increasingly aggressive gangs called Triads, which were typically based in Hong Kong but were busy expanding their operations into North America. He lowered his sneakers to the floor by way of a concession. "Yeah, Pop. We're agreed."

"Good," Chow senior replied. "*Everything* will belong to you soon, and I want you to succeed."

"Yeah, I know that."

"Will you stay for lunch?"

"No," Joe said as he came to his feet. "I have work to do."

Sam Chow knew it wasn't true, but had been expecting the reply, and kept his face empty of emotion. "Joi gin." *Goodbye.*

"Joi gin," Joe Chow said carelessly as he made his way to the door. "I'll see you later."

Sam Chow watched the doors close behind his only child, allowed himself a heartfelt sigh, and turned his chair back towards the bay. A container ship had nosed its way into the harbor from the north—and had already started to lose speed as a tug went out to meet it. There weren't very many *real* stowaways anymore but a few got through. Young men armed with little more than their wits, a desire to succeed, and a large share of courage. Perhaps one such individual was hidden aboard the newly arrived freighter. If so, the old man wished him luck.

# Chapter Three

Strangely enough, in a city known for gray days and incessant rain, the day of the funerals was sunny and clear, a boon for the hundreds of media types sent to cover the memorial service for the FBI agents who had been killed in the line of duty.

Helicopters circled Capital Hill like a flock of mechanical vultures, streets had been blocked off so that the hundred-plus vehicle procession could make its way up to the Lake View Cemetery, and specially trained elements of the SPD, the FBI's elite Hostage Rescue Team (HRT), and various branches of the military stood ready to respond should the ELA or a similar organization attempt to disrupt the proceedings.

Rossi, along with Kissler and Qwan, rode in Theel's sedan. The atmosphere inside the car was subdued, but the fact that Kissler was scheduled to go in front of a Shooting Review Board added to the sense of gloom. Theel made attempts at conversation, but met with little more than grunts of acknowledgement, he soon gave up. Qwan turned on the radio, happened on play-by-play coverage of the funeral procession, and turned it off.

Meanwhile, in the car ahead of them, Amy Haxton had little choice but to listen as her boss, Harley Demont, offered some "impressions." Nothing overt, nothing that could be construed as an old-fashioned order, but "suggestions" that were binding nevertheless. He was a relatively small man, who though in denial where his incipient baldness was concerned, kept himself in excellent shape. He had flown in the day before—and planned to be gone by nightfall. "So," Demont continued, "those are my impressions, what do you think?"

*I think you're an overly ambitious asshole who would run over his own mother if she got in the way of your career,* Haxton thought to herself, but knew better than to say so. "Yes, the amount of media hype focused on Rossi is likely to have an impact on her near-term effectiveness, but let's be fair.... She did a great job that night—and she has an outstanding record. Did you look at her file? This is a woman who spent an entire year on an undercover assignment, received an Award for Meritorious Service from the Director, and gets consistently high marks from her boss."

"As a matter of fact I *did* pull her jacket," Demont responded smoothly. "And I noticed something else as well.... Agent Rossi has a degree in Computer Science from Berkeley. A rather significant asset."

Haxton sighed. "I'm wasting my time aren't I? The decision has already been made."

Demont smiled engagingly. "Not true, Amy, it's your call. The purpose of my comment was to identify an alternative, an assignment that would take the heat off Rossi and allow her to spend more time with her daughter."

There it was. The dot over the "i" in Rossi. End of discussion. If Haxton continued to argue in favor of retaining Rossi on her team she would appear thick-headed not to mention uncooperative. "Okay," the ASAC answered reluctantly. "You make some good points. Especially where Rossi's private life is concerned."

"Glad I could help," Demont replied smugly. "Let me know what *you* decide."

The better part of an hour passed as the motorcade made its way up onto the north end of Capitol Hill, turned left onto 15th Avenue, and rolled passed the park.

That's when the cars stopped, and the passengers got out and followed guides into the lush green cemetery. Reporters were present, hundreds of them, but weren't allowed to enter. The TV crews had long lenses and Rossi could feel them zooming in on her as they took the opportunity to roll the human torch footage one more time.

The cemetery was relatively small as such things go, but enjoyed a commanding view of Lake Union, and had been chosen as the final resting place for Bruce Lee and other notables. A covered platform had been established on a rise.

The mourners wore color-coded name tags that determined how

close to the platform they would be allowed to get. They were herded into somberly clad squads, platoons, and companies, all according to their relationship with the deceased. Due to their status as co-workers, Theel, Rossi, Kissler, and Qwan were led up toward the front of the assemblage and invited to sit in the third row of folding chairs.

It was a moving service, complete with bagpipes, hymns, and a series of well-spoken eulogies. As Rossi turned to leave, someone touched her arm. The FBI agent turned to find Holly Nealy standing next to her. Tall and thin, the blonde had a regal quality. Even now, at the center of a media circus, she appeared calm and poised. She wore sunglasses which she removed. Her eyes were red from crying and her voice was brittle. "Christina, just one thing before you go."

Rossi swallowed. "Of course…. Anything."

"Val and I wanted you to know how much we appreciate what you did. There isn't anything that can bring our husbands back—but it helps to know their killers are dead. Thank you." Then, as her lower lip started to quiver, Nealy turned away.

Rossi knew the other woman meant well, that the message was intended to make her feel better, but she felt empty instead. There were things she was proud of, Missy being the foremost example, but killing people wasn't one of them.

Rossi turned, hurried to catch up with the others, and was just about to enter Theel's sedan when Haxton appeared. Demont was at her side and they wore matching smiles. "Christina! Just the person I was looking for. Are you in this afternoon? You are? Good. Could we meet at 3:00 P.M.? There's something I'd like to talk to you about."

Rossi promised to be there and entered the car. She wanted to ask Theel if he knew what the ASAC had in mind, but the fact that other agents were present kept her from doing so, and her supervisor performed a quick fade the moment they arrived at the office. The morning was over, there was plenty to do, and time passed quickly. Haxton was already at her desk when Rossi followed Theel into her office. The door closed with a definitive "click." Rossi eyed Theel but the SSA refused to meet her gaze. That's when her suspicions were confirmed. Something was up and John knew she wouldn't like it.

Haxton said, "Let's sit somewhere more comfortable," and headed for the eight-foot-long couch that one of her predecessors had installed against the long wall. A few moments later Rossi found herself sinking into the couch's floral embrace, while wishing that she could sit on a regular chair. Haxton smiled serenely. "Well, I'm sure you're wondering what this is all about, so I'll cut to the chase. You did an excellent job on the ECODOOM case, everyone agrees on that, but we have a new opportunity for you. A case that will not only take advantage of your degree in Computer Science—but allow you to spend more time with Mary."

Rossi frowned. "The terrorist thing is starting to heat up, I haven't worked on computers for years, and her name is *Missy*. But that doesn't matter does it? You want me off ECODOOM."

Haxton sighed. *Damn it to hell… Why couldn't Demont do his own dirty work? Because he didn't want to that's why.* She leaned forward. "That isn't true Christina…I don't want you off the case. But, perhaps I should. For your sake as well as the team's. Let's be honest. You can't buy a pair of socks without television crews following you to the store—not to mention your influence on the other agents."

Theel winced. He had warned Haxton not to go there and now she had. It was like launching a gob of spit into the wind. The whole mess was about to smack the ASAC in the face. "My 'influence on other agents?'" Rossi demanded coldly. "What are you talking about?"

Haxton looked at Theel. "John?"

Theel looked down at his tasseled loafers and back up again. It required effort to turn and meet her eyes. "The Shooting Review Board is coming up in a couple of days. Kissler had to meet with the shrink. It turns out that he may have been trying to make an impression on you when he shot Brenner."

There was a moment of silence. Rossi broke it. Her voice had a steely quality. "Let me see if I understand. Kissler wants to get in my pants, so he shoots someone, and *I* get the boot."

"*No*," Haxton said emphatically, "it isn't like that. A number of factors came into play and Kevin was one of them. This is a good opportunity, a case where they really need your help, and you can make a difference."

Theel nodded. His concern was plain to see. "Amy's right, Christina. We need you on the case. You won't be sorry."

Rossi looked from one superior to the other. "The case...what is it?

"We call it SNAKE EYE," Haxton answered.

"Which refers to?"

"Which refers to the people who specialize in bringing illegal aliens into the country from Asia," Theel replied soberly. "A slimy bunch commonly referred to as snakeheads."

"Except that you're going to be part of an interagency team going after *the* snakehead," Haxton put in. "A naturalized citizen named Sam Chow."

Rossi frowned. "The guy who funds the big New Year's Eve fireworks display every year?"

"That's the one," Theel acknowledged. "He also owns a trucking line, a fishing fleet, and a lot of real estate. The problem is that his other business activities aren't so pretty. Like human trafficking, extortion, and murder."

"Okay," Rossi said as she came to her feet. "Is there anything else?"

Theel looked at Haxton and back again. "No, I guess there isn't. I'll put you in touch with your team leader tomorrow morning."

"Understood," Rossi said. "I'll see you tomorrow."

The other agents watched her leave. "So," Haxton said brightly, "that went well, don't you think?"

Theel tried to come up with a tactful response and failed. He rose from the couch. "Amy, for an intelligent woman, you sure are stupid sometimes." And with that he left the room.

Rossi made her way to her cubicle, retrieved her things, and headed for the elevators. Other people were in the area but none of them yelled insults from the far side of the office or ran up to ask questions as they usually did. That was because word of Rossi's reassignment had already spread, and being unsure of how she would react, her peers were laying low. The elevator bonged, the agent entered, and the door closed. *And how am I going to react to the assignment?* Rossi asked herself as the car began to descend.

In spite of Haxton and Theel's best efforts to make the SNAKE EYE case sound important, it probably wasn't. Not compared to ECODOOM. But so what? People received new assignments every day. Some of them were happy and some weren't. They managed to deal with it and so would she.

The agent continued to think about the situation as she entered the garage and got into her car. Here was the sort of thing that she and Ed would have spent hours discussing back when their relationship was intact. And that was what she missed most, having someone to share things with, someone who cared. The FBI agent was still making her way through downtown traffic when her cell phone chirped. She picked it up. "Rossi here."

There was a moment of silence followed by the sound of screams and gunshots. It was confusing as first, then the FBI agent recognized the sounds and knew she was listening to audio from the shootout at the University of Washington. There was an audible *click* as the recording ended followed by the sound of dial-tone. She might be finished with the ELA—but it seemed as if they weren't done with her.

Dexter's office was located just off the brand new lobby. It consisted of a small waiting area, a desk for the secretary/receptionist that he hadn't hired yet, and a glassed-in area for himself. With his back to some nearly empty bookcases and a custom-made credenza, he could look across the surface of his gleaming rosewood desk to a pair of very expensive guest chairs and the window beyond. The blinds were open, which meant that he could see out onto the street where pedestrians battled a stiff breeze. Most were dressed in brightly colored REI parkas, heavy overcoats, and puffy ski jackets. Not a good time of year for girl watching.

The door to the outer office sung open, but rather than one of the tenants, the man who entered was Dexter's only employee. His name was Pasco, John Pasco, and his job was to keep the newly remodeled building in tip-top shape. The retired chief petty officer had silvery hair, a matching mustache, and wore khakis similar to those he had been required to wear in the Navy. The noncom had been in charge of maintenance for an entire hospital prior to wrapping up his twenty five-year career—which meant he had more than enough expertise to keep the Bayview Apartment complex going.

The problem, if there was one, had to do with Pasco's personality. He was rarely seen without a cell phone nestled next to his ear and had an unfortunate tendency to be both evasive and nosy. Or were such judgments premature? Good maintenance people were hard to find—and it would be best to wait and see. Pasco had just completed a telephone conversation as he entered the inner office. He flipped the phone closed and returned the device to his belt with all the panache of a gunfighter returning his pistol to its holster. The chair sighed as it accepted his weight. Dexter nodded. "Good afternoon, Chief... How's it going?"

In spite of repeated invitations to address his employer by his first name, Pasco insisted on calling the ex-officer "sir." His eyes made contact with Dexter's and slid away. "Pretty well, sir. The plumbing contractor is here...and he needs access to 6A."

Up until that point Dexter had insisted on letting workmen into 6A himself, lest someone accidentally discover the two-way mirror, but that was silly. The only way to access the other side was via the closet off his bedroom. And, judging from the other man's demeanor, Pasco was getting curious. The maintenance man had keys to all the other units... What made 6A so special?

Dexter opened a side drawer and rummaged through a box of carefully tagged keys. "Here," the businessman said, as he slid a key across the surface of his desk. "Add this to your collection."

Pasco looked slightly surprised, as if he expected some resistance, but was quick to recover. "Yes, sir. Can I meet with you later? I have invoices for you to sign."

The outer door opened to admit an Asian couple. Dexter nodded. "Sure, chief... How does fourteen hundred sound?"

That'll be fine, sir," the retired petty officer said, and turned to leave.

Dexter was on his feet by then and followed Pasco out to meet his prospective tenants. The man was tall, well put together, and wore casual clothes—expensive stuff that the ex-naval officer would never have been willing to try on much less buy. The woman looked younger, wore very little for such a cold winter day, and could only be described as beautiful. A quality that made her perfect for the viewing room. "Hello!" Dexter said as he extended his hand. "My name is Jack Dexter. I own the Bayview."

"Chow," the other man responded economically, giving the

businessman's hand a single rather unenthusiastic pump. "*Joe Chow.*"

The name was delivered with a very slight emphasis—as if Dexter should be familiar with it. The ex-naval officer wasn't but that didn't stop him from pretending to be. "Yes! Of course! You're here to look at unit 6A."

Since Chow hadn't seen fit to introduce his beautiful companion Dexter assumed they weren't married. Even though she was dressed like a street whore the woman was surprisingly asexual. The businessman thought it best to be courteous and extended his hand. "I'm Jack Dexter, and you are?"

"She doesn't speak English," Chow stated brusquely.

"Yes, well, please take a seat," Dexter responded awkwardly. "I have some literature for you to take a look at...plus a lease if you're interested."

Both guests had taken their seats by the time Dexter made it around to the other side of the desk. The woman lit a cigarette, only to have it appropriated by Chow, forcing her to light another. Dexter didn't like smokers, but knew $2,500 per month was steep, and that people with that sort of money didn't want to hear the word "no." He opened a drawer, removed the candy dish that he'd been meaning to fill, and pushed it across the desk.

The girl's skirt was so short that it barely hit mid-thigh when she was standing and went even higher when she sat. The ex-officer caught a glimpse of red panties as she crossed her legs and looked up to discover that Chow was grinning. "She looks good, doesn't she?" the snakehead observed.

It was a strange thing to say, and since the girl's expression remained the same, Dexter assumed that she hadn't understood. "Yes," the ex-naval officer admitted uncomfortably, "she does. Here's a copy of the floor plan, a copy of our standard lease, and a list of the building's amenities. We have underground parking by the way—that's a big plus downtown."

Chow exhaled a column of smoke but left the paperwork untouched. "No offense—but why stare at a floor plan if we can see the apartment?"

"Why indeed," Dexter said agreeably. "Let's go up and take a look."

The businessman followed his prospective tenants out into the lobby and pushed the elevator button. There was a chime as the polished metal doors parted. "It requires a key card to enter the building after 6:00 P.M.," Dexter explained. "And you need the same device to operate the elevator. We have cameras on every floor—and they are monitored around the clock."

"That's good," Chow allowed, as he dropped his cigarette onto the elevator's highly polished floor and stepped on it. "We had a burglary at my present apartment. They broke the door down…. We're looking for something more secure."

"You won't have that sort of problem here," Dexter assured him. "Our doors are made of metal—and they're fireproof to boot."

Chow uttered what might have been a grunt of approval as the elevator came to a smooth stop and the doors parted to reveal a marble-topped table that bore a handsome flower arrangement. The snakehead exited first, followed by Ling, and then Dexter. While it was true that the young woman's knowledge of English was less than perfect, she had been honing her linguistic skills by watching daytime television, and was momentarily hopeful. Ling hated the Chinatown apartment and hoped Chow would move into something better.

Two doors were visible—one at each end of the short hall. "That's 6A," Dexter said, pointing to the right. "It has a wonderful view of the bay."

"Who lives in the other apartment?" Chow wanted to know.

"*I* do," the businessman replied, "which means that the person who takes 6A will have a good neighbor."

It was meant to be a joke but Chow didn't laugh as he allowed himself to be ushered into the apartment where Pasco and a plumber were hard at work in the kitchen. It featured top-of-the-line stainless steel appliances, dark granite counters, and maple cabinets. The first Instahot water heater had broken down within a matter of days so a second unit was being installed. "We're still adding a few finishing touches," Dexter explained, "but the apartment will be available by Friday."

Chow ignored the workmen, drifted out into the sunken living room, and found himself looking at an unobstructed view of Elliott Bay. Though not as high as his father's condominium, the view was every bit as good, and that pleased him. The snakehead knew that a Feng Shui master would have commented on the fact that *chi*, or positive energy, would flow well through the space, but was determined to ignore his father's old-world superstition. "I'll take it," Chow proclaimed. "How much?"

Dexter, who was used to waiting through a good deal of hemming and hawing while people made up their minds, was pleasantly surprised. "That's wonderful! I'll need the first and last months' rent plus a one-thousand-dollar damage deposit. Would you like to see the rest of the unit?"

"Yeah, sure," Chow replied, but the snakehead's mind was already made up as he stuck his head into a couple of smaller rooms prior to entering the master suite. Not only was it huge, it boasted a nice view of downtown, and an oversized mirror on the wall opposite the spot where a bed would go. Chow imagined what it would be like to screw Ling from behind while he watched her face in the mirror. He felt his penis start to harden and knew he had made the right choice.

Ling knew it was important to maintain her makeup and took the opportunity to peer into the mirror. She recognized the face as being hers—but the eyes belonged to someone else.

The rain was so fine that it accumulated on the windshield as a thousand tiny dots, all of which were swept away by a single swipe of Rossi's wipers as the agent made a hard right-hand turn into the SEACON terminal. It consisted of a vast concrete wasteland presided over by orange cranes so tall that they dwarfed the white, green, and blue cargo containers stacked around their skeletal legs. The lunch that the FBI agent had prepared for her daughter slid across the passenger seat, bounced off the door, and tumbled to the floor. Missy had intentionally or unintentionally forgotten to grab the brown paper sack as she bailed out of the car in front of her school, and Rossi hadn't noticed in time, a mistake that the hyper-efficient Vanessa would never be guilty of.

Rossi was still fussing over her own inadequacies as the tractor trailer rig in front of her slowed and then stopped next to a small guard station. Security was a big concern in the Port of Seattle, and had been ever since 9/11.

Rossi pulled forward as the truck cleared the check point. She offered the uniformed security guard her credentials and was pleased to see that the man took the time required to compare the photo with her face. If he was impressed by the badge, there was no outward indication of it. He nodded politely. "Good morning, ma'am. How can I help you?"

Rossi consulted the fax that the SNAKE EYE team leader had sent her. "I'm meeting some people at SEACON B-4. Which way do I go?"

The guard gave some concise directions, and the agent followed them through a maze of stacked cargo containers and entered an open area. Yellow crime tape had been used to mark off one of the big forty-foot-long shipping containers. Patches of red rust had corrupted the gray paint and were nibbling at the four-foot tall letters that spelled "SEACON." A thick black cable led from a diesel generator to the isolated shipping container. It seemed like an odd location for a meeting, but given the presence of some sedans with tax-exempt plates, Rossi figured she was in the right place. That impression was reinforced when she saw the small group of people who stood talking under a blue awning.

Conscious of the fact that she was running ten minutes late, the agent parked in the first available slot, got out, and hurried across the worn concrete to the spot where the crime tape barred her way. She lifted the plastic ribbon high enough to slip underneath and was halfway across the open area beyond when a man came out to meet her. He wore a big hat, with a western cut gray suit and fancy boots. His face was brown, as if he had spent a lot of time out in the sun, and the sunglasses he normally wore had left white ovals around pale blue eyes. The man grinned and stuck out his hand. It was large, warm, and firm. "I'm Hawkins. You must be Rossi."

Based on what she'd been able to learn from the unofficial network that binds federal law enforcement officers together, the FBI agent knew that Assistant Special Agent in Charge Dale Hawkins was not only a customs agent, but a legendary customs agent, who had spent most of the last twenty years working to slow if not halt the flow of illegal aliens into the southern United States. There was something about his no-bullshit style that Rossi liked. She smiled in return. "Yes, I'm Christina Rossi. Sorry I'm late. It won't happen again."

The ASAC released her hand. "No problem. I figured the bureau would send me a rookie, a pencil pusher, or some old geezer who was coasting to retirement. You can't imagine how happy I was when they assigned a *real* agent to the team. Someone who can think, act, *and* shoot if it comes to that."

Rossi was used to receiving more criticism than praise and couldn't help but feel complimented, especially since her built-in bullshit detector hadn't gone off. "Thank you, Agent Hawkins. I'm glad to be here."

"Call me Hawk, or hey asshole," the customs agent said breezily. "Everyone else does. Come on. I want you to meet the rest of the team."

The rest of the team consisted of a crisp-looking Coast Guard Lieutenant named Tom Olman, Immigration and Customs Enforcement (ICE) agents Olivia Inez, Chuck Hagger, and Ellen Moller, plus a Seattle Police Detective named George Tolley. Some were already working on the illegal immigrant problem on behalf of their various agencies. All were pleasant, but reserved, as if waiting to see how the FBI agent would square with the media hype.

"All right," Hawkins said once the introductions had been made, "let's get to work. If you would be so kind as to step inside the cargo container we'll start the meeting."

Tolley was an African-American with a receding hairline, wire-rimmed glasses, and a ready smile. He motioned for Rossi to enter the metal box ahead of him. "I believe that FBI agents should always enter dark cargo containers *before* members of the Seattle Police Department."

Rossi made a face at the policeman and entered the box. The agent noticed that a table and chairs had been set up in the middle of the floor. She wondered why the enclosure smelled so bad, but was then startled when the door slammed closed. Total darkness was accompanied by the sound of Hawk's voice. "Welcome to SEACON container 7306, ladies and gentlemen. Please remain right where you are. If you have had the pleasure of visiting Hong Kong, you saw hundreds, maybe thousands of containers like this one as the train carried you from the airport to Central. Mountains of boxes frequently protected by little more than a cyclone fence. About eight million of these suckers enter the U.S. each year— and only six percent of them are inspected.

"Now, I want you to imagine that you were one of the eighteen Chinese nationals who were loaded into this particular container. You were strangers to each other at first, but you had plenty of things in common. All of you were from the Chinese province of Fujian, which is located north of Hong Kong, and only one hundred miles from Taiwan. And you weren't the first to make such a journey. ICE estimates that more than two hundred thousand of your countrymen settled in the New York area alone during the last twenty years."

It had already become close in the container, *very* close, and the smell made it worse. Light splashed the ceiling as Hawkins produced a small flashlight and positioned the device directly below his chin. The glow made him look gruesome, and Rossi was reminded of a camping trip when she had used the same technique to tell Missy a ghost story. The then-third-grader had been scared all right, *too* scared to sleep, and cranky the next morning.

"You sat in container seven three oh six for five days waiting for it to be loaded," Hawkins continued. "Followed by two weeks at sea. You had a few flashlights, like this one, but the batteries ran out after a few days which left you to live in total darkness. What little fresh air there was came in through holes and the gaps around the doors. Some of you had the runs, others were seasick, and it didn't take long to fill the five-gallon buckets that served as toilets. A corner was designated as the john, but ships roll, so the mixture of feces, urine, and vomit had a tendency to slosh back and forth."

"And it was cold, *very* cold, with no way to generate heat. Rations consisted of rice, crackers, and water. The food ran out with a week left to go. So it was no surprise when people started to die. Three in all, leaving just fifteen of you huddled together, sealed in what might become your tomb. Finally, having been unloaded here in Seattle, the Americans found you. Or what was left of you, before they carted you off to jail."

Hawkins let the words hang there, giving each member of the team the time necessary to assimilate them before bringing a small radio up to his lips. "Okay, Larry. The horror show is over. Open the doors."

There was a *clang* as a vertical locking bar was released, followed by the squeal of unoiled hinges as a heretofore unseen agent pulled the double doors open. Daylight entered the container along with a welcome surge of fresh air. Rossi drew it deep into her lungs. Hawkins grinned knowingly. "Excuse the drama, folks. But my presentation lasted about two minutes. Imagine nineteen or twenty days of that."

Inez was short, petite, and pretty. "The sonovabitch is crazy," the ICE agent muttered darkly as the generator started to chatter outside. "I'll have to burn these clothes." Rossi laughed and realized that the other woman was correct. The combined odors of decaying flesh, raw sewage, and vomit would be hard if not impossible to get rid of. The blue suit was toast.

Portable lights had been hung inside the container and they came on as someone flipped a switch. "Okay, people," Hawkins said cheerfully. "Welcome to conference room seven three oh six. Take any seat that's open. While most of this is old news to some of you, the rest need to hear it, so listen up. The background stuff is on the CDs that have been prepared for you—so there's no need to take a whole lot of notes."

The customs agent withdrew a laser pointer from an inside pocket and projected a red dot onto the surface of a large, wall-mounted map. "I got most of my experience with human smuggling down in the southwest, but having just completed a crash course on Asian trafficking, I know just enough to be dangerous. As I mentioned earlier, a lot of the illegals who come through Vancouver and Seattle originate in Fujian province. It's about the size of Delaware. The capital city of Fuzhou is home to a *liudong renkou*, or floating population of a quarter million displaced farm workers who migrated there hoping to find work, but lack the skills and education necessary to get factory jobs.

"Having heard stories about life in the United States, which they commonly refer to as the 'Golden Mountain,' many displaced workers want to come here. And that makes sense since workers in Shanghai earn eight times what the folks in rural China do—and the average worker in the United States makes twenty times more than that! Which is why criminals called snakeheads have such an easy time signing them up to come here. Never mind the fact that the would-be immigrants have to borrow between fifty and sixty grand to buy their passage, then work eighty- to ninety-hour weeks to pay the money back, all at a wage of four to five bucks an hour. Oh yeah, and did I mention that the smugglers charge interest? It all adds up to what some experts say is an eight-billion-dollar per year business worldwide."

Hawkins paused to eye those in front of him. "Task Force SNAKE EYE can't put a stop to the trade—it's way too big for that—but we can sure as hell put a dent in it. And *this* particular bastard would be a good place to start."

The little red dot wobbled across the wall and came to rest on a poster-sized mug shot of an Asian male. "For those of you who aren't already acquainted with this piece of shit, his name is Sam Chow. Over the last thirty years he's been accused of everything from spitting on the sidewalk to premeditated murder. None of the charges have stuck. He's getting old now and plans to hand the business over to his son, but it ain't over till it's over."

"Has anyone tried going after him on taxes?" Rossi wanted to know. "Maybe the IRS could help."

"They nailed Al Capone," Hawkins agreed, "but no, Chow is too smart for that. Our guess is that profits generated from human trafficking are taken out of country where they are washed through seemingly legitimate corporations prior to being repatriated. Then he pays whatever taxes are owed and uses the remainder to buy more fishing boats for his fleet, trucks for his shipping company, and lots of real estate.

"So, having failed to nail him in the past, the powers-that-be decided to create a task force that will go after Chow the old-fashioned way. We'll put some pressure on the bastard, spook him if we can, and wait for him to make a mistake, which would be good, because the intelligence folks believe that the old man has developed a *new* way to smuggle illegals into the country by sea, but we haven't been able to figure out how. A body washed ashore a few days ago. An Asian male dressed in a survival suit. But there must have been more. *Lots* more. But where are they? We have a full-court press in place but nothing to show for it. Maybe this team can come up with the answer."

"It *sounds* good," Tolley allowed cynically, "but where do we start? The SPD has been chasing Chow for years without success."

When Hawkins smiled it had a predatory quality and Rossi felt a sudden sense of sympathy for the coyotes who worked the Mexican border. "That's simple, Detective Tolley," the customs agent replied.

"We'll go after Chow the same way we would go after *you*."

Tolley raised his eyebrows. "Which is?"

"Which is through your children," Hawkins answered coldly.

Rossi thought about how much she loved Missy, and judging from the expression on Tolley's face, knew that the detective felt the same way about *his* children.

"That's right," the ASAC said knowingly, "and consider *this*: The name *Chow* comes from *Zhou*, which means to encircle. And, as it happens, the Zhou Dynasty ruled China from ten twenty-seven to two twenty-one B.C. Something Sam Chow not only takes pride in, but continues to identify with, as he prepares to found a dynasty of his own.

"And that," Hawkins said, "brings us to *this* piece of shit." Rossi watched the red dot land on a second mug shot. "This is *Joe* Chow," the customs agent added, "also referred to as 'Little Chow' by the denizens of the International District. He is not only Sam Chow's right-hand man, but his heir apparent, and chance for immortality. That makes him the old geezer's weak spot, which is why Rossi is going to bug his apartment and see what we can find out about him. Isn't that right, Rossi?"

The FBI agent looked up at the mug shot and nodded her head. "Yes, sir. Assuming we can get a judge to sign the Title III paperwork and the proprietor will cooperate."

"He'd *better* cooperate," Inez put in mischievously, "or Rossi will shoot him."

Everyone laughed, and Rossi smiled, but her heart wasn't in it. The FBI agent could still see the flames, still smell the burning flesh, and still feel the gun bucking in her hands.

The meeting broke up two hours later, but the smell followed Rossi into the rain and all the way home. A bath took care of the odor in her hair, but not the loneliness that went with an empty house and a life focused almost entirely on work. She had her job but very little else. With Snowball on her lap, and CNN for company, Rossi fell asleep.

Careful not to make any noise Dexter entered his closet, pushed his carefully hung clothes out of the way, and slid the hidden door to one side. Then, with his heart beating a little faster than normal, the businessman peered through the window into the dimly lit bedroom next door. But there are problems associated with being a voyeur, not the least of which has to do with the fact that the victim or victims determine when they will be victimized.

The reality of that served to remind Dexter of the deep recons that he and his men had carried out along the border between Iraq and Iran. Long, often boring missions during which the SEALS spent up to six days waiting for bad guys to transit a remote mountain pass, hold a meeting in an isolated cave, or hunker down around a campfire. Of course they, just like Joe Chow and his mistress Lena Ling, frequently failed to show.

Once all the paperwork had been signed Joe Chow had moved into the Bayview apartments with surprising speed. A wave of brand new furniture had been followed by some starkly modern art and a dozen cardboard boxes. Hardly anything at all compared to the tons of stuff that most tenants trucked in.

Then, once his belongings had been unpacked by two well-coiffed interior designers, Chow and a small entourage of what Dexter took to be bodyguards arrived. That was problematical since the businessman didn't want renters who needed that kind of protection living in his building—not to mention the fact that at least two of the heavies could be found slouched in their employer's SUV at all hours of the day and night, a development that annoyed Pasco no end since the maintenance man regarded the parking garage as *his* turf.

Still, if Dexter was ready and waiting when Chow and Ling decided to enter the adjoining bedroom, then the subsequent show might be worth all the trouble. The couple were home, the businessman knew that, so he dropped into his easy chair and opened a book. It was *The Fermata*, by Nicholson Baker, which seemed perfect for the occasion. There were times when the missing leg felt as though it was still there, and for whatever reason, such was the case as the businessman began to read. The ex-SEAL was well into chapter eight, in which Marian finds interesting ways to entertain herself inside a UPS truck, when the lights came up and Ling was propelled into the room beyond the glass. The young woman stumbled, tripped, and fell.

Chow rounded the corner with a beer in his hand. He smiled, said something Dexter couldn't hear, and used his left hand to release his belt and pull it free. The ex-SEAL felt his stomach muscles tighten as the leather dangled next to the other man's leg.

Having placed the beer on a night stand, Chow went over to where Ling cowered on the floor. He grabbed a handful of the girl's thick black hair and jerked her up onto her feet. Then, having ordered her to remain there, the snakehead brought the belt around. The resulting *crack* was loud enough for the apartment house owner to hear through the interconnecting ventilation system. Dexter came to his feet. His hands were balled into fists. The strap struck *again*.

But then, just as Dexter was about to reveal his presence and to hell with the consequences, the scene on the other side of the mirror changed. Chow dropped the belt, ripped Ling's blouse open, and pushed her onto the neatly made bed. The young woman made no attempt to resist, which raised the possibility that what the businessman had witnessed was consensual, and left him unsure as to what to do.

Ling knew what to expect. Chow needed to inflict pain on her, needed to demonstrate his dominance, in order to achieve an erection. Now, with his hard-on poking at the front of his jeans, the snakehead was ready to take her. She felt rough hands rip at her clothes, and knew it was important to struggle, but not too much. Because if Chow thought his victim was resisting, *really* resisting, he would take that as an affront to his masculinity and beat the crap out of her. But the sado-masochistic charade followed the unwritten script, and it wasn't long before Ling had been prodded into position.

Dexter felt a variety of emotions as he watched the couple prepare to copulate, including curiosity, anticipation, lust, anxiety, fear, and guilt. But he had felt guilty before, many times in fact, and always given into his desires. So the voyeur watched with a growing sense of excitement as Chow positioned his mistress on her hands and knees, paused to remove his pants, and prepared to take Ling doggy style, a position that would allow the snakehead to watch himself perform in the big mirror opposite the bed. A strategy that would make *Chow* a voyeur too, thereby locking both males together in what had become a strange ménage a trois.

Ling felt her master's hands pry her buttocks apart. She knew he planned to use her anally, and so left her body. It was sunny in southern California, and as she and her sister made their way across the imaginary campus Ling saw hundreds of pretty people, all wearing the latest fashions. They were happy, just as she would be happy some day, and completely oblivious to the pain that so much of the world lived with.

Dexter watched Chow flick his hips forward, knew he had entered Ling, and took a look at her face. But rather than the pleasure he had hoped to witness, the businessman saw her face go blank, and knew that her essence had gone somewhere else. And it was the knowledge of that, the *certainty* of it, that brought Dexter's experiment to an abrupt end. Because rather than the sexual excitement that he had expected to feel, the ex-SEAL experienced revulsion instead, and not just for his tenant. Because the apartment house owner knew that even though he remained in the adjoining room, *he* was guilty of victimizing the young woman too. Sickened by what he had done, and determined to eliminate the mirror the moment that Chow moved out, Dexter left the secret room.

Meanwhile, having prolonged the pleasure for as long as he could, Chow made the decision to end it. It was a powerful orgasm and the snakehead gave a bellow of satisfaction as he granted himself release.

Ling felt the final thrust, heard Chow shout, and knew the ordeal was over. Soon, within a minute or so, he would wipe himself on the bed cover, put his pants back on, and head for the living room. That was when he would tell his bodyguards what a good lay she was, bask in their approval, and pop another beer. Though not as good as California, a bath would feel good, followed by the nothingness of sleep. They were small pleasures, but all a slave could hope for, and Ling was grateful.

# Chapter Four

Americo Lopa awoke as he always did, to the gentle, *beep, beep, beep* of his battery-powered alarm clock. Even though he didn't have a job to go to it was important to make sure that he didn't spend more than one night per week in the same parking lot, a precaution that prevented the shopping center's rent-a-cops and the local police from tagging his vehicle as suspicious, or worse yet, having it towed—a potential nightmare for a man who kept all of his possessions in his van and was paranoid about his privacy.

Lopa slapped the off button on the alarm, sat up, and took a peek out through the hand-sewn curtains that not only served to screen the van's interior but blocked the harsh green glow that illuminated the parking lot at night. It was still dark, but a single glance confirmed that he was in the Mountlake Terrace strip mall, where one of his many alter-egos maintained a membership at the local gym.

In spite of the fact that he lived within the context of an extremely large city, most of Lopa's days were spent in near-isolation on the streets or in the solitude of his van. Today would be different however, since he was scheduled to meet the man who would kill FBI agent Christina Rossi for him. That being the case, Lopa was even more efficient than usual as he entered Ginny's Gym, spent thirty minutes on the treadmill, shaved while he showered, and ambled down to Starbucks where he purchased a grande mocha, a Hawaiian bagel, and a copy of *USA Today*.

Exactly thirty minutes later, Lopa entered his van and made his way onto I-5 southbound, where he entered the normal flow of traffic. As always the cell leader was careful to keep his speed at or just below the limit, signal before he changed lanes, and avoid conflicts with other drivers. Still, in spite of all those precautions it was unsettling to know that on any given day footage of his white van was likely to be captured by the news choppers that cruised overhead, the traffic cams mounted at strategic spots along the freeways, and the ATM machines that fronted most banks.

Lopa took the Mercer street exit, made a couple of turns, and lucked into an on-street parking spot. The terrorist tried to avoid lots because some were monitored. Had anyone been watching the man who exited the white van—they would have been hard-pressed to describe him later. He had black hair, that much was obvious, but everything else was a blur. He wore a tan jacket, faded blue jeans, and beat-up hiking boots, the same sort of clothes worn by students at the University of Washington, thousands of blue-collar workers, and anyone else who didn't have to wear a suit or uniform.

As usual Denny's was packed with people who liked lukewarm coffee, grand slam breakfasts, and sticky tabletops. Lopa saw the security camera that was mounted over the cash register, wished there was a way to avoid it, and knew there wasn't. He scanned the area ahead, spotted the man in the black beret, and made his way down the center aisle. The man with the rimless glasses, sunken cheeks, and sallow skin looked more like a retired college instructor than the man of violence that Lopa knew him to be. That impression was reinforced by the fact that the assassin was reading the *New York Times* and sipping tea. In spite of the fact that the ELA had no formal hierarchy and consisted of ad hoc cells, there were certain websites that could be used as message drops, which was how the man he knew as Eason had been contacted. Lopa approached the booth with the surety of an old friend joining another for breakfast, slid onto the bench-style seat, and smiled pleasantly. "Good morning! It's good to see you."

Eason lowered the paper, removed the reading glasses, and tucked them away. Rather than actually reading the *Times*, he'd been looking over the top of it, watching to see if Lopa had been followed. If the terrorist had a tail, and if left with no other choice, the assassin was prepared to remove the Ingram MAC 10 submachine gun from the briefcase on the floor beside him and spray the interior of the restaurant with 9mm bullets before exiting via the door located six paces behind him. But Lopa was clean, or that was the way it appeared, so Eason added some additional water to his cup and made a ritual out of dunking a fresh tea bag into the hot liquid. His voice was pitched intentionally low. "Thank you. It's good to see you as well."

A tired-looking waitress arrived, offered Lopa some coffee from a nearly empty pot, and slopped some of the noxious brew into his cup. "So," Eason said as the waitress waddled away, "I understand you need some help."

"Yes," Lopa agreed solemnly. "I do. How soon can you begin work?"

"Today," Eason replied laconically. "If that's convenient."

"The sooner the better," the terrorist said as he brought the coffee cup up to his lips. Having been threatened by the ELA for two months a corporate executive had been gunned down in Los Angeles two days before—and Lopa wondered if Eason had been the triggerman. Not that it mattered. The coffee tasted horrible so he put it down. "What will you need?"

"You mean what will *we* need," Eason answered levelly. "Either we work together or we don't work at all."

Though not adverse to using violence to achieve his ends Lopa preferred to let others pull the actual triggers whenever possible. But, having spent his cell on the university sanction, the cell leader was out of foot soldiers. He frowned. "Why?"

"Because I'm a pragmatist," Eason replied. "The task you have in mind involves a high level of risk. One way to control that risk is to ensure that everyone who knows about the activity participates in it. So, assuming you want my assistance, it will be necessary to stay by my side until the project is complete. The choice is yours."

Lopa understood what the hit man was getting at but didn't like the notion of providing anyone with that kind of a hold on him. Still, Christina Rossi would be a lot harder to kill than Aspee had been, which meant that he was in need of help. "I see," the terrorist responded neutrally. "Tell me something…. How did you wind up in this line of work anyway?"

Eason smiled thinly. He could see the other man's hesitancy and practically smell his fear. Lopa was stalling for time. "I put in twenty years at a nuclear waste facility. They told me it was safe even though they knew it wasn't. I'll be dead twelve months from now—but not before I send a few of them to hell ahead of me."

Now Lopa understood why the hitman looked the way he did. As for Eason's desire to get back at "them," well that was what everyone within the resistance movement wanted to do, although various subgroups were focused on different aspects of the same problem. *His* anger was fueled by a childhood spent in migrant labor camps, his politics were Che Guevara's, and his methods were those of Mao Tse Tung. "I'm sorry," the terrorist said sincerely. "That's why the battle must go on."

"Exactly," Eason agreed emotionlessly. "So, what will it be? Are we going to tackle the project together? Or should I leave you with the check?"

The knowledge that Eason was going to die, and sooner rather than later, made Lopa feel better. He smiled. "We'll do it together."

They shook on it, and when Lopa took the assassin's hand, he noticed that it was very, very cold.

Having lucked into a parking spot, Rossi fed what seemed like an excessive amount of money into the gray meter, and eyed the newly refurbished building on the far side of the street. Her face had been on TV a lot lately, so there was the risk that Joe Chow would recognize the agent should they run into each other in the lobby, but that wasn't going to happen since the snakehead was busy losing money at a tribal casino north of Everett. Just one of the habits that kept little Chow from amassing the kind of fortune that his father had.

Confident that her visit would go undetected, Rossi crossed the street, mounted a short flight of stairs, and entered a well-appointed lobby. The agent spotted the office, pushed open the door, and saw the man she knew to be Jack Dexter beyond a glass divider. He waved her in.

Dexter stood as the woman entered. He saw that she was tall, had black hair, large brown eyes, and a determined mouth. She also looked familiar although he couldn't say why. While not drop-dead gorgeous, she was very attractive, and well dressed. The businessman had been expecting an FBI agent, but this lady looked more like a prospective tenant, so he reacted accordingly. "Hello.... Can I help you?"

Rossi inspected the man on the other side of the desk the same way she inspected everyone, as a potential scam artist, thief, or murderer. Dexter didn't look like a criminal though. Far from it. He had hazel eyes, even features, and an athletic build. The last was somewhat predictable, given his special ops background, but hadn't been apparent in the photo that the Department of Defense (DOD) supplied along with the ex-officer's military record. "Yes," the FBI agent said as she offered him a look at her badge and credentials. "My name is Christina Rossi."

"Please, sit down," Dexter replied, as he updated his stereotypes of female law enforcement officers to include pretty FBI agents. "I'm Jack Dexter. Most people call me Dex."

Rossi struggled to remember whether the man opposite her was married as she sat down. "Thank you for taking the time to see me. I'm here because one of your tenants is under criminal investigation."

Dexter nodded as he returned to his chair. The agent had a hard-soft quality that he found appealing. "Can I ask which one?"

"Yes," Rossi answered, "you can. The man we're interested in is Joe Chow."

Dexter sighed. "I should have known."

Rossi raised a perfectly plucked eyebrow. "Really? Why is that?"

"Mr. Chow is the only tenant who employs bodyguards. When they aren't in his apartment they're usually sitting in his Hummer with the sound system turned up. They love hip-hop and it drives my maintenance man crazy."

Rossi nodded as she scribbled in her notebook. "Yes, well, Mr. Chow has numerous enemies, so it pays to be careful."

Dexter nodded. "What about the rest of my tenants? Are they safe?"

"As far as I know," Rossi answered cautiously. "Our experts tell me that you have an extremely good security system. So good that it would be difficult to install surveillance devices without you knowing about it. That's why I came to see you."

The news that the government was familiar with his security system was disquieting to say the least. Dexter thought about the one-way mirror, the viewing room, and the tie to his illegal sex life—all things he wanted to conceal from the FBI *and* the agent on the other side of the desk. Like all special ops warriors he'd been trained to handle interrogations and kept his voice neutral. "Are you sure that's necessary?"

"Yes," Rossi replied. "I'm afraid it is. I am not at liberty to go into the details, but suffice it to say that we need to know what Mr. Chow is up to, and we need your help."

Dexter felt the trap close around him but was powerless to object. First the sadistic episode between Chow and his mistress, now this. "Okay, if that's what you need, then so be it. Should I ask to see a court order or something?"

"Yes, you should," Rossi said, as she opened her briefcase. "Take a look at these."

The ex-SEAL scanned the documents that the FBI agent put in front of him but his thoughts were elsewhere. The woman across from him was not wearing a ring, but was far too attractive to be single, so what did that mean? A live-in boyfriend perhaps? Probably, but what if there wasn't? What if he asked her to have a drink with him and she said "yes?" That would trigger the very series of events that he had worked so hard to avoid. A successful date could lead to more, the inevitable moment would arrive, and the businessman would be expected to remove his clothes. Now, more than two years later, he could still see the expression of shock and revulsion on Kristen's face as she looked at the stump for both the first and last time. It had only been there for a moment, and had been replaced by what could only be described as a determined smile, but there was no mistaking how she felt.

Perhaps that was predictable given that she had been a prototypical high school cheerleader when they had first met, and he had been an equally prototypical jock, both focused on and celebrated for the quality of their physical bodies. But predictable or not, and second only to the moment when he'd been wounded, that had been the most painful episode of his life—one which he didn't want to repeat. But what if he let the opportunity go? There was something different about Christina Rossi, something he didn't want to take a pass on, and that meant taking a chance.

The FBI agent restored the documents to her briefcase and snapped the lid closed. "I think that covers it. Please don't share any part of this conversation with anyone else. One of our technical agents will call to set up an appointment. I appreciate you taking the time to meet with me."

As Dexter stood he felt his heart beat a little faster, wondered if his face was flushed, and knew his hands were clammy. "Agent Rossi, I know this is out of the blue, but I wondered if there was any chance that I could buy you a drink?"

Rossi experienced a feeling of surprise, followed by pleasure, followed by suspicion. Was Dexter trying to play her somehow? There was no reason other than the obvious one for him to do so. Besides, judging from the look of apprehension in his eyes, he was anything but predatory. Yes, he was hitting on her, but why not? So long as the contact was limited to a drink. She glanced at her watch, saw it was nearly 5:00 P.M., and looked up. "You know what? That sounds good… Where shall we go?"

The look of pleasure on Dexter's face was clear to see and the FBI agent was surprised by his reaction. Surprised, but pleased, since the last man who had looked at her with the same combination of relief, eagerness, and enthusiasm was her daughter's father.

It took the better part of twenty minutes for Dexter to lock his office, provide Rossi with a quick description of the renovation process, and walk to one of the small but classy cocktail lounges scattered about Bell Town. Once in a cozy corner, with drinks resting in front of them, it felt natural to ask Rossi about her work. That led to a discussion of the ELA shoot-out, the resulting media attention, and the impact on her social life. That was when Dexter realized that while he'd seen stories about the University shootout on the news he hadn't made the connection. "Sorry about that," the ex-SEAL said apologetically. "I didn't recognize you."

"Don't be sorry," Rossi answered fervently. "I'd rather be known for something other than killing people."

There was a pause while Dexter took a sip of his gin and tonic. "Yeah," he said soberly. "I served in Iraq. It's hard isn't it?"

And that was the moment when Rossi realized that unlike most of the people she came into contact with, Dexter knew how it felt to kill someone. A whole lot of people judging from the medals listed in his file. Something special came into existence between them at that moment— something that her ex-husband would never be able to understand. "Yes," the agent answered. "It is."

The conversation turned to more cheerful topics after that, and once it was pretty well established, Rossi told one of her stories about

Missy. It had been her experience that the very mention of a child was sufficient to send many men packing, but if Dexter found the revelation troubling, he showed no sign of it.

The next time the FBI agent checked her watch she discovered that more than two hours had passed without working on the paperwork in her briefcase, taking care of the laundry that was waiting at home, or talking to Missy on the phone. She informed Dexter that she had to leave, felt pleased when he looked disappointed, and said "Yes" when he asked if he could see her again. The fact that the businessman was a potential witness in an active case triggered an alarm bell but the agent didn't want to hear it. Dexter took care of the tab, held the door, and escorted Rossi to her car. It was silly, since *she* was the one who carried a gun, but it felt right.

Lopa and Eason were parked across the street, just as they had been ever since they had followed the FBI agent from her office to Bell Town, and watched the couple shake hands. There was plenty of traffic and Rossi had a lot on her mind as she pulled away from the curb and headed for the Wallingford district. That's why she didn't notice the white van, the two men who were in it, or the fact that they followed her home.

The day had dawned bright and clear. That meant it was cold, and Christina Rossi could see her breath as she locked the sedan and made her way toward the Coast Guard hangar at Boeing Field. Now that an autopsy had been completed, Hawkins wanted to interview Coast Guard personnel who were familiar with the area and learn whatever he could from the local pathologist regarding the body that had washed ashore near Port Angeles.

A petty officer directed Rossi into a hangar that was so clean it resembled a surgical suite. Dale Hawkins was already there. He wore a blue flight suit and had a helmet tucked under one arm. "Good morning! There's a pile of overalls over there... and you'll need a brain bucket too."

Rossi was glad that she had chosen to wear slacks as she selected a flight suit and pulled it on over her street clothes. It took three tries to find a helmet that fit and the FBI agent was carrying it by the chin strap as she went to join the ASAC. Lieutenant Olman had appeared by then—and was clearly pleased to be in *his* element for once.

Hawkins turned to include Rossi in the conversation. "I was telling the lieutenant that the surveillance team ran into trouble yesterday. They followed Joe Chow to a series of casinos and watched the jerk piss thirty grand down the toilet. Unfortunately the rent-a-cops in the last joint made our team, assumed they were going to rob Chow, and tipped the bastard off.

"He called in some reinforcements, they rammed our van, and the scumbag got away. We don't know where he and his merry men went from there, but they didn't arrive in Bell Town until four thirty, so that suggests that they made a stop along the way. Meanwhile the local sheriff got pissy, demanded to know what we were doing on his turf, and I had to kiss his ass for the better part of two hours before he would get off my back."

Rossi shook her head sympathetically. "That sucks."

"Yeah," Hawkins agreed wearily. "It sure as hell does. Fortunately, for reasons we don't fully understand, the operation seems to be intact. Either sonny boy believes that the surveillance team really were rip-off artists, or he forgot to tell the old man that he was wearing a tail, because it looks like business as usual for the Chow household."

"I'll bet Little Chow didn't want to tell his father about the surveillance team," Rossi put in. "That would make him look bad."

"Yeah," Hawkins nodded. "I agree."

It all sounded inefficient if not downright incompetent to Olman, who preferred a more disciplined, which was to say "military" approach to problems. "What now?" the Coast Guard officer wanted to know.

"We keep trying," Hawkins replied steadfastly. "In fact, given our strategy, what took place last night could even work to our advantage. The whole idea is to put pressure on Little Chow—and wait for him to make a mistake."

"Exactly," Rossi agreed. "And the fact that he doesn't know who was watching him will add to the uncertainty."

"Which brings us to the body," the ASAC said. "My grandpappy told me that there's at least a hundred ways to skin a cat. Who knows? Maybe dead men *can* tell tales."

Rossi raised an eyebrow. "Your grandfather went to Yale—and made a living as an investment banker. I doubt he spent much time skinning cats."

Hawkins grinned and turned to Olman. "Did you hear that? She pulled my file! I wonder what she knows about *you*?"

"He wears boxers," Rossi said calmly. "Size thirty-four."

The information *wasn't* in the Coast Guard officer's file, but the FBI agent was correct nevertheless, and the expression on Olman's face confirmed it. Hawkins laughed and the lieutenant was grateful when the helicopter's rescue diver gave the passengers a flask of hot coffee, three Styrofoam cups, and an invitation to board.

They climbed into the HH-65A Dolphin and strapped themselves in while the crewman pulled the door closed. The helicopter wobbled slightly as if took off. A few minutes later they were out over Elliott Bay on a straight, level course for Port Angeles. They could talk via the intercom system, but it was noisy, and the pilots weren't cleared for information pertaining to the operation. That left them to comment on the scenery, sip coffee, and pepper the rescue swimmer with questions about his job. The chopper arrived over Port Angeles thirty-one minutes later.

Rossi had been to the city on previous occasions, but had never seen it from the air, and never ventured out to the far end of the Ediz Hook where the Coast Guard station was located. It included a cluster of low-lying buildings, a communications tower, and a good-sized cutter moored in the lee of the hook. The Strait lay north of the station and Rossi could see the dark smudge that was Canada's Vancouver Island.

As the Dolphin turned and settled in for a landing, the FBI agent got a quick look glimpse of the harbor, the picturesque town of Port Angeles, and a busy waterfront. Having exited the helicopter, the passengers were invited to enter another scrupulously clean hangar. Then, having removed their flight gear, they were led across a small parking lot to the station's headquarters building. A retired thirty-foot Surf Rescue Boat sat cradled out front, not far from a white-washed flagpole.

Once inside Olman led the agents up a flight of stairs, through a wardroom, and into a well-equipped conference room. The long, glass-topped wooden table was surrounded by blue upholstered chairs. As Rossi took her seat, she could look out the window opposite her and see the short runway that World War II carrier pilots had practiced on, the blue water of the Strait, and the city of Victoria, Canada, in the far distance.

Thanks to some advance work by Olman C. & G. S., charts 6300 and 6401 had been taped to the large white board that dominated one wall and a chief warrant officer was present to brief them. His name was Cummings, and once everyone had been seated, the presentation began. He tapped a couple of computer keys and a chart filled the wall screen. "As you can see," Cummings said, "approximately four thousand ships pass through the Strait each year. That's a lot of vessels to keep an eye on—but we do pretty well. The Vehicle Traffic Service Center in Seattle tracks any vessel over one hundred thirty feet in length—and our Canadian friends watch everything over seventy feet."

"We're here," Cummings said stabbing one of the charts with a laser pointer, "and the body that you're interested in came ashore at the Salt Creek campground west of Port Angeles. The water temperature was approximately fifty degrees, but the victim was wearing a suit, which suggests the man survived for at least two hours before he succumbed to the cold. Given the weather on the night in question, plus the prevailing currents, I would hazard a guess that the victim entered the water right about *here*. Give or take ten miles in every direction. "

Hawkins uttered a low whistle. "That's a lot of give and take."

"Yes," the officer agreed apologetically, "it is. But that's the best that we can do."

Rossi eyed the chart. "Assuming that you're right, it looks like the point of entry was out in the main shipping channel."

"Correct," Cummings replied. "Not that lesser vessels don't pass through there too…. They do. However, had this man fallen off a fishing boat, or jumped into the water because his yacht was taking on water, you'd think someone would have reported that. Or issued a distress call. No one did."

"Which suggests that he arrived on one of the larger vessels," Hawkins observed. "Could this man have been a crew member who jumped overboard in a vain attempt to swim ashore?"

"There's no way to rule that out," Cummings answered soberly. "Many captains would be reluctant to admit that a crewman was missing out of fear that an investigation would delay them and cost their company money—especially when they could report the disappearance to a more forgiving government. But I think that scenario is unlikely. Most members of the international merchant marines are either satisfied with their nationality—or have other options should they wish to enter the country illegally. Why jump overboard if you can simply walk off your ship and never return?"

"Okay," Hawkins said thoughtfully. "So he's Asian, jumped off a large ship, and wasn't part of the crew. Inez is running his prints but odds are that we'll never find out who he was. That leaves us with the following question: Was this guy Chinese? Because if he was, then it's my bet that he was part of a larger group, which probably got through."

The agents thanked Cummings, piled into a van that Olman had borrowed from the station, and made their way into Port Angeles. They passed the 110-foot Island Class Cutter *Cuttyhunk* on the left, paused at the gate, and followed the road down the hook and between the buildings that went to make up the garishly painted Nippon Paper plant. The road curved to the east after that, giving Rossi a look at a large marina, a busy log yard, and the enormous ship *Prince William Sound*.

Then, having passed through downtown Port Angeles, Olman turned right onto Lincoln and drove past the county court house. "Clallam County doesn't have a morgue," the Coast Guard officer explained. "All of the autopsies take place at local funeral homes." Judging from appearances the building that housed the Canthy Funeral Home had been constructed by an early lumber baron or a successful fishing family because it occupied the equivalent of four city lots. Olman pulled into one of the slots intended for the funeral home's customers. A walk took them to some stairs that led to a spacious front porch. The front door opened into a large hallway where they were met by an employee who took the visitors down into the mansion's basement. A narrow hall led to a small, sparsely furnished office. "Please wait here," the employee requested. "Doctor Foley will be along in a moment."

The office was obviously shared and had very little personality outside of the framed homilies that hung on the walls, a nineteenth-century teaching skeleton that stood in one corner, and a Dell computer station.

Hawkins came to his feet as the door opened to admit a woman in her early thirties. She wore a white lab coat over a T-shirt and jeans. Pale blue eyes stared out over rimless glasses that were perched on the end of a freckled nose. She smiled. "Good morning. I'm Doctor Foley…. Sorry to keep you waiting."

"No problem," Hawkins assured her. "We've only been here for a minute or two. My name is Hawkins. I'm with ICE, Special Agent Rossi is with the FBI, and Lieutenant Olman works for the Coast Guard. We're part of a task force assigned to end human trafficking. Thanks for taking the time to see us."

"It's a pleasure to meet you," the forensic pathologist replied, and shook hands all around. "I'm not sure that I will be of much use, however…. Outside of the fact that the man in the survival suit was young, Asian, and died of hypothermia, there isn't very much to tell you. He broke his arm at some point during his teens, was suffering from mild malnutrition at the time of his death, and had very heavily callused feet. All of which is in my written report."

Hawkins frowned. "Is there some way to tell whether he was Chinese rather than Korean, Japanese, or something else?"

Foley looked thoughtful. "There are features we can look at, but while they might tell you something about where his ancestors came from, that doesn't say anything about the man himself. Not these days. There can be other indicators, however—"

Hawkins looked hopeful. "Such as?"

"Such as their dental work," the pathologist answered. "Come on, I'll show you what I mean."

The visitors followed Foley down a hall, through a pair of double doors, and past a sign that read: "Authorized personnel only." The air was cold and reeked of disinfectants. Foley led the threesome past a row of three operating tables and into a smaller room. The entire right-hand wall was occupied by stainless steel compartments, each of which bore a name card. "Here's the one we want," the pathologist said cheerfully. "Hold on while I fetch an instrument."

As the three of them stood there, waiting for Foley's return, Rossi noticed that Olman looked a little green and could imagine why. Both she and Hawkins had been forced to examine dead bodies from time to time but the Coast Guard officer had been more fortunate.

"Okay," Foley said, as she reentered the room. "Here's what we need. If you gentlemen would be so kind as to pull out that drawer, I'll show you some of the worst dentistry you're ever likely to see."

A body bag was revealed as the men pulled the long metal tray out from the wall. The doctor pulled the zipper down far enough to reveal Lok Lee's face. It was colorless, a bit waxy, and empty of all expression. Foley pried the cadaver's mouth open, made use of a retractor to keep it that way, and motioned for the visitors to take a look. "Here's what I was telling you about," the pathologist said, as she used her ballpoint pen to tap some of Lee's teeth. "See that? It's a partial denture. It's made of plastic. Dentists refer to them as 'flippers.' They use them here in the United States, but only on an interim basis, while a more permanent denture is being prepared.

"But it's different in China. A lot of people can't afford the real thing, so they buy flippers and have them wired in place. As you can see from the copper wire, plus all the gum disease, that's what happened to this man. At least that's what my dad tells me…and he's a dentist. I asked him to take a look once I saw the wire."

Olman looked away, Rossi felt sorry for the floater and Hawkins peered into Lee's gaping maw. The excitement was easy to detect. "So, let me see if I have this straight… What we're looking at is characteristic of China? Not Taiwan? Not Korea?"

"Nope," Foley answered stolidly. "Dad has done volunteer work throughout Asia. The only place he ran into dental work like this was in China."

"Bingo," Hawkins said as he straightened up. "We're going to need a copy of the autopsy report plus statements from both you and your father. A member of my staff will contact you."

The pathologist looked from Hawkins to Rossi. "So where this guy came from is important?"

"Yes," the FBI agent replied. "*Very* important."

"Good," Foley said as she looked down at Lee's corpse. "That's nice to know."

Retired Chief Petty Officer John Pasco had been a thief for most of his fifty-seven years, which was why he had let himself into unit 4B, and was busy rifling through Mrs. Tepper's belongings while she was out getting her hair done. The widow was very well off thanks to the investments her husband had made during the previous thirty years. She never bothered to put her jewelry in her safe, however, which was why Pasco had the opportunity to fondle each item before putting it back where it had been.

And it was that natural restraint, the ability to look at high-value items yet leave them alone, that had always been the hallmark of the retired petty officer's thievery. Because even at the age of seven, when he had first taken to pilfering money from his mother's purse, the little boy had known better than to take fives, tens, or twenties.

During his teenage years, the young Pasco discovered that one-dollar bills were rarely if ever missed, two cigarettes could be removed from a pack without fear of discovery, and a shot of bourbon could be poured off without his father taking notice—all of which explained why he had been able to steal what he estimated to be at least $100,000 worth of cash and goods over the past half-century.

Now, as the maintenance man plucked the occasional one-, five-, or ten-dollar bill from the hiding places that Mrs. Tepper had established throughout her apartment, Pasco had the satisfaction of knowing that his victim would not only remain ignorant of her losses, but continually refresh the supposedly secret stashes of cash that she kept in bowls, books, and drawers.

Having finished going through the over-decorated bedroom, Pasco checked his watch and saw that only thirty minutes remained before the elderly woman was due back. And, were Mrs. Tepper to return home early, some mechanical mumbo-jumbo, plus the presence of the tool box that the maintenance man had been careful to leave just inside the front door, would not only justify his presence but help ensure a Christmas tip.

Satisfied with his haul, Pasco grabbed the toolbox, and exited the apartment with the surety of someone who had every right to be there. Once clear of the crime scene, he removed the latex gloves that he habitually wore while stealing *and* performing his legitimate duties. An elevator carried the ex-NCO down to the parking garage and his office.

A quick glance was sufficient to establish that the yellow Hummer was absent from its usual parking slot, a fact that served to further improve Pasco's already ebullient mood. Because while he didn't care about Chow, the maintenance man had strong feelings about the renter's bodyguards and the loud hip-hop music they insisted on playing while waiting for their boss.

Pasco unlocked his office, put the toolbox away, and went over to his scrupulously tidy desk. One of his many duties, and the one that he enjoyed the most, was to monitor the building's security system—a task that not only gave him an excuse to watch the residents but Mr. High and Mighty Jack Dexter, too.

Pasco didn't like the Dexters of the world and never had. It was his opinion that while piss ant officers strut around, giving mostly meaningless orders, it's the professional NCOs who actually run the Navy, Army, Marine Corps, and Air Force. So, given the fact that Dexter had not only been an officer, but a *SEAL* officer, Pasco felt nothing but resentment for him, an emotion made all the more intense by the fact that the businessman came across as aloof, standoffish, and secretive—especially where his apartment was concerned. Because while the maintenance man had been given keys for all the rest of the units, 6B was the single exception—a fact that not only hurt Pasco's feelings, but limited the opportunities for petty thievery and served to stimulate his curiosity.

That was why Pasco not only kept an eye on the monitors located on the wall opposite his desk, but reviewed the security recordings after each absence and kept an eye peeled for Dexter. As the maintenance man opened his lunch bucket and removed a thick, meatloaf sandwich, he hit fast forward. Mrs. Tepper ran out of the building, a Fed-Ex delivery man ran in, and relatives of the couple in 2B seemed to jog through the parking area—all of which was not only boring, but not worth so much as a momentary pause.

That was when two men carrying what looked like identical hard-sided sample cases arrived in the lobby, where they were met by Jack Dexter and escorted up to 6A. This during a time when Chow and his bodyguards were elsewhere.

Pasco hit "Stop," followed by "Play," and waited to see what would happen next. The answer was nothing. Then, exactly twenty-six minutes later, the threesome emerged.

The question was why? The men weren't there to see Chow, and Pasco would have been notified had there been some sort of maintenance problem, so what did that leave? Nothing in so far as the ex-chief could tell—and that piqued his curiosity.

A tour of Chow's apartment was in order—followed by a visit to Dexter's. But how to enter? The maintenance man took a bite, chased the meatloaf with a mouthful of lukewarm coffee, and stared into space. "Where there's a will there's a way." That's what Pasco's mother liked to say—and it was his experience that she was always right.

The maintenance man's cell phone started to play "Anchors Aweigh," he flipped it open and said, "Pasco here." Strangely, as if the old woman had the capacity to pick up on her son's thoughts, the person on the other end was none other than Pasco's mother.

It was already dark as Rossi left home, and the fact that hers was the only house on the street that didn't boast any Christmas lights made her feel guilty. Especially since Missy *loved* the holidays, the much-delayed sleepover was coming up, and lights were part of the package. But that was for tomorrow, or if not tomorrow then soon. Tonight she was going out on a date. And not just *any* date, but the first one in five months, and with a guy who wasn't living with his mother, cheating on his wife, or in rehab.

*Not only that*, Rossi thought as she entered her car, *but Dex was clearly intelligent, funny, and something else. Cautious? Yes. Scared? Yes. Sad? Definitely.* All of which were emotions that the FBI agent could relate to.

The non-descript white van had been sitting there for hours. Eason and Lopa watched the five-year-old Maxima pull away from the curb and waited for it to get halfway down the block before pulling out to follow.

The evening rush was over, and traffic was relatively light as Rossi made her way across the Aurora bridge into downtown Seattle. She was running late, so rather than look for on-street parking, the agent pulled up directly in front of the Metropolitan Grill and got out. She gave the parking attendant a dollar along with her keys, wondered if that was enough, and fumbled through her purse for more while he drove away.

The FBI agent turned toward the door, which opened as if by magic. Once inside she found herself in an orderly universe of dark wood, glittering glass, and white linen. The steady rumble of conversation was punctuated by an occasional burst of laughter, the continual clink of glassware, and a round of applause as the people in the bar celebrated a successful free-throw.

Rossi had just stepped up to the podium-like structure that served to separate the man in the black suit from his guests, and was about to ask if Dexter had arrived when the maitre d' spoke first. "Ms. Rossi? Welcome to the Metropolitan Grill."

The agent must have looked surprised—because the maitre d' smiled. "Mr. Dexter told me to expect a beautiful brunette. And, as it happens, a rather well-known FBI agent. Please follow Kim."

Rossi felt pleased, embarrassed, and suspicious all at once. Was the compliment for real? Or part of a well-conceived plan to get her into bed? And what if it was? Other people had sex—why couldn't she? *Because he's a witness,* she told herself, *or could be. Why are you here?*

The question was left unanswered as Rossi was led back between tightly packed booths to a linen-covered table. Dexter stood as the FBI agent approached, smiled, and kissed her cheek. "You look wonderful," he said sincerely. "May I take your coat?"

Rossi surrendered her coat. The sleek black St. John's dress she wore had a V-shaped neckline, was cut in at the waist, and clung to her hips. Gold earrings, a gold necklace, and a diamond dinner ring served to complete the outfit. "Sorry I'm late," Rossi said, as she slid into the booth, "but I have a lot of excuses."

"Excellent!" Dexter replied cheerfully. "I love a good excuse. But first, how about something to drink?"

After they ordered drinks, Rossi told the businessman about her trip to Port Angeles and was surprised to find that the businessman was interested. It turned out that Dexter had been a certified SCUBA diver *before* he joined the Navy and knew the San Juan islands well. After Rossi told him about the body, and where it came ashore, he nodded in agreement. "Yeah, that makes sense. If he jumped in the shipping channel, and died of hypothermia, the body would wash up on that stretch of coastline. But, assuming there were other illegals, what happened to them?"

"That's the sixty-four-thousand-dollar question," Rossi replied, before skillfully turning the conversation away from the investigation and back to her dinner companion.

The meal went well, or that's what Dexter thought anyway, which gave him the courage to pop the question. "So, tell me," the businessman said as their plates were being removed from the table. "Are you armed?"

One of Rossi's eyebrows rose slightly. "Yes… Why? Do you want me to shoot the waiter?"

"No," Dexter replied lightly. "The service was excellent. However, given the fact that you are carrying a gun, and are therefore prepared to defend yourself, I wondered if you would be willing to have dessert at my apartment. The view is excellent—especially at night."

Rossi had enjoyed the conversation, the dinner, and Dexter's company. But who was he really? One way to find out was to see the inside of Dexter's apartment. She smiled. "Sure. That sounds like fun."

Dexter paid the bill, and having come by cab, accepted Rossi's offer of a ride. Rather than a by-the-book FBI agent it seemed as if the Maxima belonged to someone else. The center console was home to a couple of half-empty Starbucks cups. A pair of little-girl-sized gym shoes lay next to the businessman's feet and a stack of dirty clothes occupied half the backseat. "I've got to get to the dry cleaners," the FBI agent said apologetically. "There's never enough time."

Dexter agreed, but knew he was lying, because he had plenty of time. Too much time—most of which was spent by himself. The businessman directed Rossi into the private parking area beneath his building, gave her his key card so she could operate the gate, and guided the agent into one of four visitor slots.

They got out, walked past the empty slot where Joe Chow kept his Hummer, and entered the elevator. Five minutes later they were upstairs in Dexter's apartment. "Take a look around," the ex-naval officer suggested, "while I make dessert."

Rossi surrendered her coat, and left her purse on a small table inside of the front door. She followed a short hall out into a generously proportioned living room that featured high ceilings, pale yellow walls, and gleaming hardwood floors. It was not only nicely furnished but carefully conceived. It wasn't clear whether Dexter had decorated the place himself or hired someone to do it, but it spoke to his taste either way. And in spite of the black and white photos of Navy SEAL teams and the framed medals that hung on one of the walls, the room came across as masculine rather than macho. An important distinction.

Then there was the view of downtown Seattle. The high-rise residential buildings were closest, while a concrete forest of hotels and office buildings lay beyond, some of which were draped with Christmas lights. It was all part of an unintended light show that filled the big picture window.

The bay, which was off to the right, was less spectacular at night, but still worth a look as Rossi stepped up to the tripod-mounted telescope that stood poised in front of the window. As the agent peered through the eyepiece she discovered that rather than being focused on Elliott Bay as she expected it to be, the Nikon was lined up on a high-rise apartment building. Not only that, but on a well-lit living room where a young woman could be seen sitting on her couch. She was fully dressed, but it didn't take a great deal of imagination to realize that there were times when she wasn't, and Rossi was still processing that fact when Dexter entered the room.

The ex-naval officer took one look at the tableau, knew what had occurred, and swore a silent oath. He was stupid, stupid, stupid, and there was no getting around it. "It looks like I'm busted," Dexter said, as he placed a tray on a table. "Would you like some coffee?"

"She's pretty," Rossi admitted, as she turned to confront him. "But watching her through a telescope constitutes a crime. Perhaps I should take you in."

Dexter swallowed. Rossi wasn't thrilled, he could see that, but she wasn't angry either. That meant there was still a chance. He offered his wrists. "Cuff me officer…. I deserve it."

"Maybe later," Ross replied lightly. "If I don't like the dessert."

Dexter felt an enormous sense of relief as the FBI agent sat on the couch, took a cup of coffee, and brought it to her lips. "The pressure is on," the businessman said meekly. "I'll be back in a minute."

When the ex-naval officer returned, it was with two generous portions of crème brûlée, which, unbeknownst to him, was one of Rossi's favorites. "So," she said, having taken the first delicious bite. "You're a SEAL, an entrepreneur, *and* a chef."

"No," Dexter replied honestly. "The first two batches, which I made early this afternoon, are sitting at the bottom of the garbage can."

"Well practice certainly makes perfect," Rossi said as she took a second bite. "That was very sweet of you…. And, as it turns out, *very* good."

Once the dessert was finished, Dexter found himself where he wanted to be, which was next to Rossi. They talked for a while, trivial stuff mostly, but laden with the sort of details that define lives and are of interest to potential lovers.

Finally, after Rossi finished telling Dexter about her divorce, she took the opportunity to steer the conversation back towards him. "So, what about you? I know you never married…. But did you ever come close?"

Dexter remembered Kristen, the night after he had been released from the hospital, and the look of horror that came over her face when she saw the angry red stump. She had been sorry, *very* sorry, but they had never made love again. More than that, *he* had never made love again, not in the normal manner at least. "Yes," he replied. "I came close once. But it didn't work out."

In spite of his effort to conceal his emotions Rossi could see the pain in the ex-SEAL's eyes. She took his hand. "I'm sorry, Dex. It was the leg, wasn't it?"

The direct question caught the ex-naval officer off guard. He pulled his hand back. "It's that obvious?"

"The leg?" Rossi inquired gently. "Or what happened to your relationship? The fact that you lost a leg in Iraq was in your military file…. Along with a full list of the decorations you received. I guessed the rest."

The possibility that Rossi had seen his military record had never occurred to Dexter but made perfect sense. That meant she had known about the leg all along! Known, but gone out with him anyway. He opened his mouth to speak—but stopped when she put a finger on his lips. "That's right," Rossi said softly. "I didn't care."

It felt natural for Dexter to put his arms around Rossi and pull her close. The scent of perfume mixed with soap made a heady combination. It filled Dexter's nostrils and mind as her lips melted against his.

Meanwhile, sitting within a darkened living room and concealed by yards of fabric, the woman that Dexter called Glass Eye watched through her telescope, ate popcorn, and wondered what would happen next. The man she called "peg leg" *never* had guests, much less female ones, so this was a first. She giggled happily, fumbled for another handful of popcorn, and wished she was younger.

# Chapter Five

The customs agent was in the process of shaving when his cell phone started to chirp insistently. He picked it up and looked into the mirror. It seemed as though the man reflected there was older than he should have been. "This is Hawkins."

The voice on the other end was female and sounded thin as if the connection could fail at any moment. "Hawk? Moller here.... We have a problem."

The customs agent wished he had already had a cup of coffee but hadn't. Moller and her partner had been detailed to keep an eye on Joe Chow. Problems, if any, could stem from the nature of the assignment, their relative lack of experience, or bad luck. "Okay," Hawkins said stolidly. "Shoot."

She may have been a newbie but Moller knew better than to mention names on an unscrambled cell phone call. "The subject took off up Highway 2 towards Stevens Pass. A second vehicle joined him in Monroe. We estimate seven or eight subjects total. There's no way to be sure what they're up to but it doesn't look like a snowboarding expedition."

"Roger that," Hawkins said, his mind racing. Chow was a city boy.... So why head up into the Cascade Mountains in the dead of winter? It didn't make sense. It was interesting though, *very* interesting, and he wanted to know more. "Stick with them," the customs agent instructed. "And stay in touch."

"That may be difficult to do," Moller replied cautiously. "Cell coverage is iffy up here—but we'll do our best. What if the shit hits the fan? Do we jump in? Or take notes?"

Hawkins eyed the *other him*. It was a tough question. But if Chow planned to commit a violent crime there was no way that his agents could just sit and watch. Even if they were outgunned. Hawkins frowned. "You said *eight* subjects?"

"Yeah," Moller replied, "give or take. It's hard to tell without pulling up next to them for a head count."

"That's a lot," Hawkins replied. "I'll call for help. Maybe the sheriff or the state patrol has somebody up that way. Once the back-up is in place you can intervene if necessary. But don't bust them for pissing in the snow.... We have bigger fish to fry."

"Roger that," Moller replied. "Sorry to call so early."

"No problem," Hawkins answered. "Watch your six."

The call ended after that and the customs agent pressed the razor against his face. It slid smoothly down along his neck, hit a tiny irregularity, and nicked his skin. A droplet of blood appeared. Hawkins swore and attempted to wipe it away, but the cut continued to bleed until he took a tiny piece of toilet paper, placed it over the wound, and watched the tissue turn red. Another day had begun.

Mountains could be seen beyond the helicopter's Plexiglas windscreen as the KATO 8 reporter turned to look into the camera. Thanks to the extensive violence, and the high body count, the shootout in the mountains was all over the midday news casts. Supervisory Special Agent John Theel watched with considerable interest as the serious-looking journalist told what he knew, or *didn't* know, since the customs people had the lid on tight. "Authorities won't say what took place in the parking area," the reporter intoned, "only that they estimate that fifteen to twenty people were involved, ten of whom were killed in the violence. Those directly involved in the investigation won't confirm this, but one of the EMTs who responded to the scene told KATO 8 that two ICE agents were on the scene when he arrived, suggesting the possibility of a drug deal gone wrong."

"That's close," Assistant Special Agent in Charge Amy Haxton observed as she entered the office, "but no cigar."

Theel realized that his size-twelves were up on his desk and swung them down onto the floor as the ASAC plopped down in one of two guest chairs. "True," he agreed, "but it's only a matter of time before they dog it out."

"Some of it," Haxton allowed, "but not all. I just got off the phone with Hawkins. Thanks to the fact that his agents weren't involved in the fire fight, and all of the victims were known criminals, he figures it will be easier to keep the lid on."

"Maybe so," Theel agreed doubtfully. But gang bangers or not, Chow *murdered* those people. Why leave him on the street?"

"Because we don't know how he's bringing illegals in," the other agent answered. "And if illegals can enter the country—then terrorists could too. Hawkins believes that if we give his team more time they'll figure it out."

"Which brings us to Rossi."

"Yes," Haxton agreed thoughtfully. "I'm thankful she wasn't there. Here's hoping the media will leave her alone and focus their attention on the sheriff. It looks like he owns the hot seat this time."

Hawkins grinned. "Along with ICE!"

The ASAC shook her head disapprovingly but smiled as she came to her feet. "I'll pretend I didn't hear that.... Now that we have Rossi's shooting review behind us, all we have to do is get through Kissler's, and we're in the clear."

"Sounds good," Theel responded. "I'll keep my fingers crossed."

As soon as Haxton was gone Theel dialed Rossi and invited the agent to join him. Rossi had heard about the massacre from Hawkins and hurried down the hall. Haxton was going to freak, or so she assumed, and the agent was ready to lobby for some additional time.

But Theel looked relaxed as Rossi entered his office and that was generally a good sign. After listening to the SSA's account of his conversation with Haxton the FBI agent felt even better. "So," Theel concluded, "I think you'll get the time you need. But keep a close eye on Chow. Drug dealers are one thing, but if that psycho sonofabitch were to cap a citizen, then we're all in deep trouble."

Rossi agreed and was about to leave when Theel motioned for her to stay. "Hold on for a moment," the SSA said, as he thumbed through some papers. "There's something I meant to share. Ah, here it is. It seems that the Wallingford District has a block watch program. Two different people took notice of a suspicious white van and called it in. One of the boys in blue realized that the vehicle in question had been parked near your house and emailed a copy of the report to me. You owe him a doughnut."

Rossi frowned. "That's it? A white van? There are millions of them."

"Yes," her supervisor responded patiently, "but not parked on your street for extended periods of time. Not only that, but both citizens reported that while the vehicle appeared to be occupied, no one ever got in or out of it. Someone has one helluva bladder."

"Or a Pepsi bottle," Rossi replied dryly. "Okay, point taken. I'll keep my eyes peeled."

"Good," Theel replied. "That's all I ask. By the way—you look unusually perky this morning. What's up?"

Rossi shrugged uncomfortably. It was a personal question, but given the fact that she had been known to cry on Theel's shoulder from time to time, a fair one. "I had a date. It was fun. Have you got a problem with that?"

Theel grinned. "Not if he's nice to you. Who's the lucky guy?"

"His name is Dexter," Rossi replied. "Jack Dexter. He owns the building where Chow lives."

Theel's eyebrows shot straight up. "The building where Chow lives? Is that a good idea?"

"He isn't a witness," Rossi said defensively.

"Not yet anyway," the SSA responded darkly. "Be careful, Christina. You're walking a *very* thin line."

Theel *never* used her first name, not unless he was in the parental mode, and Rossi took note. Like it or not her relationship with Dexter could be questionable. And, given her recent controversial past, it was important to be careful. "I hear you, John," she said. "I'll take care of it."

"Good," Theel responded soberly. "I'm counting on it. By the way, what, if anything, has your team picked up off the wire?"

"We know that Chow is a Sonics fan, likes a lot of pepperoni on his pizzas, and treats his girlfriend like shit," Rossi replied. "But we're hoping for more."

Theel shrugged. "The bastard is a bastard, but he was raised by a master criminal, and is bound to be cagey. He'll slip up eventually though—all of them do."

Rossi wasn't so sure, but nodded agreeably, and left.

The SSA turned back to the television. It quickly became apparent that there had been a seven-car pile-up on Interstate-5 and with the prospect of good, which was to say *bad* footage in the offing, all of the mechanical vultures had flocked to the scene. Theel turned off the TV, and felt a sense of satisfaction as the screen went black.

John Pasco discovered that it was a lot easier to break into his employer's apartment than he thought it would be. The solution was to schedule a locksmith for the morning when Dexter typically left to work out, tell the tradesman a convincing lie, and get *him* to open unit 6B. The best part was the fact that Mr. Stuck-Up Dexter would wind up paying the bill! Just the kind of silent "gotcha" that the ex-chief petty officer had specialized in during his Naval service.

Having escorted the unsuspecting locksmith out of the building, Pasco returned to unit 6B. He always took pleasure in surreptitiously entering other people's homes, but never more so than the moment when he walked into Dexter's apartment and closed the door behind him. There was the sense of excitement that stemmed from being where he shouldn't be, plus a wonderful feeling of dominance, as all of his employer's belongings came under his control.

Pasco hummed to himself as he pulled a pair of disposable latex gloves down over his fingers. Then, as he passed through the open-style kitchen into the living room, his cell phone went off. The maintenance man checked to see who was calling, saw that it was one of three women that he occasionally had sex with, and let the call go to voicemail. Though not especially interested in the nicely framed prints that hung on his employer's walls or the hardcover books that filled his book shelves, the ex-CPO was immediately drawn to the black-and-white photos of a younger Dexter posed with fellow SEALs.

More than twenty years earlier, Pasco had taken a shot at the Basic Underwater Demolition/SEAL (BUD/S) program, where he battled his way through four weeks of brutal Phase One training before hitting the wall. Never had Pasco felt such a sense of shame as the moment when he placed both feet on the painted frog footprints and rang the brass bell three times. There was no disgrace in quitting, that's what people told him, but Pasco knew differently. He wanted to take the photos off the wall and smash them on the floor. But Pasco had never allowed himself to give into such impulses nor would he now.

Having turned his back on the photos, Pasco spotted the powerful telescope and the gray day beyond. He went over to peer through the Nikon and found it was focused on the bay. *Trust Dexter to look at something boring*, the maintenance man thought to himself, and swiveled the scope over to the nearest buildings.

But there wasn't much to see, and the clock was ticking, so Pasco made his way out of the living room and into the master suite, the place where people were most likely to leave a big mess *and* hide their valuables. Not Dexter though. His bed had been made with military precision, the underwear in his dresser was so tidy it could have passed an inspection, and the lowest drawers were empty.

The generously proportioned bathroom was equally empty of clutter—although it quickly became apparent that Dexter preferred to purchase his toiletries only once or twice a year. One drawer contained nothing but Crest toothpaste, another was half-filled with boxes of roll-on deodorant, and the space beneath the his-and-hers sinks was crammed with toilet paper. All of which was efficient, but something less than satisfying, since Pasco was looking for loose cash rather than toiletries.

*But it isn't over until it's over*, the maintenance man assured himself, and made his way into the closet, a place where all manner of goodies were frequently kept. Except that Dexter didn't *have* any goodies, or if he did, he had stashed them elsewhere, because outside of the clothes that hung against one wall and some neatly aligned shoes, the closet was practically empty. There was what appeared to be a gun locker however, plus a safe, and an artificial leg.

Frustrated by then, and conscious of the need to get out of the apartment before his employer returned, Pasco was about to leave when he noticed the section of maple paneling that was half-concealed by Dexter's clothes. Though not unusual in and of itself, the wood grain caught Pasco's eye because it was the *only* maple paneling in the apartment house. And that raised a question. Had the building's owner simply given himself an additional amenity? Or, was there something more to it than that?

Pasco felt a rising sense of excitement as he pushed the clothes out of the way and placed both of his hands on the paneling. It gave, the retired chief petty officer pushed it to one side, and a puff of cold chemical-scented air kissed his face. *Bingo!* the maintenance man thought to himself as he stepped through the opening into the space beyond. He noticed that the tiny enclosure was furnished with a standing lamp, a side table, and a comfortable chair. Then, much to Pasco's surprise, he found himself looking into still *another* room—a bedroom, which according to the way the apartments were laid out, belonged to Joe Chow. But how? And *why?*

The ex-petty officer's brain had just begun to wrestle with the questions when a light came on and Chow's mistress came into view. She wore a red silk robe and carried a lap top computer under one arm. When she coughed Pasco was startled by how loud the sound was and made a note to be careful.

The girl placed the computer on the bed, sat cross-legged in front of it, and opened the lid. Thanks to the fact that the building was equipped with a wireless network the young woman could access the Internet from wherever she chose.

That was when Pasco remembered the huge one-of-a-kind mirror that dominated one wall of the neighboring apartment and knew he was looking *through* it. And the reason was obvious… In spite of all appearances to the contrary Mr. High and Mighty Dexter was not only a creep but a dyed-in-the-wool pervert! Not that the ex-CPO could blame him since the woman in the next room was incredibly hot. Pasco felt a sudden sense of excitement as he came to appreciate the full import of what he had uncovered. The possibilities were mind boggling! What should he ask for? Part ownership of the building? No, petty theft was safer. A nice raise perhaps, or better benefits.

But such considerations would have to wait. The first thing Pasco wanted to do was to exit Dexter's apartment before the ex-SEAL returned. Because even though he had sufficient leverage to prevent the businessman from calling the police, the ex-CPO wanted to occupy the psychological high ground when the confrontation took place. With that in mind Pasco withdrew, closed the panel behind him, and pulled the clothes back into place. Three minutes later the maintenance man was in the elevator and on his way down. Mrs. Tepper entered the car on four, nodded politely, and wondered why Pasco looked so happy.

Had there been someone there to see it, and missed the blood-matted white hair on the back of Mrs. Pello's skull, they might have assumed that the elderly woman had simply fallen asleep in her rocking chair. But the eighty-six-year Block Watch Captain and mother of three was starting to smell. And that made sense because it was warm inside her Craftsman-style home—and she'd been dead for more than twenty-four hours.

Lopa didn't like the odor of rotting flesh and wanted to move the corpse down into the basement, but Eason wouldn't have it. The assassin thought the three-person tableau was hilarious. He delighted in addressing comments to the deceased woman and didn't seem to possess a sense of smell, all of which served to confirm what Lopa should have known all along: Eason was crazy.

Mrs. Pello had been responsible for her own death. That's the way the eco-terrorist saw it anyway, since the old biddy not only insisted on watching everything that went on in the neighborhood through a pair of antique opera glasses, but occasionally went out onto her porch for a better angle.

And it had been then, while staring at the white van, that the nosy bitch attracted Eason's attention. It took less than fifteen minutes to drive around the end of the block, cruise up the alley, and pull into the empty slot next to Mrs. Pello's 1986 Dodge Diplomat. Then, with the surety of someone on a legitimate errand, the assassin walked up to the backdoor and knocked.

There was a prolonged period of fumbling while the old lady undid all three of the locks that protected the rear entrance of her home and opened the door. Only nice people knock—or so she assumed. Eason smiled pleasantly, stepped inside, and whacked Pello on the head. Then, having carried the frail body into the living room, the assassin insisted on posing the corpse in front of the television.

All of which struck Lopa as unnecessary, until police cars began to cruise by on a regular basis, and it became obvious that Mrs. Pello had reported his van. Still, justified or not, the murder posed a problem. Judging from all the photos ranked on top of her pump organ, Mrs. Pello had a lot of friends and relatives, any one of whom could walk up and knock at the door. With that in mind, both men agreed that it would be stupid to wait any longer. The results of their research were clear: The best place to hit Rossi was in her home—and the best time to do it was at night.

"Take a look at this," Eason suggested, as he peered through the antique binoculars. "Rossi has a boyfriend."

Lopa stepped up to the lace curtains, accepted the opera glasses, and brought them up to his eyes. It was dark outside but the combination of streetlamps and Christmas lights provided plenty of illumination as a man with a bouquet of roses climbed the stairs to Rossi's porch. "Damn," Lopa said disappointedly. "There goes our plan."

"Really?" Eason countered. "Why do you say that? If the boyfriend leaves before midnight he lives. Otherwise we cap him too. A second body would help to confuse the cops."

The plan made sense and Lopa said as much. "Good," Eason replied as he returned to the burgundy-colored couch and patted the worn spot where Mr. Pello had once spent his evenings. "Take a load off. The three of us will watch TV and have a bite to eat. I don't know about you—but Mrs. Pello and I are getting hungry."

Lopa looked at Mrs. Pello and felt nauseous, but he needed Eason, for the next few hours at least, so he forced a smile. "Sure, that sounds good."

There was something about dying, about feeling his lifeforce start to leak out of his body, which granted Eason a nearly miraculous ability to access the minds of those around him. That's how the assassin knew that the eco-terrorist would attempt to kill him. Eason felt the couch cushions give as Lopa sat down. He lifted the remote and began to click through the channels. There were at least eighty of them—but Eason knew it would be hard to find something that all three of them liked.

Rossi was in the kitchen when the doorbell rang. "I'll get it!" Missy yelled, and was already pulling the front door open when the FBI agent made her way out into the small living room. She had cleaned the house in honor of Dexter's visit, and added more Christmas decorations, but knew the interior fell well short of the expensive décor that her guest was used to. Not that it made a heck of a lot of difference, since the whole purpose of inviting the ex-SEAL over was to tell him that she wouldn't be able to spend any more time with him, not until the Chow investigation was complete, and that would take months if not more. Yes, Dexter could wait if he wanted to, but how likely was that? Not very, which was why Rossi had already begun the process of sealing what she felt for him into an emotional box as she headed for the door.

"Hi!" Missy said, as she opened the door and spotted the red roses. "Are those for my mother?"

"Yes," Dexter responded. "They are. Except for this one…which is for *you.*"

Rossi watched her daughter accept the single yellow rose and felt a sense of warmth. It was a thoughtful gesture, which made her task that much more difficult. "Look, Mom," Missy said. "I got one, too!"

"Yes, you did," Rossi said as she came forward to receive her roses and a kiss on the cheek. "Dex, this is my daughter Missy."

"It's a pleasure to meet you," the ex-SEAL said gravely, as he extended his hand. He noticed that the little girl had her mother's dark brown hair and big brown eyes but a slightly rounder chin. Dexter was impressed by the youngster's firm handshake.

"Glad to meet you," Missy said formally. "And thanks for the rose."

"Why don't you put it in a vase?" Rossi suggested. "You can take it home with you."

"Okay!" the ten-year-old said brightly, and departed for the kitchen still clutching her prize.

"Her step-mom is going to pick her up in half an hour," Rossi explained. "Would you care for a glass of wine?"

Dexter indicated that he would, accepted the seat that Rossi offered, and took a moment to survey his surroundings. Something smelled good. As with the interior of her car, the living room spoke volumes about the *other* Rossi, the one who liked over-stuffed furniture, owned mismatched bookcases filled with worn paperbacks, and was reluctant to dispose of Missy's old artwork.

"Here you go," Rossi said, as she handed Dexter a glass of chilled wine. "It should have been red, since we're having lasagna for dinner, but I forgot to buy any."

"No problem," Dexter responded easily. "I like white wine better anyway."

Rossi sat down on the other end of the couch and the twosome chatted until a horn sounded and Missy peered out through the front window. "Vanessa's here!" she announced, and went to find her belongings.

It took the better part of five minutes to cram everything back into the little girl's backpack, get her coat on, and see her out onto the porch. Meanwhile, on the other side of the street, Eason peeked between Mrs. Pello's lace curtains. He was holding a peanut butter and jam sandwich in one hand and the opera glasses in the other. "There she is," the assassin said, as he watched the FBI agent appear in the brightly lit doorway. "Too bad I don't have a rifle. I could pop the bitch from here."

"Yeah," Lopa agreed from his place on the couch. "What about the man? Is he leaving too?"

"Nope," Eason said with his mouth full. "Too bad for him."

"Yeah," the eco-terrorist agreed, and turned back to the only program that the three of them had been able to agree on: *The Forensic Files.*

Rossi waved goodbye. Then, cognizant of Theel's warning, the FBI agent took a moment to scan the street. There were cars, lots of them, but no white vans. Satisfied that all was well she reentered the house.

Rossi was a traditionalist where lasagna was concerned, and in spite of the fact that she didn't consider herself to be much of a cook, she enjoyed preparing it, partly because the process was satisfying, partly because lasagna tasted good, but mostly because it reminded the FBI agent of her mother, a woman who *really* knew how to cook and had done so every day of her adult life.

The recipe called for pork sausage mixed with ground beef, chopped onion, garlic, diced tomatoes, tomato sauce, dried Italian seasoning, black pepper, dried lasagna noodles, an egg, and lots of ricotta, Parmesan, and mozzarella cheese. It had been in the oven for thirty minutes by then and was bubbling nicely as she took the casserole dish out and placed it on top of the stove. "We need to let that cool," Rossi announced. "So, let's have another glass of wine. And then, assuming that you are properly inebriated, there's something I need to talk to you about."

"Uh, oh," the businessman replied gloomily, as he poured some wine into her glass. "I don't like the sound of that."

"We'll see," Rossi said, as she sat down at the small dining room table. "Who knows? Maybe you'll thank your lucky stars."

"I doubt it," Dexter replied as he joined her. "But, go ahead. If there's a problem let's deal with it."

"Okay," the FBI agent agreed. "Here's the situation. You are a witness—or a potential witness. That means I should never have gone out to dinner with you."

Dexter felt his spirits plummet. "So, you're dumping me?"

"No," Rossi said gently. "How could I? We barely know each other. But *if* we want to see each other again it will have to wait."

Dexter took a sip of wine. "How long?"

"That's hard to say," the FBI agent responded. "At least two or three months. Maybe as long as a year."

"That's a long time."

"Yes," Rossi admitted soberly. "It is."

"And there's no way around it?"

"No. My supervisor as much as told me that he felt if I haven't already stepped over the line then I'm darned close."

Dexter was silent for a moment as he looked into her eyes. "You invited me over because of the leg didn't you? So I wouldn't go crazy and blow my brains out."

"I certainly didn't want you to think that your leg was a factor in my decision," Rossi admitted. "But there was another reason as well. And a rather selfish one. I thought it would be nice to see you again."

The ex-SEAL searched her face. "Really?"

Rossi smiled. "Really."

"Well, for whatever it's worth, I'll be waiting when the case comes to an end. Do me a favor though…."

Rossi's eyebrows rose. "Yes?"

"Wrap it up soon."

Rossi laughed and dinner was served shortly thereafter. Dexter was easy to talk to and the time flew by. Finally, once the dishes had been cleared away, the couple returned to the couch. The ex-SEAL had a fire going by then, and having kissed Rossi once before, did so again.

Rossi intended for it to end there, see Dexter to the door, and call it a night. But one pleasant thing led to another, and about the time the agent should have been removing her make-up she was being carried into her bedroom instead. It was wrong, but enjoyable, and she gave into it. What illumination there was spilled into the bedroom from the hall. Dexter laid Rossi on the queen-sized bed, helped remove the last of her clothing, and took pleasure in the way her hair fell across the pillow. He took a moment to admire the stark whiteness of her breasts, the soft curve of her stomach, and the long taper of her legs—not as an object viewed through a lens, but as a *real* person, waiting for him to touch her.

The reality of that should have made him hard, *would* have made him hard, except for one thing. In order to make love to Rossi the ex-SEAL would have to remove his artificial leg *before* he could remove his pants. Then, once he got the pants off, his stump would be exposed. The reality of that, and the possibility of how the woman in front of him might react, froze Dexter in place.

Rossi noticed the moment of hesitation and reached up to pull him down. "This is the leg that *I'm* interested in," the FBI agent whispered, and got a firm grip on the member she had in mind. The reaction was nearly instantaneous, and once Dexter removed the prosthesis, the rest was easy. They spent some time getting to know each other, but the moment came when Rossi couldn't wait any longer, and pulled Dexter in. The climax came quickly after that, swept the lovers away, and left both of them exhausted. Eventually, after everything that could be said had been said, they drifted off to sleep.

Having set a fire in Mrs. Pello's basement and positioned the van in the alley behind the FBI agent's house, Lopa and Eason were ready to complete the Rossi sanction, a murder that would recapture the headlines and prove that the ELA could strike any target that it chose.

Lopa had agreed to enter through the front door while Eason took care of the back. The terrorist heard the old wood creak as he mounted the front stairs. Once on the porch he paused. There was no noise other than the whir of the neighbor's heat pump, the drone of a distant plane, and the sound of his own breathing.

A quick check confirmed that the fire that would eventually consume Mrs. Pello's home, the woman herself, and at least some of the forensic evidence was still contained. But it wouldn't be for long, which meant that they needed to break into the house and kill the people inside before a passerby called 911.

Then, assuming that things went well, Lopa planned to pop Eason on the way out. Of course there was the distinct possibility that the assassin had similar plans—which was why Lopa wore body armor under his street clothes. Satisfied that the conditions were right, Lopa pressed the key on the Motorola walkie talkie and whispered into the mike. "I'm ready."

"Same here," Eason replied his position on the back porch. "Try the door first… You'd be surprised how many people forget to lock them."

Christina Rossi didn't strike Lopa as the type of person who would forget to lock her front door, but it wouldn't hurt to try, so he placed his hand on the knob.

Maybe it was the strange house, or maybe Rossi had just rolled over, but whatever the reason, Dexter awoke from a deep sleep. Not half awake, like when he needed to pee, but *fully* awake as if he'd had consumed two cups of coffee. He simply lay there at first, luxuriating in Rossi's closeness and the steady rhythm of her breathing. Then he heard a noise. A sound that didn't belong. Dexter fumbled for his leg, found it laying on the floor next to the bed, and pulled the limb into place. There was a positive *click* as the fitting mated with the Ferrier coupler.

With the artificial limb in place Dexter stood and limped into the hall. He wanted to tiptoe, but that was impossible, so he did what he could. Once in the living room he paused to listen. A streetlight projected blue-green rectangles across the front room, the refrigerator chose that particular moment to turn itself on, and a siren could be heard in the distance. Old houses make noises, Dexter knew that, and had already turned back towards the bedroom when the front door knob rattled. Certain that something was amiss the ex-SEAL went to wake Rossi. The FBI agent felt the bed give under Dexter's weight and heard him whisper her name. She groaned. "What time is it?"

"About 3:30 A.M.," Dexter whispered. "Were you expecting anyone?"

"No," the agent said, sitting up in bed. "Why?"

"Because there's someone on the front porch. He just tried the door."

"You're sure?"

"Yes, I'm sure."

Rossi swore, opened the drawer in her nightstand, and grabbed the Glock.

"You wouldn't happen to have another one of those, would you?" Dexter inquired, suddenly feeling even more naked.

Rossi started to say, "No," having no desire to have an amateur firing at shadows, but then remembered Dexter's military background. The ex-SEAL probably knew more about firearms than she did. "There's a shotgun in the closet—but don't fire unless I say you can."

"Is it loaded?"

"Of course it's loaded!" the agent whispered emphatically. "What good is an unloaded gun?" And with that she was gone, a shadow attired in a T-shirt and panties headed for the front of the house.

Dexter opened the closet, which due to its small size, was absolutely crammed with Rossi's clothes. He felt around the right side of the door, came up empty, and was still probing around when he heard the sound of shattering glass followed by the words, "FBI! Hold it right there!"

That was the moment when Dexter's fingers encountered cold steel. He heard a second crash from the rear of the house and knew there were at least *two* intruders. He pulled the Mossberg pump-action 12-gauge out into the open.

Rossi fired as the first man came through the broken window, saw the muzzle flash as he triggered a semi-automatic weapon, and dove for the floor.

Dexter heard the exchange of gunfire, thumbed the shotgun's safety into the "off" position, and approached the bedroom door in time to see the second intruder exit the kitchen. A few more steps and he or she would be positioned to back-shoot Rossi. The ex-SEAL shouted, "Hold it right there!" He saw a gleam of metal as the hooded figure swung his way and pulled the trigger. The Mossberg jumped as the double-ought buck tore into its target. The man uttered a loud grunt, hit the wall behind him, and slid to the floor.

There was a loud double *clack* as Dexter chambered another shell. Meanwhile the businessman heard the steady, "Blam! Blam! Blam!" as someone fired a .9mm handgun. "Christina? Are you okay?" Dexter turned towards the living room.

That was the moment when Eason managed to fight off the impending darkness long enough to fire another burst from the MAC-10. Dexter felt plaster spray the side of his face, cursed himself for being stupid, and turned back. The shotgun boomed, Eason's face disappeared, and more blood splattered the wall and floor.

Rossi heard her opponent grunt as a 10mm round hit him above the sternum. She saw him stagger and bring his weapon back up. Body armor! It seemed like everyone had it. The FBI agent tried to make a head shot, missed, and rolled as her opponent's 9mm slugs dug splinters in her hardwood floor. Firing low, Rossi emptied the Glock at her attacker's legs and prayed for a hit. The nearest back-up magazine was in her briefcase and might as well have been on the moon for all the good it would do her.

Lopa swore as a slug slammed into his thigh. He fired a bullet into the ceiling which the agent had worked so hard to paint and toppled over backwards.

Rossi scrambled on all fours, pounced on the man's chest, and grabbed for the gun. The would-be assassin not only refused to let go, but made use of his superior strength to tilt the barrel towards her chest. The FBI agent could smell his sweat as the weapon inched her way. Was this how she was going to die? Wrestling with some lunatic in her own living room?

Then a pair of legs appeared in Rossi's peripheral vision. Dexter shoved the shotgun barrel into the intruder's gaping mouth and said, "Let go of the weapon."

That was when the eco-terrorist attempted to say "Fuck you!" discovered that it was extremely difficult to talk with a shotgun barrel in his mouth, and twisted the 9mm pistol back towards himself. There was a loud *boom* as the weapon went off. The 9mm slug smashed through the terrorist's brain and painted Rossi with warm gore.

The FBI agent pushed the body away and staggered to her feet. "There could be more of them. Give the shotgun to me and call nine-one-one."

Sirens could be heard and flames had erupted from Mrs. Pello's house "I don't think that will be necessary," Dexter said dryly, as a roof full of flashing lights appeared out front. "I think the neighbors took care of that for us."

"Get my briefcase," Rossi ordered. "I'll handle the police."

Dexter left and was on his way back when a uniformed cop appeared in the doorway. He had his service pistol out and it was aimed at Rossi. "Police! Drop the weapon!"

"Gladly," Rossi replied, lowering the shotgun to the floor with exaggerated care. "My name is Rossi. Special Agent Rossi, FBI."

Dexter sensed movement behind him, heard a woman say "Freeze!" and knew that the first cop's partner had entered the house through the shattered back door. "Drop the briefcase. Put your hands on the top of your head and kneel," she said grimly. "Do it *now!*" The businessman obeyed, remembered the leg, and was astonished to realize that he had been completely unaware of it during the firefight, something that provided scant comfort as he knelt with his hands cuffed behind him.

After fifteen minutes the police were able to verify Rossi's identity. That, plus the fact that the intruders had been found *inside* the residence, caused the police to remove Dexter's cuffs.

All the lights were on and the house was full of cops when Theel showed up. The SSA was dressed in jeans, a sweatshirt, and an "FBI" raid jacket. He took a long, slow look around then shook his head. "Damn, Rossi. You are one lucky woman. Come on, I'll take you downtown. Once the reports are filed you're coming home with me. Marlene wouldn't let me back in the house if you went to a hotel."

Rossi gave his hand a squeeze. "Thanks, John. Give me a moment will you? I need to say goodbye to someone."

Theel watched the agent make her way over to where Dexter was standing. Like Rossi, the businessman had more clothes on by then. He watched her approach. They smiled at each other. She took his hand. "Are you okay?"

The ex-SEAL nodded wordlessly.

"What are you going to do?"

Dexter smiled. "The police want a statement. After that I plan to go home and hit the sack."

Rossi smiled a crooked smile. "I'm sorry, Dex, I really am. You remember what we talked about? Well, this will make it even worse. The press will have a field day, my boss will chew me out, and *his* boss will chew *him* out."

A tear rolled down her cheek and Dexter used a thumb to blot it out. "I'm sorry about all the trouble this will cause you, but I'm not sorry about last night, and I'll be waiting when the smoke clears. Call me when and if you can."

Rossi nodded. "Thanks. You saved my life."

Dexter smiled mischievously. "I didn't ask for permission to fire the shotgun."

"No," Rossi agreed solemnly, "you didn't. We'll discuss that breach of etiquette later."

"I'm looking forward to it."

"So am I."

And with that Rossi was gone. The alley and the white van that blocked it were both part of the crime scene, which left Theel with no choice but to escort his agent out into the full glare of the television lights. The FBI agents were subjected to a barrage of questions as they hurried down the steps, made their way between the fire engines, and entered Theel's sedan. Rossi opened her briefcase, located her cell phone, and thumbed the speed dial. Thankfully it was Vanessa who answered instead of Ed. She sounded sleepy. "I'm sorry to call so late," Rossi began, "but there's something you need to know."

It was mid-afternoon by the time Dexter rolled out of bed, took a shower, and made his way downstairs. The plan was to check his mail, see if there were any bills that had to be paid, and return to his apartment. A trip to Starbucks would have been nice, but having flipped through the cable news channels, the businessman knew he would be ambushed. His phone rang constantly, his voicemail had maxed out, and half-a-dozen reporters were camped in front of his building.

Most of the focus was on Rossi, but once the press discovered that what one of the earliest reports had referred to as "Agent Rossi's male house guest" was actually an ex-SEAL, and had killed one of the intruders, the feeding frenzy intensified.

The businessman could see the TV trucks through the front windows as he left the elevator, made his way across the spotless lobby, and unlocked the door to his office. The phone rang in steady bursts, but the ex-naval officer ignored it, and was busy sorting through his mail when Pasco arrived. The timing could have been a matter of coincidence, but Dexter wondered if the maintenance man had been waiting for him—and if so why? He nodded as the other man entered. "Good afternoon, Chief. Sorry about all the ruckus. Is everything okay?"

Pasco dropped into one of the guest chairs and produced what could only be described as a shit-eating grin. "Yes, sir," the maintenance man responded. "Everything is fine. One of the reporters tried to sneak in along with the UPS truck, but I caught the bastard and escorted him out."

"Good work," Dexter said warily. There was something different about Pasco, something *very* different, but what? And why hadn't the maintenance man made mention of the shoot-out? It was as if he didn't care. The businessman placed his forearms on the desk. "So, Chief, what can I do for you?"

"Well," Pasco said, as he savored the moment. "I would like a raise. A substantial raise. An increase of a thousand per month should do it."

Dexter frowned. "In light of the fact that you haven't even been on the job for six months yet, I suggest that we defer this conversation to a later time."

Even now, with everything going his way, Pasco found it difficult to confront authority. His eyes slid away from Dexter's and it took act of will to bring them back into contact. "I'm sorry, sir, but that ain't going to cut it. Either you give me the raise, or I march out through the front door and tell those reporters about your secret room."

The blow was so unexpected and fell with such swiftness, that Dexter was left speechless. By means unknown, Pasco had discovered the room! Something that would have been bad before, but could be disastrous now, since the press would connect it with Rossi. Not only that, reporters would want to know if she had been aware of the secret viewing room, or worse yet, used it with him. He could tell them the truth—but would they believe it? Especially given all the controversy that already surrounded the agent.

What felt like liquid lead trickled into the pit of Dexter's stomach and some of the concern he felt must have been visible on his face, because Pasco nodded in mock sympathy. "I know it's a tough break sir, but you'll notice that I kept the payment down, so you'll be able to afford it."

That was when Dexter realized just how calculating Pasco really was. Rather than run the risk of killing the golden goose, the retired CPO was determined to nurture the poor bird, and thereby maximize his profit. Not only that, but he expected his victim to feel a sense of gratitude regarding the way in which the blackmail would be carried out, a notion that struck Dexter as laughable. But he *couldn't* laugh, not so long as Pasco could harm Rossi. "Yes," Dexter said humbly, "that was very thoughtful of you. All things considered I think a raise is definitely in order. Is there anything else?"

"Yes, there is," Pasco replied, his eyes gleaming with satisfaction. "Given the fact that you're a trained killer and all, I took the precaution of writing up a description of the room, which I placed in my safety deposit box. Should something happen to me, my dear old mother will find it and go to the police. Oh, and don't make any alterations to the viewing room unless you discuss them with me first. I plan to use it from time to time."

Dexter's eyes narrowed and for one brief moment Pasco knew he was staring into eternity. "Stay out of my apartment," the ex-SEAL growled, "or I may decide to take my chances with that letter."

Pasco was frightened but determined to hide it as he came to his feet. It required all the courage he could muster to push back. "And you can kiss my ass, pervert. Truth is that I will go anywhere I please…and that includes your apartment."

There was nothing Dexter could do as the other left his office, except think about the room and wish that it didn't exist.

# Chapter Six

There was a profound emptiness in the pit of Rossi's stomach as she took the elevator up to Haxton's office, where she was forced to wait for a good ten minutes before being invited to enter. Theel was present, which was to be expected, but so was Harley Demont—a surprise, and a not-altogether pleasant one, especially if the administrator had flown in because of the shoot-out. Haxton, who was concerned for both herself *and* Rossi, hurried to smooth the way. "Good morning," she said brightly. "The SAC and I both wanted to talk to you."

"Sure," Rossi replied neutrally, and shook the SAC's hand. Demont's grip was firm, almost *too* firm, as if the administrator was attempting to compensate for his relatively small stature. Rather than take her cue from Demont's carefully calibrated smile, the agent looked into his eyes. They were like chips of obsidian. "Hello, Christina. How's your daughter?"

The question had a manipulative quality, so rather than give Demont credit for remembering Missy, Rossi felt resentful instead. She forced herself to remain civil. "She's fine, sir. Thank you."

"Please," Haxton said, as she pointed toward the dreaded couch. "Have a seat."

Rossi had little choice but to circumnavigate the coffee table and lower herself onto the couch. Theel, who was seated next to her, turned his head. That allowed him to deliver a wink without Demont being able to see it. The gesture was intended to reassure her but didn't.

"Well," Haxton said awkwardly. "We know the past few weeks have been very difficult for you, especially given all the media attention you've had to endure, but there are some important matters to discuss."

"Yes," Demont added ominously. "That's correct. I'm the kind of guy who tells it like it is, and John tells me that you're the kind of person who likes to know where she stands. So, here's the situation: All of the preliminary data points to a good shooting. Even *with* the involvement by your houseguest. The technicians are still in the process of examining Lopa's van, but we're pretty sure that he was behind the attack on Rigg Hall, and carried out the Aspee murder as well. If so, that will deal a significant blow to the ELA, for which you deserve a great deal of the credit.

"In fact your boss put you in for a *second* Award for Meritorious Service. And I would support his submission, if it weren't for a serious breach of ethics."

Theel started to object at that point but Demont raised a hand. "Hold on, John. I know how you feel about your team—but Christina needs to hear this. It was a mistake to enter into a personal relationship with a potential witness. I know you were going to break it off—but that doesn't alter the facts. When the ELA gunmen broke into your house, Mr. Dexter was sleeping in your bed. The press aren't aware of the SNAKE EYE investigation, but that could change, and the ethical issue could become public. But even if it doesn't the matter must still be dealt with. That's how I see it," Demont finished matter-of-factly. "Is there anything you would like to say?"

Rossi was numb by then. The facts spoke for themselves and she was guilty. It took all her strength to hold her head up. "No. Everything you said was true."

"No excuses," Demont commented approvingly. "I respect that— and so will the folks at headquarters. So enough about the past. Let's talk about the future. The press are a fickle lot, and some of the same bozos who used to refer to you as 'Rambo Rossi,' now praise your skill and courage. That's good for the Bureau, especially given the size of this year's budget request, and could be helpful to you so long as you don't let the notoriety go to your head.

"So, given the fact that these two believe in you, it looks like you're off the hook for now. Hopefully, if things go well, the ethics thing will never show up on the six o'clock news. Don't look for a second award though," he added sternly. "Not while I'm pulling a paycheck."

Theel, who knew how contentious Rossi could be, held his breath.

Would his agent accept what amounted to a pardon? Or charge in and screw everything up? His fears were misplaced. Rossi nodded. "Yes. I understand boss."

"Well then," Haxton said, clearly happy to have the whole thing over. "It's settled. Agent Hawkins tells us that he has plenty for you to do… and the SPD is going to keep an eye on your house. Watch your back, though. There might be more wackos out there."

The statement was made as a dismissal and Rossi recognized it as such. She stood, and had just edged her way around the coffee table when Demont cleared his throat. "Christina…."

"Yes?"

"Stay away from this Dexter guy until the SNAKE EYE investigation is over. What you do after that is up to you."

Rossi gave a short jerky nod. "Can I tell him that?"

Demont opened his mouth to say, "No," but Haxton spoke first. "*Yes*," she answered without looking at her boss. "You can."

Rossi said, "Thank you," and left the office.

Demont waited for the door to close and shook his head. "She won't make SSA. Not in a million years."

"No," Theel replied quietly, "but I don't think she cares."

It was just past 1:00 P.M. The sun had broken through the clouds and thousands of people were in the process of returning to their offices as Rossi hurried towards the King County Jail building at 500 Fifth Avenue. The fact that the store windows were decorated for Christmas, and many of the people around her were heavily burdened with packages, combined to make the FBI agent feel guilty all over again. Because even though Vanessa had already completed her shopping *and* wrapped the family's presents, Rossi had yet to start. Something which was of considerable concern to Missy, who feared a repeat of the year before, when her mother returned from Arizona just in time to go shopping on December 24. *Maybe tonight*, Rossi thought to herself as she pushed her way through the door and entered the lobby.

Special Agent Olivia Inez was waiting for her FBI counterpart and had been for five minutes. She was small, only five-five or so, and had an elfin face. She wore her hair back, and her ears stuck out, which served to emphasize how cute she was. The ICE agent was dressed in a nicely tailored blue overcoat, a business-like gray suit, and low heels. The oversized bag that hung from her right shoulder was open at the top, which meant she could access her 9mm Glock quickly should she need to—a fact that had surprised more than one suspect during the past seven years.

The two women hadn't had an opportunity to work together since being introduced inside Container 7306—but that was about to change. "Sorry I'm late," Rossi said. "I was trapped in conference call hell. The good news is that they let me return to work." That wasn't completely true of course, since the FBI agent remained on administrative leave, but what was she supposed to do, sit in her hotel all day?

"It was a good shoot," Inez replied sympathetically. "Everybody knows that. The whole team was glad to hear that you weren't hurt. As for being late, don't worry about that. The gentleman we're going to talk to has plenty of time on his hands."

"Thanks," Rossi replied. "What can you tell me about this guy? I got an email from Hawk but he didn't provide much detail."

Inez nodded understandingly. "We're still in the process of putting the information together. Here's what we have so far: The suspect, a guy named Hector Battoon, is a citizen of the Philippines. He arrived in Seattle on the ship *South Wind* more than two weeks ago, went ashore after the ship's cargo was unloaded, and wound up in a knife fight. Have you ever run into a perp armed with a balisong? No? Well, I have, and don't let them get in close.

"Anyway, it seems that Battoon got into an argument with a wino down in Pioneer Square and cut the poor bastard up. Then, rather than return to his ship where he was almost certain to get arrested, our knife fighter went to ground. The only problem was that he chose the wrong people to hide with. Someone dropped a quarter on him and he wound up in the slammer. Now, after talking to his court-appointed lawyer, he wants to cut a deal."

Rossi's eyebrows rose. "What does he have to offer?"

"That's what we're here to find out," the ICE agent countered. "He claims to have information regarding human trafficking, but that could be a load of you know what, so we'll see what he says."

Rossi nodded and followed Inez to security where they were required to surrender their weapons and cell phones before being led to a small holding cell where Battoon and his attorney were waiting. The Filipino had restless brown eyes, long black hair, and Rossi noticed that his left ear lobe was missing. Lost in a knife fight? The FBI agent would have been willing to bet on it.

The Filipino's attorney was extremely young, most likely just out of law school, and appeared to be a bit unsure of himself. Having already lost a great deal of hair, he wore what remained extremely short, and even though it was early afternoon he had a distinct five o'clock shadow. When he stood, the lawyer turned out to be quite tall. "Hello," he said as he extended his hand. "I'm Larry Farley—and this is Mr. Battoon."

Both women shook his hand. "I'm Agent Inez," the shorter of the two women announced, "and this is Agent Rossi. She's FBI and I'm with ICE."

Both agents removed their coats and draped them over the back of a tired-looking plastic chair. "We would like to tape this conversation," Inez said, as she removed a small mini-cassette recorder from her bag and turned it on. "Is that okay with you?"

Farley frowned. "What about the deal?"

"There isn't any deal," Rossi said firmly. "And there won't be unless your client tells us something of value. Then, assuming that he does, the prosecutor will get involved."

Farley wasn't pleased, but produced a short jerky nod and turned to Battoon. "Go ahead. Tell them what you know."

The Filipino looked from Inez to Rossi and back again. There was fear in his eyes. Like most of his countrymen he spoke good English. "The people you're after have a very long reach. There's no place to run in here, and if they find out that I have been talking to you, I'll be dead within days."

"We'll put you in isolation, then move you to a different facility," Inez responded. "*If* you're worth the effort. Are you?"

Battoon wrestled with the question for a moment, decided that there wasn't much of a choice, and nodded his head.

"Good," Inez said. The ICE agent checked to ensure that the recorder was taping, and ran through the usual preamble regarding his rights before placing the device on the table in front of Battoon. "So, tell us about the *South Wind*."

Inez, Rossi, *and* Bowen all listened as Battoon described how the illegals had been brought aboard the ship in Hong Kong, locked into a storage compartment for the duration of the voyage, and rousted as the freighter entered the Strait of Juan de Fuca. Then the crewman told his audience how the survival-suited men had been ordered to walk out onto a rain-lashed plank prior to jumping into the sea. He had heard the roar of an outboard motor, but only for a moment, and had never seen the pick-up boat.

When Battoon made mention of the survival suits Inez glanced at Rossi and both agents felt a sudden surge of hope. The suit was a unique detail, something that could tie the *South Wind* to the body that had been found near Port Angeles, and might help move the investigation forward. But it wasn't to be. Yes, the crewman was in a position to finger the ship's captain, first officer, and purser; unfortunately he had no idea who had received the illegals, where they had been taken, or what had happened to them since. And, given the fact that the *South Wind* had left port more than a week before, the agents knew it would be a long time, if ever, before they had an opportunity to interrogate the ship's officers.

Nevertheless, it was important to squeeze everything they could out of Battoon, so the women spent the better part of an hour questioning the crewman before finally bringing the session to a close. Then, having ensured that Battoon would be placed in isolation, they returned to the lobby. "So," Inez said, as they prepared to part company. "What do you think?"

"I think we have the officers of the *South Wind* right where we want them," Rossi answered. "Providing that we can extradite the bastards. But we aren't any closer to Chow."

"I agree," Inez replied. "Take care of that, would you? It's about time the FBI started to pull its weight."

Both women laughed and Rossi felt a blast of cold air press against her face as she pushed her way through the door and stepped out onto the sidewalk. She passed a clothing store a few minutes later. Judging from their expressions the manikins were ready for Christmas.

It was evening and most of the day-people had already gone home, leaving Seattle to those who lived there or on one of the adjacent hills. Like most of those who existed at the city's core, Dexter preferred to use mass transit for local errands, or to simply walk. And that's what the businessman was doing as he headed south along Fourth Avenue towards the Westlake Mall, a small open area that fronted a shopping complex and was surrounded by retail stores. That was where he had agreed to meet Rossi. It was an appointment he had been both looking forward to and dreading.

A few days had passed since the shoot-out in Rossi's house and the press attention had finally died down to the point where the businessman could leave the apartment building without being harassed. That didn't mean Rossi would be free to see him on a regular basis. *But maybe that's for the best,* Dexter thought to himself. *Until I can find a way to get Pasco off my back.*

It seemed that with each passing day the blackmailer became more obnoxious. Pasco's previously slimy, almost-servile manner had been replaced by what could only be described as an attitude of breezy contempt. In fact, when the two of them were alone, Pasco took great pleasure in addressing Dexter as "Pervert." Not only that, but the ex-CPO had taken to spending increasing amounts of time in the illicit viewing room, watching Joe Chow abuse his mistress.

All of which brought Dexter back to Rossi, because if it hadn't been for her, the ex-naval officer would have been tempted to simply turn Pasco into the police, and to hell with the consequences. But that was impossible if he hoped to continue his relationship with the FBI agent— and protect her from negative publicity.

The whole thing was a mess and the businessman pushed it out of his mind as he crossed Fourth Avenue and entered the mall. The Christmas carousel had been in operation for the better part of a week by then and a small crowd of adults and children were waiting to ride it. Music filled the air, lights whirled, and the steady clang, clang, clang of a nearby bell ringer could be heard as the businessman paused to survey the area.

Rossi had a tendency to be late, Dexter knew that, which was why he was surprised to see her standing not twenty feet away. She wore a long overcoat with the collar turned up and was facing the carousel. Colored lights played across her face as the merry-go-round turned and a girl about Missy's age waved to her mother. Then the moment was over as the youngster laughed and rotated out of sight.

And it was during that brief moment that the businessman imagined a different life. One in which he had met Rossi rather than Kristen, been a banker instead of a SEAL, and never gone to Iraq. *How precious such a life would be*, Dexter thought to himself, and waved as the FBI agent turned.

Rossi had made use of the hour between getting off work and the appointment with Dexter to do some Christmas shopping. That made the ensuing hug awkward but enjoyable since every time the FBI agent saw Dexter her stomach went flip-flop. Which was silly given the fact that she was a grown woman rather than a lovestruck teenager. "Here," Dexter said, "let me give you a hand with those."

Rossi surrendered her shopping bags, slipped an arm through his, and thought how pleasant that was. The Westin was only a couple of blocks away—which meant it was a convenient place to have a drink and get a bite to eat. Once they were inside and seated, Dexter looked Rossi in the eye. "Okay, Christina. Let's get the bad stuff over with. Tell me the worst."

So Rossi did, and even though Dexter was expecting to hear bad news, it was disappointing nevertheless. In an effort to find out how long it would be before they could see each other again the businessman inquired about the Chow case. Although Rossi was understandably evasive, Dexter got the impression that things weren't going as well as the authorities had hoped, a fact that didn't bode well for their relationship. Unless something broke soon that is—and the possibility of that gave the ex-SEAL an idea. Something that Rossi wouldn't approve of, but couldn't do any harm, and might help. He filed the notion away.

The next couple of hours went by quickly, and it seemed like only minutes had passed before it was time for Rossi put her packages into the trunk of her car. She kissed Dexter on the lips. Nothing had been said, no commitments had been made, but the kiss was full of promise. And as the FBI agent made her way home she knew Dexter would be waiting when the SNAKE EYE team was disbanded.

But that was then—and this was now. And, rather than looking forward to going home, Rossi had come to dread it. The forensic team was done, which meant she could return, but to what? The thought of having to deal with bullet holes, blood-drenched walls, and violent memories was depressing to say the least.

The agent pulled into her rickety garage twenty minutes later, saw that some of her lights had been left on, and removed her packages from the trunk. The mish-mash of clothing that had seen her through the last few days would be brought in later.

The first sign that something was amiss came when Rossi noticed that all the recyclables that had piled up on her back porch had mysteriously disappeared. Then, as Rossi went to unlock the brand new backdoor, the smell of fresh paint assailed her nostrils. Not only that, but the faint strains of Christmas music could be heard, as if someone had left the stereo on. That was so unexpected that the FBI agent placed her packages on the floor and removed the Glock from her purse.

With the weapon pointed at the ceiling, the FBI agent kicked off her shoes and tiptoed through the house. Two of the living room lights were on, and that was when Rossi realized that the bullet holes had miraculously disappeared under a fresh coat of paint. Not only that, but her front window had been replaced, and her Christmas decorations had been restored. Except better than before. But who would have done such a thing?

The agent lowered her weapon, spotted the envelope propped up on the mantle, and walked over to inspect it. Someone had written "Christina" across the front, and when Rossi tore it open, there was a card inside. It said, "Welcome Home," in childish cursive, and had been signed by both Vanessa and Missy.

Rossi took the card over to the couch and sat down. Then, with both the gun and the card laying on her lap, she cried. That was when Snowball emerged from the bedroom, performed a long deliberate stretch, and padded across the room. Her human was home—and all was right with the world.

It was cold outside the camper, *damned* cold, and Hank Stanton's bladder was full. That meant the retired trucker had to choose between trying to hold it till morning, which was unlikely given the fact that daybreak was still a good eight hours away, peeing in his trusty 7-Up bottle, which was already half-full, or facing up to the fact that the time had come to haul his sorry old ass out into the cold. "Okay," Stanton said out loud. "It looks like it's time for EVA (extra-vehicular activity.)"

Petey, who was curled up on his bed next to the door, looked up at the sound of his master's voice and barked approvingly. The fact that the human was pulling his boots on meant they were going outside, which from a doggie perspective was always a good thing to do.

Like the sleeper Stanton had spent so many years in back during his long-haul trucking days—the camper's cheerful interior was neat as a pin. The amenities included a bookshelf filled with second-hand science fiction novels, a battery-powered radio, pictures of his family, a two-burner stove and stainless steel sink, the table he used for just about everything, some storage compartments, and his bunk up over the cab. Everything had a place, and everything was in its place, partly because of the fact that Stanton was a very disciplined man, but also because the seventy-six-year old ex-trucker had simplified his life. It might have been different had Carol survived her leukemia, but she hadn't, and once she was gone it seemed natural to sell the house, let his daughter take what she wanted, and sell the rest. Getting rid of a lifetime's worth of junk had been a liberating experience and one he didn't regret.

So, outside of dropping in on his daughter once a month to catch up on what she was doing, Stanton was a nomad. Three nights in the camper, followed by one night in a cheap motel, was his routine. And Ebey's Landing on Whidbey Island was only one of his haunts. There were at least two dozen more, some of which lay in sunnier climes and were on the calendar for late January.

There was a sudden rush of cold marine air as Stanton opened the door—followed by a joyful bark as Petey exploded out into the darkness. The waves made an insistent *swish, swish, swish* sound as they ran up onto the beach and a southbound freighter uttered a mournful moan as it churned its way through the off-shore fog.

The first step was a lulu, but the ex-trucker was used to that, and took his time. He used one hand to hold the 7-Up bottle and the other to steady himself. Once both feet were on the ground Stanton became aware of the light breeze that was coming in from the west, and gave thanks for his polar fleece–lined Gortex parka. It was practically bullet-proof and his pride and joy.

Spacious pockets held his keys, a small flashlight, and a half-used roll of toilet paper. And a good thing, too, because the unisex restroom at Ebey's Landing was locked to discourage overnighters like himself and therefore of no use to the ex-trucker. Of course such inconveniences were to be expected, especially if one chose to ignore the "No overnight camping" signs, and stay anyway. Stanton had been ticketed on a couple of occasions, but not often, and the retiree enjoyed playing hide and seek with the police.

But, outlaw though he was, the retiree didn't think it was acceptable to do his business near the parking area, which was why he followed the flashlight's glow north along the gravelly beach. Petey, his nose to the ground, cut back and forth through the oblong-shaped pattern of light as the ex-trucker made his way towards a tangle of sun-whitened driftwood. There had been mountains of the stuff back when he was a boy but it was a rare log that found its way onto a beach anymore. As for the smaller stuff, most of that was burned in campfires or hauled off to sit in front of someone's tract home. A travesty in so far as Stanton was concerned.

The old man had just stepped behind the pile of driftwood and was in the process of emptying the 7-Up bottle down a crevice when a pair of headlights appeared up on the bluff. The beams disappeared momentarily as the vehicle they belonged to made its way down Ebey Road towards the beach, but were quickly followed by a second pair of lights, and then a *third* as what appeared to be a small convoy descended on Ebey's Landing.

In spite of the fact that his daughter never stopped worrying about his safety, the ex-trucker always felt secure in the camper, especially since he had modified the back wall of the pick-up's cab so he could crawl into the front and drive away without going outside. But now, separated from his vehicle, Stanton felt a sudden stab of fear. It was December for God's sake, and colder than the bulldog perched on the front end of a Mack truck, so why would anyone other than a wacko like himself go to the beach in the dead of winter?

There was no obvious answer, not one the old man was comfortable with, so rather than return to the camper and thereby reveal his presence, Stanton whistled for Petey. Once the terrier appeared out of the darkness the old man took hold of the dog's collar and fumbled for his belt. Once freed from its loops the leather strap made a serviceable leash. The ex-trucker had just secured one end to the terrier when a pair of extremely bright headlights swept across the parking area. The boxy vehicle pulled up about ten yards away from Stanton's camper and came to a stop. The ex-trucker, who had extinguished the flashlight by then, wrapped his fingers around Petey's muzzle. "Quiet boy," the old man whispered, and watched to see what would happen.

Joe Chow was seated in the front passenger seat as Paco brought the Hummer to a stop. The pick-up with the piggyback camper was both a surprise and an annoyance. "Look at that old piece of shit," the snakehead said disparagingly. "Just what we don't need.... Some guy humping his best friend's wife. Give the bastard fifty bucks and tell him to find another place to drill her."

"And if he refuses?" Paco asked, as he ran the zipper up his coat.

"Then offer him a hundred," Chow answered. "We're only a fifteen-minute drive from the old man's house. He'll go ballistic if we pop some bozo right in his own backyard. Not to mention the fact that the holding tank is right off shore."

Paco nodded, opened the door, and made his way over to the camper. What Little Chow said made sense—but what if the guy who owned the camper was armed? With that possibility in mind Paco removed the 9mm from the waistband of his pants and held the flashlight well away from his body before he thumbed the device on. The other vehicles had pulled into the lot by then and the knowledge that there was plenty of back-up helped ease the snakehead's mind as he approached the camper. While it was old, and the paint was faded, Paco noticed that the vehicle had been well cared for. "Hello there!" the gang member shouted. "Is anyone home?"

But there was no answer other than the continual rush of the wind. A quick check confirmed that the truck's cab was empty and the doors were locked. Then, having made his way to the rear of the vehicle, Paco knocked on the door. There was no response. He brought the pistol up, turned the latch, and felt the door swing open. The beam from his flashlight swung across the tidy interior and stabbed into the darker corners.

Paco pushed the door closed, put the pistol back where it belonged, and felt a sense of relief as he made his way back to the Hummer. There was a whirring sound as Chow lowered the passenger side window. "So? What's up?"

"There's nobody home," Paco replied. "Probably a dead battery or something."

"Okay," Little Chow replied, "Let's get on with it. Our friends should be topside by now. Tell them to come on in."

Paco's fingers were starting to get numb as he fumbled the two-way out of a pocket and brought the radio up to his lips. The response was nearly instantaneous as a cold diver heard the code phrase and made the appropriate reply.

Then, as Stanton continued to watch from concealment, the distant roar of an outboard motor was heard. Minutes passed as the sound grew louder, until a fully loaded Zodiac appeared in the glare of the combined headlights and nosed its way in through the surf. Then the motor came up and the old man watched in amazement as two dry-suit clad divers jumped into the water and held the inflatable in place so that six individuals could scramble out of the boat and splash their way up onto the rocky beach.

The first thing that came to mind was some sort of drug-smuggling operation, but while the newly arrived people were busy removing their rubber suits, there was no sign of any contraband. Bundles of clothes were provided to the shivering men who hurried to put them on. Meanwhile two of what the ex-driver assumed to be their comrades struggled to turn the Zodiac around and push it back out. One of them positioned himself in the stern. The outboard came back to life, the second man rolled into the boat, and water churned as the Zodiac got underway. The operation was complete.

Stanton pressed a button on his Timex, saw the time appear, and was surprised to learn that the entire sequence had taken no more than fifteen minutes. But to what end? There was no way to know as the newly landed individuals were herded into various vehicles, engines roared, and the convoy departed. Their headlights disappeared over the top of the bluff a few minutes later, but Stanton waited long enough to be sure they weren't coming back before allowing himself to relax.

The ex-trucker had just freed Petey from the makeshift leash when he remembered what he had come for. His pecker shriveled when confronted with the cold air, but it felt good to empty his bladder, especially with a long night ahead. As for what he had already come to think of as the beach party—the old man saw no reason to report it. Not unless he wanted to report himself as well and answer a whole lot of stupid questions. "Okay, Petey," Stanton said. "Let's go home. The last one to arrive is an old geezer." The terrier barked excitedly, dashed away, and left the human to bring up the rear.

Thanks to the fact that she was with Haxton and Theel, Rossi arrived a full ten minutes early. Unlike the FBI, which had a building of its own, ICE was housed in a regular office tower, which explained the lack of security in the spacious lobby. A painting that consisted of red, green, and gold swooshes on a black background hung above the empty reception desk. After a brief wait, a half-empty elevator carried the FBI agents up to the twenty-third floor, where they got off and made their way down a short hall. The door said "Immigration and Customs Enforcement" on it and opened into a tiny reception area. A locked door blocked access to the offices beyond and a glass partition protected the receptionist. She checked IDs, asked the agents to sign in, and made a quick phone call. Hawkins appeared a few moments later and led the visitors to a conference room that overlooked downtown Seattle.

Agent Inez gave Rossi a cheerful wave. Detective Tolley pumped her hand and Lieutenant Olman offered a mock salute. Refreshments were available, so there was a pause while the newcomers removed their coats and poured coffee into Styrofoam cups. Then, with her notebook open in front of her, Rossi had an opportunity to scan the maps, photos, and schematics that covered two of the four walls. The forensic work related to the Cascade shootout site was just about complete—but the overall investigation continued.

"Okay," Hawkins said, "I know all of you are busy so let's get to it. My computer skills are pretty limited—so don't look for any fancy stuff during this presentation."

Inez dimmed the lights, Hawkins tapped a series of keys, and a Power Point presentation blossomed on the flat-panel display. "I know you've read the reports," the ASAC continued, "but I'd like to walk you through a quick chronology of what took place. The reason for this will become apparent later."

Rossi and the others eyed a map as Hawkins spoke. "When Little Chow left his apartment, and followed Highway 520 across Lake Washington, Agents Moller and Hagger figured he was on his way to Bellevue Square to unload more of his daddy's money. But once he broke north on 405, then east on Highway 2, they knew he had something else in mind. They called for instructions, I told them to stay with the bastard, and they did."

The ICE agent paused at that point to look around the room. His eyes were bright and his voice was serious. "I wish I had an alternative explanation for what took place next, but the simple fact is that the turds caught us flat-footed, and for some rather simple reasons. Never, in the whole time that we had him under surveillance, had Joe Chow shown an interest in the mountains. The result was that Moller and Hagger were driving the wrong vehicle, wearing the wrong clothing, and were seriously outgunned as they headed up into the Cascades."

Although Haxton couldn't help but admire the no-excuses manner in which her peer had accepted full responsibility for sending two agents into a bad situation, the FBI official wondered if such a *mea culpa* was truly necessary. After all, she reasoned, there had been no hint of such a trip in the material picked up off the listening devices, so how could anyone predict such behavior? Still, if Hawkins had a need for self-flagellation, then so be it.

"Meanwhile," Hawkins continued, "A plane loaded with drugs and illegals had slipped across the border and was making its way south. We now know that the aircraft, plus its cargo, was the property of the Chinese triads. Or, to be more accurate, an especially ambitious group called the Wo Sing Wo, which is headquartered in Hong Kong but has a branch in Vancouver, British Columbia. Their traditional lines of business include drug smuggling, protection rackets, and karaoke bars. But now, if our analysis is correct, it looks as though they hope to move illegals into this country as well."

"In direct competition with the Chow family," Theel observed.

"Precisely," Hawkins agreed. "And that, as it turns out, is why Little Chow went up into the mountains. The plan was to wait for the plane to land on the frozen lake and ambush the triads as they brought their illegals and drugs down to the parking lot below."

"While our people were busy digging their car out of the snow," Theel put in.

The ASAC started to reply—but the FBI agent raised a hand. "Don't get me wrong, Hawk. It wasn't their fault. Or *yours* for that matter. But it rankles nonetheless."

"Yes," the ICE agent agreed solemnly. "It does. Fortunately none of the casualties were what you would call 'good citizens.' And, with one exception, all of them were triads."

Rossi looked up from her notes. "'With one exception?' Is there something new?"

Hawkins nodded. "Yeah… Moller and Hagger had a count on the Chow contingent, or believed they did, but had no way to be sure of it. So even though we thought we might be one body short, there was no way to verify that. But late yesterday we got a break. Some guy and his son went up a logging road looking for a Christmas tree and happened across a shallow grave. The body had been uncovered by animals. The King County sheriff's department processed the scene, and it looks like the body belongs to one of Chow's foot soldiers, an ex-Army noncom who took a round right between the eyes. The news people haven't made the connection to the ambush yet, which is fine with me." Rossi nodded and made a note.

"One other item," the ICE agent added. "Even though Moller and Hagger followed Chow to the scene, or thought they did, a good defense attorney could cast doubt on that—especially given the fact that they weren't present when the ambush took place. But I'm happy to announce that the bastard left some cigarette butts on the scene. Three contained DNA identical to samples collected from various items collected in Seattle."

"That's terrific," Lieutenant Olman put in enthusiastically. "So, let's arrest him!"

"That would be lovely," Detective Tolley observed. "So, why do I have a feeling that it isn't going to happen?"

"Because it *isn't*," Hawkins answered somberly. "Not yet anyway. And here's the problem. As many of you know, Inez and Rossi conducted an interview with a knife-wielding gentlemen by the name of Hector Battoon. He claims that the body that came ashore near Port Angeles originated from a vessel named the *South Wind*. Which, according to him, took on ten illegals in Hong Kong. But that isn't the worst of it. The concept of bringing illegals in by sea is hardly new, but most of the people who come in that way are caught soon after they arrive, and the other nine haven't been. Not so far at any rate, and we don't have any idea how many more may have arrived *before* the *South Wind* shipment, or since. And that's in spite of redoubling our efforts to find out what's going on."

"Okay," Olman agreed, "but why wait? If you arrest Chow he might be willing to cut a deal."

"Most people would," Hawkins replied. "Especially if they were facing murder charges. But Little Chow is likely to be the exception. He was raised to be a criminal, and while there is friction between Joe and his father, we believe they remain loyal to each other nevertheless. The same goes for the Chow family foot soldiers—only more so, since they know that some very bad things could happen to them *and* their families should they cooperate with authorities. And the stakes are very, very, high. This is more than an immigration issue. There are some very dangerous people who would like to enter the United States—and they have no intention of slaving away in a sweatshop. What if the Chows brought in members of Al Qaida or a similar group via their pipeline? The results could be disastrous. Amy? Would you like to comment on that?"

Haxton remembered her last phone call with Demont, a rather one-sided exchange in which the administrator had been careful to offer "suggestions" rather than orders, so that both he and his career would be well-insulated should the SNAKE EYE case go critical. She manufactured a smile. "I think you summarized the situation rather well. The folks in the Department of Homeland Security are concerned that terrorists might take advantage of this particular vulnerability. And, because of that, they want us to figure out how the pipeline works *before* we shut it down."

Rossi looked skeptical. "And if Little Chow decides to shoot some regular citizens? What then?"

Haxton sighed. "Then we'll be sorry. *Very* sorry."

"But that's *if* things go wrong," Hawkins commented. "And it's our job to make sure that they don't. And we have some new leads. A woman named Letisha Jones was with Pong's mother when she came in to ID the body. She described herself as a 'friend,' but we have it on good authority that she had been one of Pong's customers, and was his mistress when he died. That raises the question of what, if anything, does she know? I would like Rossi and Inez to follow up on that."

Both agents nodded. The meeting continued for another hour. Once it was over, Rossi followed Theel and Haxton out into the rain. "So," Theel said as he held the door for her. "What do you think?"

Rossi thought about the recordings she had listened to over the last couple of weeks. It was pretty clear that Chow was a sadist, if not a psychopath, and very unstable. His father had been able to hold him in check—but for how long? "I think Chow is a grenade," she answered. "If someone or something pulls the pin he'll go off. Shrapnel will fly in every direction and people will get hurt."

"Yeah," Theel agreed soberly. "It won't be pretty."

Haxton looked from one agent to the other and made a wry face. "Thanks. No wonder I have an ulcer. I work with two prophets of doom. Come on, let's find some lunch."

It was night, but many predators *love* the night, and Dexter was no exception as he parked his SUV on the gently winding street and killed the lights. Cars passed on a regular basis, but no one took notice of the 4-Runner, nor was there any reason to. The north slope of Capital Hill was a desirable area and nice cars were the norm. The houses to his right were perched on top of the steep slope and looked out over Portage Bay, which was part of the passageway that linked Lake Union to Lake Washington.

The businessman waited for traffic to clear, got out of the truck, and went around back. Had anyone been paying attention they might have noticed that he was wearing a black jacket, black Levis, and black boots. He pulled the long, soft-sided case out of the rear cargo compartment, brought the hatch down, and touched the remote. Lights flashed and the SUV was locked. Then, walking with the assurance of someone who knows exactly what he's doing, the ex-SEAL faded into the night.

Even though a number of houses had been constructed along the street, there were a number of areas where the clay soil was subject to slippage, and people couldn't get permits. Having scouted the area two days earlier Dexter knew that one such lot lay directly above his target. That was the good news. The bad news was that good though his prosthesis was, it lacked the flexibility of the original limb, and the steep decent would be difficult. And, due to the fact that it was a hassle to get footwear on and off the artificial leg, he was wearing street shoes, an additional handicap that he now regretted.

Clumps of maple trees dominated the hillside, along with large patches of ivy and isolated bushes. The ex-SEAL had slung the case across his back by then, and a good thing, too, since both hands were required in order to secure temporary grips on the smaller tree trunks, which served to slow him down. Dexter instinctively placed his good leg in next to the hill. A series of small jumps took him steadily downwards. But there was a lot of loose material on the slope, including construction debris that had been dumped there, and it wasn't long before the ex-naval officer landed on some loose boards. They slid. Dexter lost his balance, and fell. He landed on his butt, skidded for a ways, and collided with a half-rotten stump. The impact hurt, but the pulpy wood was softer than a tree trunk would have been, and brought the slide to an end. The ex-SEAL ignored the pain as he eyed the dwelling below.

John Pasco was a man of habit, and habits get you killed. That was just one of the many pearls of wisdom that Dexter had acquired during his years as a special ops warrior. But the saying was true, since habits made people predictable, and predictable people are easy to hit. *Very easy,* Dexter thought to himself as he eased his way further down the hill and settled in behind some bushes.

The house nestled into the hillside below him was listed on the tax rolls as belonging to Helen Pasco, John Pasco's mother, who was still part of his life on Thursdays at any rate, when the retired CPO came over for dinner and she took care of his laundry. The kitchen had windows. The blinds were up and the pair of them were seated across from each other eating. That made them targets, *easy* targets, that any half-competent marksman could hit. And Dexter was a lot better than that.

The businessman unzipped the case, removed the bolt-action rifle, and screwed the homemade silencer onto the carefully threaded barrel. Not the sort of thing that most people could fabricate—but the ex-naval officer wasn't most people. He placed the rifle across a convenient limb, brought the Leupold scope up to his eye, and panned the target. The old woman and the middle-aged man were talking at the moment, profiles exposed, with the light behind them. Pasco pretty much deserved to die—but the only crime the old woman had committed was raising a scumbag. Shooting Helen Pasco still made sense though. She would call the police if he didn't, and given the amount of time it would take the ex-naval officer to climb the hill, the cops would arrive before he could reach the Toyota.

*Besides*, Dexter thought to himself, *Pasco is a dumb fuck. He figured I might come for him, but it never occurred to the stupid bastard that I might kill his mother, too. That would give me plenty of time to combine my closet with the viewing room before the estate goes through probate and some relative opens the box. Then, once the police come by, I'll open the apartment for inspection. They won't find a thing. End of story.*

Confident that the plan would work, Dexter worked the bolt and swung the crosshairs onto Pasco. The first shot would break the glass and might even hit the target. The second would kill the ex-chief petty officer if the first didn't. With him out of the way Helen Pasco would be easy.

Dexter lifted the weapon in order to get a more comfortable grip and brought it back down again. The rifle had been inherited from a long-dead uncle who bought it used. That meant the long gun couldn't be traced to him unless he left fingerprints or DNA on it. Mistakes he didn't plan to make.

The trigger mechanism was too stiff for Dexter's liking, but not worth fussing over since the businessman planned to dispose of the weapon immediately after the hit. As the crosshairs settled over Pasco's left temple, the unsuspecting ex-NCO took a big bite of mashed potatoes. The trigger was stiff, but eventually gave, and there was a *click* as the firing pin hit an empty chamber. The ex-SEAL whispered, "Gotcha!"

but it wasn't true. Not really, since in all truth it was Pasco who had him, and by the balls at that.

Which brought Dexter back to the situation at hand. Should he reach into his pocket, remove the necessary rounds of ammunition, and load the rifle? Or haul his ass back up the hill? The internal debate lasted for a good three minutes, but when it was over, the ammo remained where it was.

It took the better part of an hour for Dexter to work his way up the street above, wait for a break in the traffic, and aim the remote at the 4-Runner. The lights flashed as he crossed the open area, opened the rear hatch, and eased the case into the back. The businessman drove away two minutes later. The Pasco problem remained, but he hadn't made it any worse, and there was reason to hope. *If* he did all the right things, *if* he found a way to put the wrong things right, maybe God, the fates, or good karma would allow him be with Rossi. The hope of that, the possibility of that, put a smile on his face.

# Chapter Seven

The temperature had dropped well below freezing the night before, which meant that the entire cemetery was covered with a layer of frost. That, plus a ground-hugging layer of ectoplasmic mist combined to create a sense of other-worldliness as Rossi steered her car through a series of gentle curves and marveled at how many markers there were. Not just hundreds, but *thousands*, each signifying a life lived. She wasn't old, not yet, but the seemingly endless rows of headstones served to remind the FBI agent that she wasn't getting any younger either.

"It kind of brings you down, doesn't it?"

Rossi glanced at Inez and nodded. "Yeah, it does."

The ICE agent examined the map on her lap. "Take the next right… and watch for the canopy."

Rossi did as she was told. Where was her last will and testament anyway? In her desk at home? Or the beat-up suitcase in her closet? It hadn't been updated in quite a while, not since the divorce, and probably should be. Missy was older now—and there was college to consider. And what about Dexter? *No*, the FBI agent told herself, *it's too early to even think about that.*

"I want to be cremated," Inez said, as she peered out through the half-fogged window. "My family has instructions to scatter my ashes in Nordstrom's."

Rossi laughed out loud. She had never been teamed with a female agent before—and the more time she spent with Inez, the better she liked the woman. "In Point of View or Lingerie?"

"Neither one," the ICE agent replied. "I have a thing for shoes."

"There it is," Rossi said. "Up on the right. Just past those cars."

Inez looked and saw that the FBI agent was correct. Mo Pong had been in charge of the triads who had been slaughtered up in the mountains and his tomb was commensurate with his rank. It stood about six-feet high, was made of highly polished granite, and clearly weighed a couple of tons. "That's a lot of monument for a drug dealer," Rossi observed, as she pulled over to the curb. "Especially one who pulls such a small group of mourners."

"Yeah," the ICE agent agreed. "But it makes sense. You can bet that Pong's triad paid for the monument, both as a sign of their respect, and as a way to recruit new gang members. Yeah, it's a strange incentive plan by our standards, but their employees like it. As for the mourners, don't be fooled. A lot of Pong's friends are wanted, so they can't attend, but a banquet will be held somewhere in Seattle or Vancouver."

Rossi turned off the engine. "How come you know all this stuff?"

"The DEA folks deal with them, too, but ICE bumps up against the triads on a regular basis, so you learn things," Inez said modestly.

"Good. Maybe you can teach me how to use chopsticks," Rossi replied, as she got out of the car. "Lord knows I need the help."

The grass was short. The frost made it slippery and both agents were wearing pumps. But, by watching where they placed their feet, both women were able to reach the top of the slope without falling. To justify their presence the agents went to a neighboring grave. Rossi had purchased some flowers, which she lay next to a weather-worn headstone.

Now that she was closer, Inez could see that Pong's box-shaped tomb was supported by four well-carved tortoises, each of which symbolized immortality and life after death. At least thirty wreaths, each representing one of the deceased's relatives, friends, or associates, had been hung around the sides of the stone container, as if to embrace it. Six mourners were present, and thanks to the description that Hawk had provided, Rossi recognized Letisha Jones. She had coffee-colored skin, and a truly massive bosom. She wore a long fur coat, an above-the knee black skirt, and a pair of shiny patent leather boots. An Asian woman stood next to her. Pong's mother perhaps? Yes, the FBI agent thought so.

The service was in Chinese but the mother's grief didn't require translation. Jones bent over, as if to whisper a few words of comfort, as she took Mrs. Pong's arm. Both women went forward to place flowers on the tomb.

Satisfied that they had accomplished their mission, the agents went back to their vehicle. They were pulling away from the curb when a forlorn looking six-man band appeared ahead of them and a rhythmic *Thump! Thump! Thump!* was heard.

The musicians wore black bowlers, black overcoats, and represented a variety of ethnicities. The music had a discordant quality, to Rossi's ears at least, and seemed to have three distinct components: The steady *Thump! Thump! Thump!* of drums, a sort of bleating sound that was reminiscent of bagpipes, and the occasional seemingly random blare of horns. "Don't tell me," the FBI agent said as the car passed the men. "The burial plan includes a band."

"Bands are a regular part of Chinese funerals." Inez confirmed.

"Terrific," Rossi replied sarcastically as the band fell away behind them. "Let's hope they have one waiting for Pong when he arrives in Hell."

Letisha Jones was living in the house that she shared with Pong prior to his death. It was located in the Central District (CD). Not the part that was increasingly gentrified, but the area to the south, which had long been plagued by a high crime rate. It was dark by the time Rossi and Inez entered the neighborhood. Rather than drive the Crown Vic, which looked like the cop car that it was, Rossi was behind the wheel of her Maxima.

"There it is," Inez commented, as the car rolled past a two-story frame house. "The one that doesn't have any Christmas lights."

The FBI agent nodded, saw a parking spot, and pulled in behind a decrepit pick-up truck. The outside air was cold, and Rossi's breath was visible as she followed the broken sidewalk. A narrow path led up to the house. A pair of very aggressive pit bulls charged the cyclone fencing to the right of the house and barked madly as the agents made their way up concrete steps and onto the front porch. A rotting couch sat to the left of the door next to a broken bicycle. As the FBI agent knocked on the door she noticed that iron bars covered the windows. A must-have for drug dealers and regular citizens alike.

The agent heard the sound of footsteps, followed by a moment of silence, and knew she was being eyeballed via the peephole. Finally locks rattled, the door swung open, and Letisha Jones peered out at them. She wore a pink turban, pink bathrobe, and matching flip-flops. Her manner was belligerent. "Didn't I see you two at the cemetery?"

Rossi nodded. "Yes, you did."

"So you're cops," Jones concluded contemptuously.

"My name is Christina Rossi, and I'm with the FBI," the agent replied, and held her credentials up for Jones to see. "This is Olivia Inez. She's with ICE."

Jones looked from one agent to the other. "So," she said, "what you want with me? I ain't done nothing."

"That's true," Inez replied soothingly. "If you don't count possession of crack cocaine, shoplifting, and prostitution. So, given that you're such a good citizen, I'm sure we can count on your help. May we come in?"

Though not thrilled with the idea Jones knew that it wasn't a good idea to talk with the police out where everyone could see. She stepped to one side. "Yeah… You can come in. Watch your step though. One of the dogs crapped on the floor and I ain't had time to clean it up. There ain't no dope in the house if that's what you're after."

Once in the hallway there was no invitation to go further so the agents stopped where they were. "We're glad to hear that," Rossi replied. "But that isn't why we came. It's like Agent Inez said, we could use your help."

"What kind of help?" Jones inquired suspiciously.

"Mr. Pong was murdered," Rossi replied. "As were a number of his associates. We're looking for the people who did it."

"Really?" Jones asked skeptically. "Why? He was a drug dealer."

"That's true," Inez put in. "But there are laws against murdering people. Even drug dealers."

"Okay," Jones said cautiously. "What do you want to know?"

"Let's start with the simple stuff," Rossi answered. "Like who killed him?"

Jones opened her mouth as if to speak, apparently thought better of it, and closed it again. Then, after taking a moment to consider the question, she spoke. "I don't know who killed Mo. But there's a good chance that his previous girlfriend would. Her name is Tina, Tina Nafino, and I heard she was there when everything went down."

Rossi frowned. Jones knew something, or thought she did, but what? "Don't lie to us Ms. Jones. Mr. Pong and his associates were killed. No one survived to tell you anything. That means you have reason to believe Ms. Nafino was there."

Jones shrugged. "Mo had something going with Tina back before I came along. Then, when Mo dumped Tina, she was pissed. She knew about the load—and how he planned to bring it in. People were waiting for it. *You* figure it out."

The agents spent another ten minutes trying to wring additional information out of the woman, but it soon became apparent that either she didn't have any more to give, or didn't want to. They thanked Jones, returned to the Maxima, and drove away. The car hadn't traveled for more than a block when Inez wrinkled her nose. "Something smells."

Rossi sniffed, recognized the odor, and swore. "Somebody stepped in some dog shit."

"I think you're right," the other agent replied, "and given your recent history, it's bound to be *you*." They laughed—and it felt good.

The road that followed along the north edge of Lake Union was a narrow two-lane affair that had been built to service the many businesses that had once flourished there. Thanks to the Chittenden Locks, boats and ships had been able to access the fresh water lake since the 1930s, and there had been a time when the north shore had been almost entirely industrial. But that was back before the railroad tracks had been paved over to make way for the Burke-Gilman Trail, the Gas Works had been transformed into a lake-front park, and dozens of small boat yards, commercial docks, and marine outfitters had been forced to make way for condos, restaurants, and marinas. Someday, in the not-too-distant future, Dexter figured that the entire shoreline would be gentrified. But, for the moment, there were still pockets of commercial activity along the muddy shore.

The businessman paused at a four-way stop, waited for a garbage truck to turn in front of him, and followed the winding street west. The objective was simple enough. The sooner Rossi's case was closed the sooner he could see her. And, truth be told, he didn't have a whole lot to do. The apartment house was a part-time endeavor, and now that Pasco felt free to invade his employer's apartment any time he chose, the ex-SEAL no longer felt comfortable there.

So, rather than sit around and feel sorry for himself, Dexter had chosen to launch his own investigation into the Chow family's business activities. And, once it became apparent that Samuel Chow owned fishing boats, tugs, and barges, the naval officer in him was intrigued. That led to online research, a visit to the downtown branch of the Seattle Public Library, and a growing interest in the 150-foot long *Zhou Spring*, a factory trawler which sank after being sideswiped by a mystery ship off Whidbey Island. The subsequent investigation found that the collision opened a forty-foot long gash in her hull, which compromised three different water-tight compartments and allowed tons of seawater to enter—so much seawater that the *Spring* went down within a matter of minutes. In spite of the Coast Guard's best efforts, the second ship had never been identified.

Once the fuel had been pumped out of the factory ship's tanks, the story faded away. But questions remained, lots of them, which was why Dexter had gone looking for members of the *Zhou Spring's* crew. One was dead of natural causes, another was serving a long stretch in prison, three had moved on to parts unknown, and the two who remained in the Seattle area refused to meet with him. That was one of the reasons why the ex-SEAL was determined to visit the shipyard where the ill-fated vessel had undergone repairs prior to her final voyage. Perhaps the people who worked there would be more forthcoming.

If Dexter hadn't been paying attention, Scotty's Marine would have been easy to miss. There was only one sign and it was so faded that the white-on-blue letters were nearly impossible to read. Perhaps that was because the yard had fallen upon hard times, Scotty's customers arrived via the lake, or he didn't give a damn.

There wasn't any parking in front of the boatyard, so Dexter left the 4-Runner on the right side of the street and crossed over. A low, one-story building fronted the road, and while the outer wall boasted a row of grimy windows, there was no door. That left the businessman with no choice but to follow the structure west to the point where a driveway slanted down to the yard. The entryway was secured by a half-open gate, an unmanned guard station, and a sign that proclaimed "No unauthorized personnel allowed."

Beyond that lay what could only be described as a jumble of equipment, salvage, and just plain junk. The driveway continued straight out to where a huge orange crane presided over the pier like an insect preparing to consume its prey. The left, or east side of Scotty's Marine was dominated by what had once been the superstructure of a small merchant ship that now served as office space. A modern tug sat directly in front of that, within the rusty embrace of a dry dock capable of handling a ship twice its size. The west side of the pier was home to a seventy-five-foot-long fishing trawler. Judging from appearances, and the barge loaded with scrap metal snuggled up to it, the fishing boat hadn't left her slip in many years.

Dexter decided to ignore the sign. He passed through the gate and was twenty-five yards out onto the gear-strewn pier before a man wearing a yellow hard hat, plaid shirt, and greasy coveralls emerged from a blue sanikan. "Hey, mister! Who you looking for?"

"I'm looking for Scotty," the businessman replied. "Where would I find him?"

"Heaven would be your best bet," the ship worker replied sagely. "Or maybe Hell. He died about a year ago not five feet from where you're standing. One minute he was standing there, screaming at the crane operator, and the next minute he was dead. I ain't never seen nothing like it."

"I'm sorry to hear that," Dexter replied politely. "So, who's in charge?"

"That would be Lonny. He's running the place for Scotty's widow. You'll find him up on the bridge." The man pointed up toward the white superstructure.

Dexter said, "Thanks," and turned away. The path to Lonny's lair led between a couple of rusty cargo containers, past a pile of old netting, through a maze of enormous propellers, and terminated in front of some metal stairs. They made a clanging noise as the ex-SEAL climbed the equivalent of three stories and arrived in front of a sign that read, "Office. Watch your step."

There was no point in attempting to knock on solid steel so Dexter opened the hatch and stepped over the raised coaming. In a marked contrast to the rest of the operation, the interior of the wheelhouse had clearly been painted within the last few years, and the office furniture looked relatively new. There were three desks but only one was occupied. Lonny, if that was who the man was, appeared to be in his forties. He was dressed in a Hawaiian shirt, khaki pants, and a pair of tasseled loafers sans socks. He eyed his visitor but continued to talk on the phone that was half-concealed under a whiskered jowl. "Hey, it's up to you," the man said. "You can do the work now, or wait until the engine goes belly-up in Alaska and pay twice as much there. Personally, I'd take care of it now."

Dexter turned to look out through the windows and realized that Lonny had an excellent view of both the yard and the ship canal beyond—or would have had someone taken the time required to clean the filthy glass. "Well, screw you, *and* the horse you rode in on," Lonny finished, and slammed the phone down. "He'll come around," the shipyard operator predicted. "We're cheap compared to the assholes up in Anchorage. So, what can I do for you?"

Dexter noticed that the big man hadn't made any attempt to introduce himself or shake hands. "I'm looking for some information about a ship," the businessman replied. "A vessel called the *Zhou Spring*."

"Never heard of it," Lonny replied loftily. "But that's not surprising. Hundreds, if not thousands, of vessels have come through this yard since the place was founded back in thirty-four."

"According to the *Seattle PI,* this yard carried out an extensive refit on the *Zhou Spring* about three years ago," Dexter explained. "Then, on her way north, she sank off Whidbey Island."

Lonny frowned. "So, where do you come in? Because if some two-bit insurance company is trying to shift the liability to us you can forget it! Our attorney will cut your balls off and serve them to you for breakfast."

"No," the businessman responded patiently. "It's nothing like that. I represent a group of investors who might want to raise the *Zhou Spring*. But, before we sink our money into a salvage operation, we want to learn everything we can about the ship."

"That makes sense," Lonny admitted grudgingly, "but you're out of luck. There was a fire back before I joined the company. The office was gutted. Damned near all the files were destroyed."

Dexter took another look around. The relatively new paint suddenly made sense. "A fire? How did it start?"

Lonny shrugged. "Beats me. Burglars I guess. They came looking for cash, didn't find any, and torched the place."

It didn't sound likely, not to Dexter at least, but how to know? Perhaps the Chows had arranged for the fire—or maybe it was a coincidence. "So, how 'bout your employees? Could I talk to one or more of them?"

"No, all our people are newer than that. There was a lot of turnover after Scotty died."

That left Dexter with no place to go, so he said, "Thanks," and was halfway to the hatch when the shipyard operator stopped him.

"Wait a minute. There is one possibility, assuming he's alive that is. His name is Willy. Scotty liked the old geezer, lord knows why, and kept him around. I hear he was a pretty good ship fitter back in his day, but he was drunk most of the time, so I let him go."

The businessman felt a renewed sense of hope. "Do you have an address for Willy? Or a phone number?"

"Yeah," Lonny replied, and proceeded to rummage through a drawer. He called once looking for some of his tools. I think he wanted to hock them. Here you go."

Dexter accepted a scrap of paper, saw that a phone number had been scrawled across it, and tucked the information away. "Thanks. I'll give him a call."

The phone rang and the shipyard operator waved prior to picking it up. "This is Scotty's Marine. George? I thought you'd call back."

Dexter left the office, made his way back across the street, and unlocked the Toyota. The visit to Scotty's Marine had been less than satisfying, and if that was how FBI agents spent their time, the businessman was glad to be in a different line of work.

It was as he pulled out onto Northlake Way that Dexter realized how close Rossi's home was. He *shouldn't* go there, he knew, but the impulse was too strong to resist. A right turn put him on Stoneway, another took him into the Wallingford district, and a left turn carried him up the street the FBI agent lived on. It was a weekday, so Dexter felt sure Rossi wouldn't be there, and he slowed as he neared her house. The burned-out remains of Mrs. Pello's home was already in the process of being torn down. And there, on the other side of the street, sat the little yellow house with the scruffy yard. Just the sight of it made Dexter feel better and worse. *Okay, Willy,* the businessman thought to himself as he pulled away. *If you're out there then I'm going to find you.*

Dozens of Chinese males had checked into Seattle's Fairmont Olympic hotel during the preceding two days—so there was no reason to pay particular attention when two more arrived. Even if one of them was confined to a high-tech wheelchair. And, because Samuel knew the hotel so well, it was he who led the way with his oxygen mask hanging down onto his chest. Like his son, the elder Chow was dressed in an expensive business suit and looked every inch the successful entrepreneur. Bodyguards weren't allowed, not at the sort of event that they were attending, so Kango and Hippo were left in the lower lobby. They looked like guests at a party that they should never have been invited to. Meanwhile their superiors followed the signs towards the shopping arcade and the elevators would that carry them up to the main lobby.

Joe Chow hated such occasions, but knew they were important to his future, and struggled to look interested as his father launched into one of his rants. "The hotel was built in nineteen twenty-four," Big Chow began. "So it was only twenty-three years old when I came ashore. I knew some English, so I was able to get a job washing dishes in the kitchen, and I slept in one of the storage rooms."

"Which is how you saved enough money to open a laundry," Joe Chow added. "And by dint of hard work, grand larceny, and no small amount of luck, Chow Enterprises came into being."

It was a good story, no a *great* story, and Samuel Chow didn't like having his son cut it off. "I know you've heard it before," the older man commented as they entered an elevator, "but it wouldn't hurt for you to hear it again. A great deal can be gleaned from the past. Remember, our family once ruled a significant portion of China!"

"Yeah, and we could again," Joe Chow said flatly as the elevator doors parted and an elderly couple stepped out.

"Yes!" Samuel Chow insisted when they were gone. "And, assuming that things go well, our plan to reestablish our family on the Chinese mainland will take a great step forward this afternoon. In order to succeed we will need to rely on our *quanxi*, our network of relationships, and that is where the *Lung Tik Chuan Ren* come in. Then, once in place, we will take what we want."

Little Chow knew that the *Lung Tik Chuan Ren*, or Descendants of the Dragon, more commonly referred to as the Dragon Society, had been established during the middle 1800s "…for the purpose of advancing Chinese culture in the west." Or so its newly arrived members claimed. But, as had been explained to him *ad nauseum*, the farsighted founders had other ambitions as well. Now, after more than a hundred years of evolution, the exclusively male society was part fraternal brotherhood, part business association, and part political alliance.

Every male who was of any importance to Chinese society belonged, and not just in the United States where the *Lung Tik Chuan Ren* had been founded, but all around the world. That made the organization powerful, and *very* influential, which was something the younger Chow could relate to. Because while different from each other in many respects, both father and son shared a common lust for power, and that bound them together.

Samuel Chow took air from the mask as his son touched a button. The doors closed and the elevator jerked into motion. "I hear you, Pop," Joe Chow said lightly. "We need to hook it up, plug it in, and get it on."

Big Chow looked up at his son, and was just about to object when he saw the familiar grin. The old man laughed, and for that brief moment in time, the Chows were one. Once the elevator came to a stop the twosome made their way into the Parliament Room, which was already half-filled with people. Security was tight and no members of the press were allowed as the general session began. It was boring. Especially the keynote speech, which focused on the question of Taiwan, a controversy that Little Chow found tedious. It was difficult to stay awake. But finally, after the seemingly endless presentation ended, dozens of smaller meetings began. And it was within these more-intimate gatherings of four or five people where disputes were resolved, deals were done, and alliances were formed.

The conference room that Joe Chow had reserved on his father's behalf was one of many that lined the second-floor gallery. It looked out over the main lobby and a beautifully lit two-story-tall Christmas tree. As they entered the Belvedere Room the younger Chow was pleased to see that a uniformed waiter was fussing over a table loaded with refreshments. It was important to offer guests good food in order to maintain face.

Agent Moller, who had been chosen for the assignment by virtue of having worked as a waitress while in college, turned and smiled. As she looked into Joe Chow's black, seemingly bottomless eyes, Moller felt something cold trickle into her veins. "Good afternoon!" she said brightly. "The kitchen ran out of shrimp—but the chef sent crab at no extra charge. I hope the substitution will be okay."

"Yeah," Joe Chow responded, as he pulled a chair out of the way to make room for his father's scooter. "That'll be fine. How can we reach you if we run out of something?"

"Just grab the house phone," Moller replied, "and ask for catering. My name is Annie."

The snakehead peeled a twenty off the roll that he kept in his pocket and passed it over. "Good job, Annie. We'll call you if we need you."

Moller offered up her best smile, made the Jackson disappear, and was on her way out when a pair of well-dressed Asian males appeared at the door. They stepped aside to let the agent pass and pulled the door closed once she was gone. There hadn't been enough time to memorize their faces but Moller took comfort from the knowledge that the conference room was thoroughly wired. By the time the meeting was over, the technoids would have plenty of footage of both the Chows and their guests.

The moment that the door closed the introductions began. "It's good to see you again, Mr. Peng. This is my son, Joe."

Peng had short hair which had already started to thin, a high forehead, and quick, intelligent eyes. The suit he wore had been cut by one of the best tailors in Hong Kong and shimmered slightly when the light struck it just so. As an assistant to the consulate general of the People's Republic of China in San Francisco it was his job to deal with trade issues. And, while thousands of foreign firms were interested in doing business in China, Chow Enterprises was especially interesting. Not because of the ethnicity of its owners, which though a positive, wasn't considered to be especially important, or its size, which was relatively small, or the technology it could bring to bear, which was nil, but because of a unique skill set that made the family-owned business unique: The ability to successfully smuggle people into the United States of America.

Peng produced a business card and held it face out, right side up, with both hands. Little Chow was prepared for formality and did likewise on behalf of both himself and his father. "It is a pleasure to meet you," the official said politely. "Please allow me to introduce my associate, Mr. Tian."

More business cards were exchanged, followed by handshakes all around, and plates were loaded with food. Then, at Samuel Chow's invitation, everyone took their seats. That was when Mr. Tian opened his briefcase, removed a black box, and placed it on top of the conference room table. A simple flick of a switch was sufficient to activate the device. Meanwhile, in a room two doors down the hall, a pair of technicians looked at their monitors in alarm. "Uh, oh," one of them said. "I don't like the looks of that."

"What?" Hawkins demanded, as he flipped his cell phone closed.

"*That*," the second technoid said, as he pointed at the black box. "It could be…"

"…A jammer," the first tech finished for him, as the video feeds went black, and static blasted through the speakers.

"God damn it to hell!" the ICE agent said angrily, and threw his cell phone across the room. It shattered against the wall. Pieces flew every which way and what remained beeped pitifully from somewhere on the floor.

"Yup," the second technician said evenly. "That pretty well covers it."

Samuel Chow had always been very fastidious about his privacy, and he found the fact that Mr. Tian had similar values to be reassuring, especially since the matters they were about to discuss would have been of keen interest to the CIA, FBI, *and* ICE. Because, in spite of credentials that listed him as the Wu Financial Group's vice president of marketing, Mr. Tian's *real* name was Kong. His *real* employer was China's Military

Intelligence Directorate (MID)—and his *real* objective was to facilitate espionage within the United States. Or so Samuel Chow's sources told him—and they were rarely wrong.

The Intel officer had slightly hooded eyes, unusually long earlobes, and pitted skin. He had a BA from USC, an MBA from Harvard, and chose to speak Mandarin. Because of many years spent in the U.S., and his knowledge of the local culture, he came right to the point. "Mr. Peng tells me that you and your company would like to do business in China."

"Yes," Samuel Chow agreed. "My son and I believe that the time has come to return to the home of our ancestors."

Kong looked from one Chow to the other. According to information gathered by his staff, the old man was corrupt, but dependably so, while his son was something of a loose cannon, a self-indulgent playboy who could produce results when forced to, but who lacked self-discipline and wasn't very reliable. Still, once Samuel Chow died, adjustments could and would be made. The kind of adjustments that would place the family's smuggling operation into more trustworthy hands. *His* hands. "I agree with you," Kong said smoothly. "This *is* a good time to reintegrate your family into Chinese society. And, as a repatriated citizen, I'm sure you will find ways to support your country's government."

Samuel Chow took a deep draught of air from the mask. He was a citizen of the United States and felt a sense of loyalty to it. But, if he hoped to relaunch the Zhou dynasty, sacrifices would have to be made. He let the mask fall. "Of course," he replied simply. "Nothing would please us more."

Everett, Washington, which was located just north of Seattle, had long been home to paper mills, a Boeing plant, and elements of the Navy's Pacific Fleet. Inez knew the area so it was she who guided the FBI agent into a neighborhood characterized by old wood-frame houses, unkempt yards, and beat-up cars. "Take a right," the ICE agent instructed as they passed an alleyway. "We're almost there."

After the conversation with Letisha Jones it seemed like a good idea to interview Tina Nafino. But, like so many people who live outside the boundaries of the law, Nafino had plenty of things to hide from, including a parole violation, a felony drug warrant, and a whole lot of creditors. So it took some detective work, but it wasn't long before they came up with an address for Nafino's sister, and that's where they were presently headed. Rossi made the turn as Inez checked the numbers posted on the front of the nearest house. "Okay, this is the block. Pull over and let me out."

The FBI agent pulled over to the curb as Inez readied both her weapon and her hand-held radio. A quick check was sufficient to ensure that they were on the same frequency. Inez opened the passenger side door. "Hold until I call."

Rossi nodded. "Watch yourself."

The ICE agent grinned. "Always." Then she was gone.

Rossi checked her mirror, pulled out, and rolled past Inez. The ICE agent looked slightly out of place in her business suit and long overcoat but nobody was paying any attention. Or that's what Rossi hoped as she continued up the block. Two out of three houses boasted some sort of Christmas decorations—most of which were bound to look better at night than they did during the day. The address they were looking for turned out to be the same as that of the Little Stars Day Care Center. Not only was that a surprise, but a potential problem, because the children could be at risk if things turned nasty. But the FBI agent was confident that Inez would take such factors into account.

Rossi paused at the end of the block, took a right, and turned into the alley that ran behind the day care facility. It was barely one car wide, pitted with muddy pot holes, and bordered by all manner of fences, rickety garages, and tarp-covered boats.

The possibility that Nafino had been present during the ambush was enough to make the FBI agent's heart beat a little bit faster as she drove down the alley. *What if she was packing?* Another shoot-out was the last thing Rossi wanted.

There weren't any street numbers to go by, but the agent knew that the house she sought was about halfway down the block, and the brightly colored toys in the fenced backyard made it easy to spot. Rossi stopped the car next to the back gate, left the engine running, and got out. There hadn't been so much as a peep from Inez so far and Rossi was just starting to wonder about that when the ICE agent's voice came over the radio. "Watch out! Here she comes!"

Rossi saw the back door fly open and a young woman emerge. She was holding what appeared to be a two-year-old girl in her arms as she ran towards the rear gate and began to fumble with the child-proof lock. Rossi had circled around the front of the car by then. She held her credentials up where they could be seen. "FBI! Hold it right there—"

Nafino turned, and was about to run back towards the house when Inez appeared in the doorway. A worried-looking woman who held an infant in her arms could be seen just inside the back entryway. "That's right," Rossi said. "There's no place to run. I want you to put the little girl down and keep your hands where I can see them. She's cute. Is she yours?"

Nafino nodded as she placed the toddler on the walkway and looked down into her face. Her breath fogged the air. "Go inside, honey. It's too cold out here. I bet Aunt Carol will give you a cookie if you asked her for one."

The little girl looked doubtful, but went willingly enough, and soon disappeared into the house. Tears ran down Nafino's cheeks as she offered her wrists. "Cuff me and let's get out of here. I don't want to make trouble for my sister."

Inez ordered the suspect to put her hands over her head and kneel down. Once she was in the correct position, Rossi cuffed the suspect from behind. With that out of the way the agents helped Nafino back to her feet and led the young woman over to the sedan. The ensuing search turned up five pieces of bubble gum, a rat-tailed comb, a recently expired driver's license, twenty-two dollars and sixty-five cents, and a color photo of the girl who had been taken into the house. The young woman eyed the pocket litter that had been spread out on the hood in front of her. Somehow she still managed to look pretty in spite of the bad hair, overdone make-up, and the mascara tracks that ran down her cheeks. "Could I have a piece of my gum?"

"Sure," Rossi said thoughtfully as she unwrapped a square of gum and popped the pink square into the suspect's mouth. "Now, if you would be so kind as to get in the back of the car, we'll take you downtown. I suspect you've heard them before. But Agent Inez will read you your rights."

Nafino *had* heard them before, and while seemingly impassive, was busy thinking her way through the situation as Inez read aloud. "So," the ICE agent finished, "do you understand your rights?"

Nafino popped her gum as Rossi guided the sedan out of the alley and onto a side street. "Yeah, sure. I have the right to remain silent—or spill my guts to some low-rent hack. Can I ask a question?"

"Fire away," Inez answered indulgently. "What's on your mind?"

Nafino looked from one agent to the other. "You're Feds, right? What's up with that? I didn't rob no bank."

Inez peered into the backseat. Maybe, just maybe, Nafino was smarter than she looked. "No," the ICE agent agreed. "But you had a pretty serious relationship with an international drug smuggler."

"Where did you hear *that*?" Nafino demanded. "They're lying!"

Rossi made an adjustment to the inside rearview mirror. Nafino was probing, trying to figure out what kind of information they had, and looking for a way to cushion her fall. All of which made sense. "Really?" the FBI agent inquired. "That's funny. Letisha didn't seem like a liar to me. What do you think, Agent Inez? Is Ms. Jones a liar?"

"Certainly not," the other law-enforcement officer replied, confidently. "Ms. Jones comes across as a very trustworthy woman."

"That bitch?" Nafino inquired. "You've got to be kidding!"

"So you know her," Rossi said gently.

"Yeah, I know her," the young woman admitted. "She has big boobs. And Mo liked big boobs. That's why he dumped me."

"So you shot him," Inez said conversationally. "I can't say as I blame you, but murder is illegal, so you're going down. That's too bad because a death sentence will be hard on your daughter."

"You're trying to trick me!" Nafino said accusingly. "I never said I shot him."

"That's true," Rossi said agreeably. "You didn't say that. But who else would shoot the guy in the balls and leave him to bleed to death? Besides, I think we can prove you were there."

Nafino frowned. "Prove it? How?"

"You chew bubblegum," Rossi answered. "And, if memory serves me correctly, three or four wads of bubblegum were found at the crime scene in the mountains. Nice, juicy samples that were full of DNA. I'm betting that after the forensic people swab the inside of your mouth and run their tests, they'll come up with a match. The prosecutor will love it! Tina Nafino had a motive—and Tina Nafino had an opportunity. Case closed."

"No!" Nafino objected vehemently. "I was there. I admit that. But it was Joe Chow and his gang that did the shooting!"

Having missed the bubblegum connection, Inez looked at the FBI agent with a heightened sense of respect. "Really?" she demanded. "Well, I suppose that *could* be true. Why don't you tell us more?" And Nafino did.

The Hathaway Home for Men occupied what had once been an old office building before it had been gutted, sub-divided, and converted into semi-permanent housing for street people. But for reasons not obvious, there was no sign out front. A stiff breeze tugged at Dexter's parka and tried to snatch the piece of paper out of his grasp as he paused to check the address that the Social Services director had given him over the phone.

Then, sure that he had the right place, the businessman went down to the corner, crossed with the light, and made his way back to the middle of the block. The Hathaway's front door opened into a sizeable lobby. It was home to a dozen well-worn chairs, most of which were occupied by men who Dexter assumed were residents, and a scattering of tired-looking potted plants. Black-and-white photos of Seattle's early days decorated the walls and a counter was visible towards the back.

Dexter felt at least a half-dozen eyes follow him as he made his way back to the desk where a weary-looking man in a black sweatsuit sat perched on a stool. He had disinterested eyes, thick dreadlocks, and wore gold rings on all of his fingers. "May I help you?"

"Yes," Dexter replied. "I'm here to see Willy Bock."

"Is he expecting you?"

"No, he isn't."

Light glinted off gold as the receptionist wrapped thick fingers around the receiver. "Your name?"

"Jack Dexter. Tell him Lonny sent me."

The receptionist nodded, punched a series of numbers into the keypad, and turned away. Finally, after a muffled conversation, the black man turned back. "Willy doesn't remember a Lonny, but he hasn't had a visitor in a long time, and would be happy to see you. May I see what's in the bag?"

Dexter lifted the paper bag and held it open for inspection. "Fig Newtons. The Social Services director told me that Willy likes them."

The receptionist smiled. He had a gold tooth as well. "We don't allow alcohol or drugs in the building—but Fig Newtons are fine. Take one of the elevators up to nine. Willy lives in nine oh five."

Dexter said, "Thanks," and made his way back to the elevators just as one of the doors opened. He was forced to wait while a frail-looking man maneuvered his walker into the car before stepping aboard. The resident punched "4" and shuffled off when the elevator came to a stop. The businessman hit the "close door" button and waited for the trip to continue.

Once on the ninth floor Dexter saw an arrow followed by the numbers "900–910" and followed that down the hall to room 905. Willy was waiting at the door. He was sixty-five, but due to a lifetime of alcohol abuse and intermittent medical care, he looked ten years older than that. The ex-shipfitter was relatively short, no more than five-seven or so, and very thin. What hair he had was combed straight back. It had been two days since his last shave—and his clothes were too large for him.

However, in spite of his less-than-perfect physical condition, the shipfitter's mental faculties were intact. He had bright blue eyes and they locked with Dexter's. "So," he demanded, "who the hell is Lonny?"

"He runs Scotty's Marine," the businessman replied. "He's a big guy with an affinity for Hawaiian attire."

"Oh, *him*," Willy said disgustedly. "I guess that was his name. I always referred to him as 'the asshole up in the office.' Maybe that's why he fired me."

"I'll bet that was a factor," Dexter agreed mildly.

Willy started to laugh but it quickly turned into a hacking cough. "Cigarettes," he explained. "About a million of them. You can't smoke here though. Or drink. About the only thing you *can* do is jack off, but I can't get it up anymore. Come on in. The room ain't much but it beats the hell out of sleeping in a doorway."

The ex-naval officer entered to find that while plain and clearly designed to withstand heavy use, Willy's room was more like a studio apartment than a room. It included a small bathroom, a walk-in closet, and a living area large enough to accommodate a single bed, an easy chair, and a dresser with a TV perched on top of it. Light entered the room via a large window that looked out onto the street.

"You take the chair," Will instructed. "I'll sit on the bed. So, what can I do for you?"

The second-hand Barcalounger had belonged to Willy for so long that it had taken on the shape of his body, and the experience of lowering himself into the recliner was, for Dexter, akin to sitting on the old man's lap. "Here," the ex-naval officer said from the depths of the chair, "I hear you like Fig Newtons."

"I *do*," Willy said brightly, as he accepted the paper bag and peered inside. "Not as much as I like booze—but I like 'em just fine. Now, like I said before, what can I do for you?"

"I'm looking for information," the businessman answered. "About a ship named the *Zhou Spring*. The asshole up in the office said that you might have worked on her."

Willy cackled appreciatively. "I like you, Jack, I really do. Sure, I not only worked on the *Zhou Spring*, I worked on her just before she took her final voyage. Tell me something, Jack. Are you a seagoing man?"

"I was a naval officer," Dexter admitted.

"I thought so," Willy said knowingly. "I served in the Navy too, except I was enlisted. So, what do you want to know about the *Spring*?"

Lonny had accepted the salvage lie so Dexter saw no reason to invent a new one. "I'm part of a group that is looking into the possibility of raising the *Zhou Spring*."

"And you want to know what kind of condition she was in," Willy interjected. "Well, you came to the right man. That was one helluva a strange refit, that was."

Dexter's eyebrows rose. "Really? Why do you say that?"

The paper bag made a rattling noise as Willy's hand plunged down inside it. "Rather than work her over the way we normally would, Scotty ordered the crew to concentrate on constructing an airtight chamber inside the main hold."

The businessman frowned. "A water-tight chamber? Whatever for?"

"That's what *we* wanted to know," the ex-ship fitter replied, as he ripped the cellophane open. "They told us it was for some kind of marine research—but that was bullshit. The chamber included a lock, just like what you would find on a submarine, plus living quarters for twelve men. We're talking a galley, fresh water showers, and bunks. Plus an air supply and everything to go with it."

Willy finished the sentence by stuffing two Fig Newtons into his mouth. A look of satisfaction came over his face as he chewed and Dexter posed the next question. "You're sure of that?"

The old man swallowed. He was clearly resentful. "Sure, I'm sure! I may have been a lush, but I served as a machinist's mate on two different subs, so I know an airlock when I see one." A conspiratorial look came over his whiskered face. "Do you know what I think?"

Dexter shook his head. "No, I don't."

Willy looked left and right and lowered his voice to little more than a whisper. "If I were you I would check to see if she's really there—before I paid one red cent to raise her! There was something weird about the people who owned her."

"Chow Enterprises?"

"Yeah, that's the bunch. What if they're a front for the CIA? What if the spooks took the *Zhou Spring* up to the Gulf of Anadyr, scuttled her just off some naval base, and made the rest up? Navy SEALS or the like could use that chamber as an underwater base! The Russians would never know."

It had been quite a while since the Cold War, and the ex-naval officer wasn't sure the United States government cared what the Russians were up to in the Gulf of Anadyr, but that didn't matter. What *did* matter was the sudden realization that there was still another way the airtight chamber could be used, one that might be worth sinking a perfectly good ship for—especially since the *Zhou Spring* had been fully insured. What if the Chows had created an underwater environment where illegal immigrants could be held—*and* recovered all of their costs from an unsuspecting insurance company? A brilliant scheme if there ever was one. "What about the investigation?" the businessman inquired. "Did anyone interview you?"

"Hell, no," Willy replied. "Scotty took care of that sort of stuff."

Dexter got up to go. "Thanks, Willy. You've been a big help. Some other people might want to speak with you. Would that be okay?"

"Sure," the old man replied brightly. "Tell them to bring Fig Newtons."

# Chapter Eight

The silver Mercedes pulled off I-5 and headed west toward Bell Town. It was a cold, gray, Seattle day, the kind that often put Joe Chow into a bad mood. But, thanks to a profitable night at the gaming tables, the snakehead felt pretty good. All he needed now was a good fuck, some decent food, and eight hours of sleep. Such were his thoughts as the car pulled over to the curb and Paco waited for him to get out. "Pick me up at seven," Little Chow instructed. "We have work to do."

Paco nodded. "I'll be here, boss."

Joe Chow got out, made his way into the apartment building, and entered one of the elevators. Meanwhile, John Pasco was one floor down, sitting at his desk when the tenant appeared on the security monitor. That gave the maintenance man an idea. Rather than sit at his desk, composing a letter to the tenants, why not have some fun?

Ten minutes later Pasco let himself into Dexter's apartment, checked to ensure that the ex-naval office wasn't there, and made his way back to the master suite. There was no way to know if Chow and his mistress would put on a show for him, but not knowing was part of the fun, as was the possibility that he would be there when his employer came home. His presence never failed to get a rise out of the ex-naval officer, which pleased the maintenance man to no end.

Pasco pushed Dexter's neatly hung clothes out of the way, slid the panel to one side, and stepped through the opening. The room beyond the glass was dark, but that could change, and the retired petty officer had high hopes as he settled into the chair. He had been fortunate enough to watch Chow screw his mistress on three different occasions by then and was looking forward to a fourth.

Nothing happened for a while, and Pasco had started to doze when the lights came on. The maintenance man sat up as Joe Chow and his mistress entered the room opposite him. Both were naked, and judging from the fact that Ling's legs were wrapped around her lover's waist, were already well into what promised to be a rather athletic quickie.

Pasco watched Chow position his mistress on the bed, and the retired CPO had already dropped his pants when "Anchors Aweigh" started to play. The ex-Navy man felt the bottom drop out of his stomach as he bent to retrieve his cell phone. His first attempt to remove the device from the belt clip failed and the Navy anthem was still playing when Joe Chow approached the mirror. His formerly erect penis was limp by then but the 9mm semi-automatic pistol that the snakehead kept next to the bed was ready for action.

Pasco looked up at that point, saw the side of Chow's face pressed against the glass, and said "Oh, shit!" He quickly wished that he hadn't as the other man raised a pistol and began to back away. Ling brought a pillow up to hide her breasts as Little Chow fired, not just one round, or two, but an entire magazine as the Browning spit fire and Ling released the pillow in order to cover her ears. Glass shattered and fell in sheets as the gun jumped in the snakehead's hand and the first of two slugs struck Pasco's chest. The maintenance man was still in the process of falling backwards when a third bullet removed the thumb from his left hand. Four shots followed, but they went wide, as Chow finished drawing a line from left to right.

Then, with a halo of gray gun smoke floating around his head, Little Chow moved forward to inspect his handiwork. There was a lot of broken glass on the floor so the snakehead had to watch his step. The last person Joe Chow expected to see in the room beyond was the building's maintenance man, but there he was, laying on his back with his trousers bunched around his ankles. The bastard was a pervert, not that it made much difference, since there were laws against shooting unarmed people. And, if he were to be arrested, the younger Chow knew that the authorities would try to hang all sorts of other shit around his neck. So, like it or not, the only thing he could do was run. "Get dressed!" Joe Chow ordered as he turned towards Ling. "We have to get out of here."

Later, after being interviewed by the police, two of the building's tenants would admit to hearing the sound of gunfire. But the sounds had been muffled, and the residents had been unsure, which was why more than two hours passed before Dexter came home from interviewing Willy, let himself into his apartment, and discovered the murder. The first indication that something was amiss was the sound of tinny music, which the businessman followed to his closet, and then into the viewing room beyond. That was when he saw the shattered glass, plus Pasco's dead body, and realized what had taken place. The ex-SEAL wasn't shocked, not after all the bodies he'd seen in Iraq, but he was saddened. Not for Pasco, who Dexter detested, but for Rossi. Because the truth about both the room and his secret sex life were about to become public and it wouldn't take the press very long to make the connection.

Slowly, like a man in an old-fashioned diving suit, the ex-naval officer bent over to retrieve the phone. He flipped it open, cleared the incoming call, and cut *Anchors Aweigh* off in mid-stanza. Then, phone in hand, he thumbed 9-1-1. It rang twice before a woman answered. "This is nine-one-one. How can I help you?"

"I have a murder to report," the businessman said heavily, and the downward spiral began.

It had been a long, hard day and Rossi was still in the office. The pale yellow winter sun had faded hours earlier, but there were plenty of lights, and the stores would be open until nine. And a good thing too, because in spite of the fact that Rossi had done a better job of getting ready for Christmas than the year before, there was still some shopping left to do. Ed and Vanessa had invited her over for Christmas dinner, which was very nice of them, although it was probably based on a request from Missy. So, in spite of the fact that Rossi didn't really *want* to go, she felt she *had* to, both to please her daughter and avoid the rather depressing prospect of spending the evening alone.

Such were the FBI agent's thoughts as she turned her computer off and prepared to leave the office. It was satisfying to take a person like Tina Nafino off the street, but no good deed goes unpunished, and the better part of the afternoon had been spent dealing with the paperwork related to the arrest and the subsequent confession. Or *partial* confession, since both Rossi and Inez believed that Nafino had been more than just a cheerleader during the mountain ambush, and was withholding information that could incriminate her. Later, once they had a chance to interview others who had taken part, the truth would come out.

But that matter aside, the weight of Nafino's statement added to the other evidence had been sufficient to tip the balance where Joe Chow was concerned. Despite concerns about a possible connection between the Chow family and the Chinese Military Intelligence Directorate, and the fact that certain aspects of their smuggling operation continued to be shrouded in mystery, the decision had been made to arrest Little Chow. Everyone agreed that the snakehead was too dangerous to leave on the streets, a decision Rossi endorsed because it would put a wacko behind bars *and* hurry the day when she could see Dexter. That was when her phone rang, and on the chance that it might be a call from Missy, the agent answered. "Rossi, here."

The voice on the other end of the line belonged to Theel. "Christina. I'm glad I caught you. Amy's here. Could you stop by?"

Theel sounded serious, but that wasn't unusual, so Rossi wasn't especially concerned as she grabbed both her coat and briefcase before making her way to the SSA's office. Theel was seated behind his desk and Haxton occupied one of the guest chairs. In spite of the twelve-hour day she had just completed, the ASAC looked fresh as a daisy. "Have a seat," Theel instructed. "There's a new development that you need to be aware of."

"Uh, oh," Rossi said, as she put her briefcase on the floor and threw her coat over the back of the remaining chair. "Why do I have a feeling that I'm not going to like this?"

"Because you aren't," Haxton answered honestly. "Did you meet a man named John Pasco when you visited Jack Dexter?"

Rossi felt something cold start to trickle into her veins. "No, I don't think so."

"Well, there's no particular reason why you should have," Theel put in. "Pasco was Dexter's maintenance man."

Rossi looked from one face to the other. "*Was?*"

"Joe Chow shot him earlier this afternoon," Haxton responded. "That's the way it looks anyway—but the SPD's homicide detectives are still working the scene. George Tolley will make sure that we're in the loop."

"Damn," the FBI agent said regretfully. "And we were just about to pick him up. He's a crazy bastard. What set him off?"

Haxton looked uncomfortable so Theel took over. "Yeah, well, this is where everything gets weird. According to what Tolley told me, Pasco was found in a secret room that was accessed via Dexter's apartment. A room equipped with an interrogation-style one-way mirror."

Both supervisors went silent at that point giving Rossi an opportunity to absorb what she had heard. Slowly, bit by bit, the pieces fell into place. The effect that Dexter's war wound had on his sex life, the telescope in his living room, and now this. She felt anger, followed by revulsion, followed by embarrassment. How could she have been so stupid? Some aspect of Rossi's emotions must have been visible on her face because Haxton hurried to intervene. "You mustn't be too hard on yourself Christine. How could you know? None of us did."

"That's right," Theel chimed in. "It was just one of those things."

Rossi battled to maintain her composure. "Thanks, but I hope they throw the book at him."

"Well," Haxton replied tentatively, "I don't think there's much chance of that. It's pretty clear that Dexter wasn't there at the time of Pasco's death. And the people that Dexter victimized, which is to say Chow and his mistress, are wanted for murder. With that in mind I doubt he'll be charged."

"There is a problem however," Theel added soberly. "Not for him— but for *you*."

"All the stations have the story," Haxton explained. "And they drew the line from Dexter to *you*. Not only that, but it gives them an excuse to replay the footage from the shoot-out at the University of Washington, the Aspee homicide, *and* the attack on your home."

Rossi thought about the impact that would have on Missy and bit her lip in an effort to hold back the tears. "Can I go now?"

"Yes," Theel said gently, "but don't return home. The media will be all over the place. We'll put you in a hotel."

"Thank you," the FBI agent replied gratefully. "That sounds like a good idea. But I need to call Missy first."

"I'll wait," the SSA said. "Come get me when you're ready."

Rossi returned to her cubicle, checked to ensure that no one else was around, and allowed herself to cry. Five minutes. That was all the time the agent was willing to grant herself before she blew her nose, dabbed at her eyes, and lifted the receiver. There was a quick series of tones as speed dialer did its work. It was Vanessa who answered. "Hello, Christina. I was expecting your call."

"Yeah," Rossi said. "I suppose you were. How's Missy?"

"She doesn't know yet," the other woman responded. "Ed heard the news on the way home and picked her up. We're going up to the cabin. We'll tell her there and wait for the media frenzy to die down."

"Thank you," Rossi said humbly. "I'm sorry."

"Don't be," Vanessa said evenly. "It wasn't your fault. Take care of yourself."

"I'll try," Rossi promised, and the conversation was over.

Later, laying in a strange bed in a strange room, the FBI agent watched the eleven o'clock news. A reporter had ambushed Dexter out on the street and the businessman looked shell-shocked as he waved the camera off. "Why?" Rossi demanded out loud. "Why did you have to be so messed up?" But the face disappeared, a story about a traffic accident came on, and the question went unanswered.

It was nearly noon on the day after John Pasco's rather inglorious death when the press were invited into the lobby of the building that bore Samuel Chow's name. Now, as the reporters addressed their questions to the family's lawyer, the old man sat in the high-tech wheelchair and clutched an oxygen mask to his face. Everyone knew that the businessman couldn't answer questions directly because of his health but his concern was plain to see.

Meanwhile, as the press focused their attention on the attorney and the body double, the *real* Sam Chow was being whisked away inside a black utility van. It left the underground garage unobserved, wound its way onto the freeway, and sped south on I-5 at a steady sixty-three mph. The last thing the snakeheads needed was a speeding ticket.

Traffic was heavy, so a full forty-five minutes passed before the van exited the freeway, and headed west into the suburb of Federal Way, a once-rural area that had seen a significant influx of Asian immigrants over the past twenty years. Most were hardworking citizens who wanted nothing more than an opportunity to carve themselves a slice of the American pie.

And that was one of the reasons why Samuel Chow had real estate holdings there, good investments that had appreciated over the years and served him in other ways as well. Earlier, before the *Zhou Spring* had been equipped for use as an underwater way station, most of the illegal immigrants that his organization brought into the US came through Canada. Once across the border, cars and vans were used to bring them down to Federal Way where it was easy for the newly arrived Asians to blend in. Then, within weeks, if not days, they were shipped south to the sweatshops of California.

Knowing that, Joe Chow had gone to ground in one such house, which though held under an employee's name actually belonged to Chow, Sr. The younger man felt a variety of emotions as he watched his father's van roll up the drive and into the garage. The old man would be pissed, no doubt about that, but what else was new?

Joe Chow turned away from the window. Paco was there, as was Skinner and a new man named Kwong. All were heavily armed. "Remember what I told you," the snakehead instructed. "I don't plan to take any shit from Kango or the other morons who work for my father. So, if they start to get up my ass, then pop them."

Paco grinned. "No problem, boss. Kango belongs to me. We got your six."

Meanwhile Samuel Chow took a pull from his oxygen mask as Kango and Weed made use of the van's lift to unload the wheelchair. Then, once the door to the house was open, the crime boss steered himself into what turned out to be the kitchen. The combined odors of garlic, soy sauce, and fermented *gochu Jang* chili paste filled the air. A family of four terrified Koreans kept their eyes on plates as even more armed men arrived to join those already in control of their home. The elder Chow was barely aware of the renters as he trundled past the pathetic tableau and turned into the shabby living room.

The first thing the crime boss saw was his son, who, in spite of the circumstances, was trying to look cool. And behind him, positioned to provide support if called upon to do so were Paco, Skinner, and a man he hadn't seen before. Big Chow frowned. "Hello, son. This is between us. Tell your boys to take a break out in the garage."

It was hard to stand up to his father, *very* hard, but the younger man forced himself to do so. He managed a smile. "Sure, Pop. You send Kango and Weed out of the room—and my men will follow."

It was a reasonable request, framed in a respectful manner, yet Samuel Chow hesitated. And, when he asked himself why, the old man was forced to confront the terrible truth. Slowly, as his own powers started to fade, he had come to fear his son. *Not* because of the younger man's strength, as should have been the case, but because of his weakness. The truth was that Joe had a hidden flaw, evidence of which could be seen in his addiction to gambling and general lack of focus.

It was a horrible realization, made all the worse by the extent to which it had so long been denied, and what it meant for the future. Yet there it was. His son, the boy on whom his hopes for immortality rested, was not only unfit to lead, but so unstable as to be dangerous. Even to his father. The older Chow spread his hands. "It shall be as you say—everyone will stay."

His father's apparent capitulation seemed like a victory at first, until the true implication of his words began to sink in, and Joe Chow felt a chill run up his spine. His father thought he was crazy! So loony it wasn't safe to be alone with him! A lump formed in his throat and he struggled to swallow it. His father was a predator, had *always* been a predator, and still was. To what lengths would such a man go in order to protect himself? Would he murder his own son if he believed such an act was necessary? The answer was obvious.

Tension filled the room as the representatives from both sides tried to stare each other down. The Korean family continued to eat with desperate intensity and the family dog scratched to get out. No one responded. "Tell me what happened," Samuel Chow began. "Tell me everything."

So Joe did, and once he was finished, his father frowned. "You could have called the police...or had Paco beat the crap out of him. Why shoot the bastard?"

Little Chow looked down at his feet and back up again. "People had been following me for weeks. I thought some triads were hiding behind the mirror."

Samuel Chow started to respond, discovered he couldn't, and was forced to take a long pull from the oxygen mask before he spoke. "You should have told me that people were following you."

Mild though the response was, it constituted a rebuke and Joe Chow was quick to respond. "You're the one who wants me to take charge," he said defensively. "I did what I thought was right."

*And you were wrong,* the elder Chow thought to himself, but chose to keep the criticism to himself. "Assuming that you have been watching the news you know that the man who owns the apartment house you lived in has been sleeping with an FBI agent named Christina Rossi. Is there any chance that the people who have been following you work for the government rather than the triads?"

Suddenly Little Chow knew that his father was correct, but he didn't want to admit that in front of the others. "Sure, anything's possible. But the triads seem more likely. Especially since we greased Pong and stole his dope."

The crime boss remained unconvinced but saw no reason to say so. "Okay, son. It's water under the bridge at this point. We need to get you out of the country. And, now that we have a footprint in China, that's the safest place to go."

Ling knew Joe Chow's moods by that time and saw anger in the way the snakehead held his body. "China?" the snakehead demanded incredulously. "I don't want to live in China. The place is a shit hole."

"You can't remain here," the elder man responded patiently. "It's either China or an American jail, assuming you escape the death penalty. A ship will arrive in a week or so. Kango will take you aboard. One of my agents will meet you in Shanghai. Later, after the furor dies down, I will join you there."

Joe Chow eyed Kango for a moment before switching his gaze back to his father. "That's bullshit, Pop. I'm not going anywhere with no duck-tail-assed, shade-wearing geezer."

Samuel Chow experienced a rising sense of anger as he paused to take some much-needed oxygen. Had Joe been anyone else he would have been dead by then. "Have you got a better idea?"

"Yeah," the younger Chow replied. "I do. You give me the name of the ship, and the person I'm supposed to contact, and I'll take care of the rest. And, once you arrive in Shanghai, we'll talk. Maybe Hong Kong would suit me better. I like the movies they make."

Samuel Chow sighed. "Okay, but lay low. Don't use your cell phone, your computer, or your credit cards. And change cars."

"Yeah, yeah," Little Chow said dismissively. "I can take care of myself."

It was a stupid statement given the circumstances, but the crime boss allowed it to pass and removed an envelope from the inside pocket of his jacket. "All the information you need is here. Memorize the note and burn it. And don't gamble the cash away. There won't be any more until you arrive in China."

A somewhat awkward hug followed. Joe Chow left first, quickly followed by Ling and his bodyguards. Rubber squealed as the Mercedes left the driveway,

Samuel Chow went next. Once he was in the van, and it had been backed out of the garage, he ordered the driver to stop. His eyes swung around to make contact with Kango's sunglasses. "Go back and clean things up."

The bodyguard nodded, motioned for Weed to accompany him, and the two of them went back inside. The silencers worked well. A clean-up crew would drop by later to pick up the bodies, and because the Koreans were illegals, there was no one to report them missing.

Meanwhile, in downtown Seattle, the press conference was nearly at an end. The TV crews had already started to tear down their gear when a pert little print reporter posed a final question. "In light of the fact that the police are looking for his son in connection with John Pasco's death, does Mr. Chow plan to go ahead with the fireworks display scheduled for New Year's Eve?"

It was a good question and one that had been lost in the give-and-take around the murder. The New Year's Eve fireworks display was a Seattle tradition—and one that Chow Enterprises had supported for the last three years. One of the TV crews hurried to turn their camera on as the lawyer pretended to conference with the double. Finally, after some muffled whispering, the attorney straightened up. He had good teeth and didn't hesitate to put them on display. "Mr. Chow is pleased to announce that his family's promise to the city of Seattle will be kept.

That will be all." The press conference was over.

Having watched the Samuel Chow press conference in the meeting room closest to her office, and desperately in need of a break from the SNAKE EYE case, Rossi went out for lunch. A few members of the press corps had been seen hanging around the building's main entrance earlier that morning but Big Chow's nicely choreographed presentation had been sufficient to pull them away. The elevator was crowded with lunch-hour traffic, and Rossi followed her coworkers out through the sparsely furnished lobby and onto the sidewalk, where the agent discovered it was raining. And not just a misty rain of the sort seasoned Seattleites tended to ignore, but a steady downpour.

Rather than return to the office and get her umbrella, the agent decided to make a run for it. The light changed, traffic came to a halt, and Rossi made a mad dash for the far side of the street. Once there she kept on going. The restaurant was halfway down the block. Though not cheap, it wasn't expensive by downtown standards, and claimed to be Italian. The front door opened as a group of women left and the FBI agent entered. No one seemed to recognize her, which was perfect, and she was shown to a two-person table.

And that's where Rossi was, menu in hand, when Jack Dexter appeared in front of her. His hair was plastered to his head, water streamed off his Northface parka, and he looked absolutely miserable. For one brief moment Rossi felt sorry for him. Then she remembered the secret room, what it meant, and who she was dealing with. Her voice was hard and unyielding. "What are *you* doing here?"

"Hoping to see you," Dexter replied honestly. "May I sit down?"

"*No,*" Rossi answered emphatically. "Not now—not ever."

"The room was wrong," Dexter said desperately. "I admit that and I'm sorry. Then I met you, and everything started to change for the better."

"Get out," Rossi said coldly. "Or should I call the police?"

The tenor of the conversation had attracted the attention of other diners by then, and there was the sound of scraping chair legs as people sought to put some distance between themselves and potential trouble. "No," Dexter answered sadly. "There's no need to call the police. But I have some information about the case that you're working on. Something that might be helpful."

Rossi was in the process of reaching for her cell phone when Agent Kissler materialized next to her table. He had been cleared by the shooting board by then, still had a thing for Rossi, and had been watching from the far side of the room. Here was the sort of opportunity he had dreamed of. "Hey, Rossi. Is everything okay?"

*"No,"* the FBI agent answered adamantly. "It isn't. Would you be so kind as to escort Mr. Dexter to the door?"

Kissler grinned. "I'd be happy to." Then, having turned toward the ex-SEAL, he said, "So, bud, how would you like to go? Vertically? Or on a stretcher?"

For one split second Dexter considered decking the pompous FBI agent but pushed the thought away. "I don't want any trouble. And I can find the door on my own."

Kissler watched to make sure that the man was truly gone before turning back to Rossi. The face had been familiar but he wasn't able to put a name with it. "Who was that jerk anyway?"

"He was a possibility," Rossi answered cryptically. "One that didn't pan out."

There had been a time when anyone who wanted to travel north to Canada, or south to Oregon, had been forced to use old Highway 99. But those days were long gone, and during the forty-odd years since Interstate 5 had been constructed, the once-vital route had fallen on hard times. Starting down in Tacoma, and extending past Seattle to Everett, 99 had gradually been transformed into an endless assembly line of strip malls, car dealerships, and second-rate motels. Some, like the one that Joe Chow had chosen to stay in, harkened back to the good old days when such establishments were independently owned and boasted monikers like the Rip Van Winkle, the Four Leaf Clover, and the Conquistador.

But if the Prospector's Palace had ever been palatial it had been a long time ago, back before its elderly owners had been forced to rent their rooms out by the month, and a seemingly endless stream of down-at-the-heels drifters, part-time whores, and crack addicts had come to stay.

Still, it was the rundown motel's seediness that made it a good place to hide, which was why one of Paco's many cousins had been kind enough to sign the guest register on Little Chow's behalf.

That had been six hours earlier, shortly before the snakehead and his bodyguards had gone out to "take care of some business," leaving Ling to entertain herself. Besides the water-stained walls, a ragged green rug, and some beat-up furniture, the room boasted an ancient television. The illegal watched that for a while, lost interest, and went looking for Chow's computer. The machine was buried under the pile of mostly dirty clothes at the center of the queen-sized bed. There was a phone, and thanks to all of her previous experience, the illegal knew how to establish a dial-up connection. Ling was online three minutes later.

The first ten minutes were spent visiting her favorite sites, but it wasn't long before the illegal became bored and began to play what she thought of as "the open game." By choosing "file," and pulling down to "open," Ling could see which sites Chow had been to by entering each letter of the alphabet. She often began with "A," which typically produced links to various sports teams, but on that particular day Ling went with "Z." But it wasn't until the illegal entered "X" that she got a series of links that included "XXX."

Though not interested in pornography herself, Ling had reason to know that the snakehead was, because looking at pictures of people having sex never failed to make him horny. And, having seen a particular act online, it wasn't unusual for Chow to insist that his sex slave help him recreate whatever he had witnessed.

So, curious as to what sex acts she might be forced to perform, the illegal chose the first link. A page called, "Asian Fuck Toys," appeared. Ling hit "enter," saw the page dissolve, and was amazed when footage of her sister May Ling appeared! Not dressed, as in the still photos Chow had given her, but naked. And not just naked, but performing oral sex on one man, while another awaited his turn.

The shock of it took Ling's breath away. Then, as the full realization of what had happened to them began to sink in, the young woman began to cry. The sobs started somewhere deep down, racked her entire body, and left her gasping for air.

Finally, her face still wet with tears, Ling retrieved her jacket, and the small stash of money she kept hidden in a spike-heeled boot, and walked out into the night. Meanwhile, as the door slammed behind her, the digitized version of May Ling continued to service her *bao* debt. The only question was whether life on the gold mountain was worth the price. Eventually, after sixty seconds had elapsed, the video faded to black.

It was cold and foggy as Dexter pulled into the Mukilteo ferry dock, paid the fare, and followed the car in front of him into lane two. A ferry had arrived ten minutes earlier and steel clanged as a stream of vehicles passed over the ramp. Most of the early morning traffic consisted of people commuting to jobs on the mainland. As for the folks headed in the opposite direction, that was a little more difficult to figure out. But, judging from the trucks that were lined up ahead of him, Dexter assumed they were transporting goods to small towns like Clinton, Langley, and Coupeville, which was where the ex-SEAL was headed.

It was a crazy idea, no a *stupid* idea, but one which would get him out of town and away from the press. Something he very much wanted to do, especially in the wake of the disastrous confrontation with Christina. It had been a mistake to wait for her and follow her into the restaurant. What he needed to do was accept the fact that the relationship with Rossi was over and put the whole thing behind him.

And he had, except that he hadn't. Because truth be told, the entire trip up to Coupeville and Ebey's Landing was part of a boyish fantasy in which he would locate the *Zhou Spring*, prove that the wreck had been equipped with an underwater habitat, and thereby secure Rossi's forgiveness—all of which was not only patently absurd, but pathetic.

The sudden blare of a horn, plus the realization that the car in front of him was halfway to the ferry, caused Dexter to hurriedly start the Toyota's engine and pull ahead. There was the usual bump, thump, and *clang* as the 4-Runner came down off the metal ramp, followed by a turn to the right as a uniformed crewman directed the businessman up onto a slightly elevated deck.

After the relatively short trip across the water, and a pleasant drive through partially wooded farmland, Dexter entered Coupeville, a small but picturesque town that attracted numerous tourists during the summer but was pleasantly empty during the winter months. From there it was a ten-minute drive to the western shore of Whidbey Island and the stretch of beach called Ebey's Landing. There were only two vehicles in the parking lot at the foot of the bluff, a white Subaru with California plates and an old but well-maintained pick-up with a camper on the back.

Dexter pulled in about ten feet away from the truck, got out, and took a moment to enjoy the sharp tang of the sea. The SUV's cargo compartment was full of diving gear. Some of it, like his mask, snorkel, and weight belt had been purchased while in college, but the rest of the equipment had been acquired shortly after he had been discharged from the Navy. The entire notion of proving himself had been important back then, but after some successful dives, he gradually lost interest in the sport as the apartment house claimed more and more of his time. Now, as the ex-SEAL began to organize his gear, he realized that more than a year had passed since he had last put it on. A terrier came racing in from the north, skidded to a stop, and barked. "He won't bite," Hank Stanton said reassuringly, as he rounded the back end of his camper.

"Good," Dexter replied, as he bent over to pat the dog on its head. "He looks pretty vicious."

Stanton laughed and extended his hand. "I'm Hank Stanton."

"Jack Dexter."

"Pleased to meet you, Jack. It looks like you're going SCUBA diving."

"Yup," the businessman replied agreeably. "We'll have a slack tide in thirty minutes or so. I thought I'd go out and take a look around."

"Sounds like fun," the ex-trucker allowed solemnly. "But be careful out there."

The words had a slightly ominous ring, which caused Dexter to examine his new acquaintance a little more carefully. He was dressed in a Mariners ball cap, a heavy-duty parka, and jeans. Judging from his face Stanton was in his late sixties or early seventies. His eyes were penetratingly blue, and based on the intelligence that the ex-naval officer saw there, he knew the other man was no fool. "It's always a good idea to be careful when diving," the ex-SEAL agreed mildly, "but did you have something special in mind?"

"Oh, nothing in particular," the older man responded vaguely. "But you should keep an eye out for boats. There's some pretty decent fishing out there, or that's what they tell me, so it's a rare day when you don't see at least one boat off-shore. Here, take a look." Stanton removed a small pair of binoculars from a pocket and handed them over.

Dexter brought the instrument to his eyes, panned the area directly offshore, and saw what he knew to be a C-Dory sixteen-foot fishing boat. It had a cabin forward, lots of open deck in the stern, and was equipped with a large outboard motor. Two fishing rods had been deployed but no people were visible. "It looks like they specialize in remote-control fishing," the ex-SEAL observed dryly.

"Yeah," Stanton agreed. "Maybe that's why they never catch anything."

Once again the other man's words had an edge to them, or so it seemed to Dexter, but it was difficult to be sure. Stanton and his dog departed soon after that, leaving Dexter to don his custom-made DUI drysuit, tank mount, and emergency life vest. His mask, snorkel, and flippers completed the load. Thanks to the drysuit, he could wear his regular prosthesis and that made everything easier.

Once the ex-SEAL had geared up and locked the rest of his possessions into the truck he had to make his way through a maze of driftwood and across a rocky beach before arriving at the water's edge. Then, having paused for a moment, he waded out into the cold water. The tide was slack, and there was a minimal amount of wind, which meant that the incoming waves could easily be dealt with. Dexter turned his back to them, gave thanks for the relative warmth of the drysuit, and ran his final checklist.

Then, having found everything to his liking, the ex-SEAL unlocked the Activankle that joined the upper part of his prosthesis to his foot. That made it possible for him to swivel his foot into a hyperextended "point" position and lock it in place. With that accomplished it was a simple matter to pull both fins into place and turn to face the waves. The plan called for him to snorkel out to the point where the *Zhou Spring* had gone down before using any tank air. Though slower than he had been back in his Navy days, the ex-SEAL made good progress and found that he enjoyed the exercise.

Dexter could see the bottom at first, but it wasn't long before the starfish-covered rocks were lost in the encroaching gloom, and he was left to stare down into the gray-green depths. There were occasional fish, cruising the edge of the darkness, but nothing of any size. It was tempting to aim his lamp downwards, but the ex-naval officer knew he would need the device if he found the wreck, which meant it was important to conserve power. By monitoring his dive console, which consisted of two gauges and a compass, the businessman could navigate without having to raise his head. The occasional peek made sense however, especially since he was diving without benefit of a support craft, and it would be difficult for boaters to see him. A quick check revealed that the C-Dory he'd seen earlier was no longer in the area—and that was a relief.

Ten minutes later the ex-naval officer was in position. It would have been difficult to tread water without the extra buoyancy of the drysuit. But, with that to rely upon, Dexter was able to recheck his gear prior to biting down on the salty mouthpiece and pulling tank air into his lungs.

The act of sliding down into the mysterious liquid atmosphere never failed to thrill the ex-SEAL. It was like entering another universe. The added pressure pushed the drysuit in against the polypropylene long johns he wore, thereby making him aware of all the laces where the fabric had gathered, was wrinkled, or seamed. But the sensation wasn't unpleasant and he quickly became used to it.

And it was then, right at the point when he was about fifteen feet below the surface, that Dexter heard the unmistakable roar of a marine engine. He was already deep enough to escape small craft but instinct drove him deeper as the outboard crossed above his head. The C-Dory? Yes, he thought it was, and wondered if the person at the wheel knew that a diver was in the water.

At twenty-five feet Dexter had just paused to look upwards when the boat returned. He could see the bottom of its hull and the turbulence produced by the big prop as the sixteen-foot fishing boat skidded into a tight turn. It was almost as if the boater or boaters knew he was there and were intent on throwing a scare into him. Of course that was preposterous, unless the *Zhou Spring was* being used as an underwater waystation for illegals—in which case it made perfect sense. The last thing the Chows would want was to have a diver poking around their carefully positioned wreck.

The easiest way to test his theory was to swim laterally and see what happened. Dexter did so—and it wasn't long before the C-Dory made the necessary adjustment. Whoever was at the controls was definitely aware of his presence and intent on chasing him off. But how? That was when the ex-SEAL remembered the fish finders that many fishermen mount on their boats—and felt sure that they were tracking his movements electronically.

That left Dexter with two choices: Press ahead, which was to say *down*, or return to shore. Could the people on the C-Dory communicate with personnel aboard the now-submerged *Zhou Spring*? It seemed unlikely, given all of the technical problems involved, but there was no way to be absolutely sure. If they *could* communicate, a group of well-armed divers would be waiting for the ex-naval officer once he arrived over the wreck. And Dexter was under no illusions about who would win the subsequent battle. He could imagine the subhead in the *PI*: "Controversial businessman Jack Dexter drowns during solo-SCUBA dive off Whidbey Island." The police would figure they had one less pervert to cope with, fellow divers would wonder how an ex-SEAL could be so stupid, and the smuggling operation would continue.

Convinced that discretion was the better part of valor, Dexter turned toward the east, and the return trip began. He hadn't traveled more than fifty feet before the C-Dory broke the circle, cut power by half, and cruised toward the west. A clear signal if there ever was one.

Hank Stanton watched from the beach as Dexter paused to remove his fins, unlock his ankle, and return his foot to its normal position. Once he was back on his feet, the ex-SEAL made his way back up onto the beach. Petey dashed back and forth barking excitedly. "So son," the old man said, "did you have a nice swim?"

There was something about the way he said it, and the glint in the old man's eye, that suggested Stanton knew about the C-Dory. "Here," Dexter said, as he paused to release the tank harness. "Perhaps you would be kind enough to carry that for me. Thank you, Mr. Stanton. I appreciate it."

"Friends call me, Hank."

"Thanks, Hank. No offense, but if I didn't know better, I'd think you had been watching me. More than that, I might even come to the conclusion that you know something about that C-Dory and the folks who own it. So, supposing that I'm right, what would it take to get a download?"

The gravel made a crunching sound and gear clinked as the two men continued to make their way up the gently sloping beach. "That depends," Stanton countered cautiously. "Are you a cop?"

"Nope," the businessman answered simply.

"But you came looking for some sort of underwater installation?"

Dexter nodded. "Yes, I did. And assuming that you have some actionable intelligence, I can put it into the right hands."

"Good," Stanton replied. "In that case the price of a complete download consists of a steak dinner and a cold beer."

"You're on," Dexter replied, as he took another hop forward. "And let's make that *two* beers."

Rossi pushed the unmarked Crown Vic up to fifty-miles per hour. Not all that fast for the freeway—but the equivalent of light speed on old Highway 99. Even though it was just past one in the morning there was still plenty of traffic on the road and it had to be dealt with. The flashing blue light on the dashboard certainly helped, as did the occasional burp of sound from the car's siren, but some of the drivers were slow to pull over. That forced the FBI agent to weave her way between them. She kept both hands on the wheel and was ready to brake.

Seedy car lots, second-class strip malls, and fast food joints blipped past, their lights smearing into a continuous blur as Rossi left them behind. Although the press was still tracking the case, the Pasco murder had slipped down to page six in the *PI*, and rarely came in for mention by the local TV stations. That had enabled Rossi to reoccupy her previously besieged home, which was where the agent had been when the phone rang, and she'd been forced to roll out of bed. Hawkins had gone to D.C. to attend a meeting of the Undercover Review Committee, and since Rossi was the principal relief supervisor, that put her in the proverbial hot seat.

According to what she'd been told, Joe Chow had been stupid

enough to go on-line via a dial-up connection. The call had been traced to a motel called the Prospector's Palace. So, assuming the snakehead was still there, it was a wonderful opportunity to put the cuffs on him. There were two cars in front of Rossi, both traveling side-by-side while communicating window-to-window. Neither one seemed to be aware of the Crown Vic or the blue beacon. The FBI agent swore, tapped on the brakes, and goosed the siren. She was gratified to see the vehicle in front of her pull away, then surprised to see it accelerate, and swerve into the right-hand lane. The driver was trying to escape! A stolen car? Probably, or a fugitive who was on the run from something.

But the FBI agent didn't have time to follow as tires squealed and the badly spooked driver made a poorly executed right-hand turn. She continued north instead, killed the siren two blocks prior to arriving at her destination, and pulled over behind a pair of marked SPD patrol cars. Detective George Tolley was waiting for Rossi as she got out of her car. The federal agent wore an FBI ball cap, a raid jacket over a bulletproof vest, and a pair of blue jeans. Her Glock, plus two extra magazines, rode high on her hip. "Welcome to the party," Tolley said. "We have the entire dump sealed off."

"The dump," as Tolley referred to it, was marked by an ancient neon sign. It was yellow and consisted of a grizzled prospector leaning on a shovel. "Good," Rossi answered. "Have we got some sort of diagram?"

"Right here," a uniformed sergeant said, as he slapped a sheet of graph paper on the hood of her car. The map was hand-drawn but clear. A blob of light from a flashlight was sufficient to illuminate it. The motel was shaped like a capital "L." The rooms lay along the long axis with the office down at the end. Someone had marked the box labeled "Unit 3" with a large "X." "We have an officer with the owners," the policeman continued. "They say the room in question is registered to a man named Martinez. But they did see a male matching Chow's description enter the unit earlier today. An Asian female and two other men were with him."

"That sounds like our favorite snakehead alright," the FBI agent agreed. "Have we got the search warrant?"

"Right here."

"Good. What about the other guests? Have they been secured?"

"There are four of them," Tolley replied. "One works nights and the rest have been evacuated by plainclothes personnel. There's lots of action around here at night—so we're hoping that the evacuation went unnoticed."

"That would be nice," Rossi agreed. "Okay, let's get this done."

Thanks to the fact that a perimeter had been established, and the rest of the units had been secured, it was relatively easy to move in on unit three. Once Rossi had received confirmation that the bathroom window had been covered by the SPD she edged up to the door. Tolley took his position on the opposite side of the entryway. Like the FBI agent, his weapon was up and ready.

Rossi could feel her heart try to pound its way through her chest wall as she prepared to knock on the door. Would Chow put up a fight? Not if he was asleep—and they could enter quickly enough. The FBI agent took a deep breath as she rapped on the door. "This is the manager. Did you report a plumbing problem?" There was silence as Rossi counted off the seconds in her head. "Okay," she said loud enough for those around her to hear, "hit it!"

Two heavily armored members of the SPD stepped around the agent and positioned themselves in front of the door. Once they had their boots planted they pulled their tubular battering ram back before swinging it toward the door. There was a loud *bang*, followed by the sound of splintering wood, and a *thud* as what remained of the obstacle slammed into one of the walls.

It was dark inside. Rossi went through the opening first, weapon at the ready, with Tolley close behind. He hit the lights, and although both were prepared to fire, there was no one to shoot at, just a shabby room, a bed with clothes piled on it, and a laptop computer. A quick check confirmed that the bathroom and closet were empty, too. "So," Tolley said, as he returned from the bathroom. "What do you think?"

"I think we missed the bastard," Rossi said, as she made use of a ballpoint pen to touch the computer's mouse pad. "But not by much."

The computer, which had long since gone to standby, came back to life. The FBI agent watched as the picture of a young Asian woman reassembled itself on the screen. "Don't let anyone mess with the laptop until we get a warrant and the techies have a chance to examine it,"

Rossi instructed as she stared at the screen. "Odds are that Chow was just surfing porn sites but you never know. Maybe he's connected to this girl somehow. And let's get the forensics folks in here. Who knows what they left behind."

It was more than an hour later when Little Chow, plus three of his bodyguards, left the strip club they had spent the evening in, and cruised north along 99. They were a block away form the motel when Paco spotted the police cars. "Holy shit, boss! Look at that! The cops are all over the place."

"Keep it cool," the snakehead advised. "And slow down. That's what most people would do."

The order made sense, even if it was counter intuitive, and Paco complied. Chow, who was seated in the rear on the passenger's side, had an excellent view of the sidewalk as the newly acquired car slowed to fifteen mph. He could see the cop cars, followed by an official-looking van, and two people standing directly below the motel's yellow neon sign. One was a black male and the other was a white female—an FBI agent judging from the letters on the back of her jacket. And not just *any* agent, but the one he'd seen on TV. The one who had been sleeping with Dexter.

The snakehead felt a rising sense of anger as he stared out through the glass. It was starting to look like the FBI bitch was determined to get up his ass. Well, two could play *that* game. "Hey, Paco," Chow said as the black caddy pulled away.

"Yeah, boss?"

"Have someone get me the down-low on that FBI bitch. You know the one. Ross, Rosso, or something like that. I want to know where she lives, who she hangs with, and what she had for dinner last night."

"Sure, boss," Paco said, as he eyed the rearview mirror for any sign of pursuit. "I'll put my cousin Tony on it. He's into computers and shit like that."

"Good," Chow said. "And one more thing. I figure they have Ling. But what if she got away? See what you can pick up from the media. If she's out there we need to find her before the cops do."

"I'll put the word out," Paco assured him. "So what about Big Chow? Are you going to tell him?"

"Hell no," the snakehead replied dismissively. "They have taps on his phone by now. No, we're on our own until that ship comes in. Shanghai could be a drag—but you'll like Hong Kong. That's where Jackie Chan hangs out."

Paco, who wasn't of Chinese ancestry, and didn't speak Spanish much less Mandarin, wasn't all that eager to live in Hong Kong. But the train had left the station, he was on it, and there was no way off. "Yeah, boss. That sounds good."

Meanwhile, back at the Prospector's Palace, Rossi was getting into her car and pulling away. The raid had been a disappointment, but not a disaster, since it was bound to turn the heat up on the Chow family. So why did she feel such a sense of impending doom? As if something really bad was about to happen? There was no logical reason for it—and logic is what counted. "Merry Christmas!" the sign on a store front read, but she had her doubts.

# Chapter Nine

The Toyota's headlights bored twin tunnels into the night as Dexter guided the four-by-four down Ebey Road to the visitor's area where Stanton's truck was parked. The businessman heard the boat trailer rattle as he turned into the parking lot, brought the rig to a halt, and killed the engine. A rectangle of buttery light appeared then vanished as Stanton peeked through a window before leaving the comparative warmth of his camper for the cold night air. Petey raced ahead and barked a greeting as Dexter made his way back to the boat trailer. "Well, it looks like you found one," the ex-trucker commented, as he played the beam from his flashlight across the old aluminum boat. A pair of wooden oars lay lengthwise on the seats.

"Yeah," Dexter replied. "It belongs to the cook at the restaurant where we had dinner. I paid him fifty bucks to let me use it."

"He should have paid *you*," Stanton observed, as he eyed the much-abused hull. "It looks heavy. How are we going to get this monster down to the water?"

"With *this*," the businessman replied, and hoisted a metal contraption out of the boat's stern. The device consisted of a U-shaped tubular framework, a pair of set screws, and two wheels. "It clamps onto the stern right where an outboard would go," Dexter explained. "Once it's in position you flip the boat over, grab onto the bow, and tow it down to the water."

"I can hardly wait," the older man said dryly. "Why did I let you talk me into this insanity anyway?"

"Because you have a weakness for steak dinners," Dexter replied lightly. "Come on. You aim the flashlight while I release the tie-downs."

Ten minutes later the boat had been freed, the wheels had been attached, and Dexter was ready to go. The idea for the excursion had come to him shortly after Stanton had described the mysterious doings at Ebey's Landing. Had illegals been brought ashore that night? And if so, had they been warehoused aboard the *Zhou Spring*? Dexter felt sure that the answer to both questions was yes.

But given the fact that his credibility was at an all-time low, and having failed to view the wreck first hand, the ex-SEAL needed some tangible proof before taking his theory to the authorities. The most obvious thing to do was to attempt another dive, and the businessman had been toying with that idea when an alternative came to mind. The sub-surface habitat was similar to a submarine in many respects, and having been trained to operate from submarines, Dexter knew that a good air supply would be critical. And that raised an interesting question. How did the underwater facility renew its air supply? Could the bad guys manufacture oxygen? The way modern subs did? Or were they reliant on something low-tech? Something they could release during the hours of darkness? His guess was yes, and pictures of such a device would go a long way toward supporting his story. And Stanton, bless his soul, had volunteered to help.

All of which explained why the two men swore and Petey barked excitedly as they struggled to drag the twelve-foot aluminum boat through a maze of driftwood and onto the rocky beach. Once they reached the edge of the water there was a pause while Stanton took Petey back to the camper. When the ex-trucker returned he found a pair of tall rubber boots and an orange life jacket waiting for him. The price tags were still on them. "Put those on," the ex-naval officer instructed. "But, if the boat tips over, kick the boots off. Otherwise they will fill with water and take you down."

Stanton nodded as he sat on a corner of the boat's stern and pulled his hiking boots off. "But it's dark out there. How are we going to find our way back?"

"This will act as our beacon," Dexter explained, as he thumbed the switch on a portable spotlight. "I'll place both it and the transporter above the tide-line. And, if that fails, I have a compass."

"Good thinking," the older man replied. "Here, put my boots next to the other stuff. I'll be able to find them again that way."

Dexter did and ten minutes later metal scraped on gravel as the men pushed the rowboat out into the low waves. The surf was light but made regular smacking sounds when it hit the bow and threw droplets of cold water back over the gunwales. Dexter entered the boat first, grabbed hold of the pre-positioned oars, and pulled as Stanton came in over the stern.

The boat bucked and scraped bottom before finally breaking free of the land. Spray hit his back, and Dexter gave thanks for his parka as he braced his boots against Stanton's seat and pulled harder. The artificial leg was working well, the beacon was visible over the ex-trucker's left shoulder, and the moon was playing hide 'n' seek behind the quickly scudding clouds. The oarlocks made a regular *clacking* sound, but no one was present to hear them, and there wasn't much he could do about the problem anyway.

Finally, when the beacon was little more than a pinpoint of light, and the ex-naval officer estimated that they were over the wreck, he began to ship his oars. But the waves started to push the boat around forcing Dexter to row in order to remain in position. "Okay," the ex-SEAL announced, "let's take a look around."

Stanton, who was armed with a flashlight, switched it on. Then, mindful of how easy it would be to miss what they were looking for, the ex-trucker established what he hoped was an effective search pattern.

Dexter alternated pushing and pulling on his oars as a way to keep the bow into the wind-blown waves—and watched the beam of light sweep back and forth across the oily looking water. The whole thing was absurd. He realized that now and wondered how he could have been so stupid. Even if he was correct, and the people in the habitat below sent some sort of snorkel up to the surface, who was to say when that would occur? Perhaps the process took an hour, or even less, and occurred every forty-eight hours. It could take days if not weeks to catch the smugglers in the act. Stanton completed the search, turned the light off in order to conserve his batteries, and shook his head. "Sorry, Jack. I didn't see a thing."

"Me neither," Dexter agreed soberly. "Are you okay? Should we go in?"

"I'm fine," the older man confirmed. "Here, see if you can rest those oars long enough to take a pull from this. And watch out—it's hot."

Dexter brought one oar inboard and made use of the other to keep the boat positioned. Then, having accepted the aluminum thermos bottle, he took a tentative sip. The coffee had been laced with whiskey and warmed his stomach. "Thanks," Dexter said gratefully as he returned the flask to its owner. "That hit the spot."

Stanton nodded, took a swig, and screwed the top back on as the ex-naval officer went back to rowing. A gentle but persistent current seemed determined to push the boat north relative to the shore beacon. Dexter was pulling against the flow when Stanton touched his leg. "Hold on, Jack. What the hell is that noise? Can you hear it?"

Dexter stopped pulling and turned an ear into the wind. That was when he heard something akin to a groan. It seemed to originate from the west, although it was hard to tell, given all the other noise. Dexter pulled on the starboard oar until the bow was lined up with the sound. Then, pulling with both oars, the ex-SEAL rowed out to sea. It didn't feel right, not if the wreck was where he thought it was, but maybe he was wrong. "There!" Stanton said excitedly, as his flashlight pointed forward. "I see something in the water!"

Dexter turned to look back over his shoulder, but that made it difficult to row, and he was forced to watch Stanton as one of the larger waves momentarily lifted the boat up prior to letting it drop again. "We're almost there!" the ex-trucker exclaimed, his face alight with excitement. "Go left a bit."

The ex-naval officer could hear the sound more clearly by then—and realized it was more like a roar than a groan. And then they were right next to the brightly lit object. The "snorkel" looked like a big black inner tube, and Dexter would have been convinced that it was one, had it not been for the noise generated by sub-surface machinery and the fact that it was stationary. Some quick work with the oars was required to bring the float alongside where Stanton managed to get a grip on the structure. "It's inflatable!" he exclaimed. "All they have to do is fill it with air and it will float to the surface."

"Along with a flexible hose that leads down to the wreck," the businessman added. "Hang onto that hummer while I snap some pictures."

The ex-naval officer was equipped with two disposable cameras—both having been purchased in Coupeville. There was a sequence of bright flashes as Dexter shot the snorkel from a variety of angles, even going so far as to half-stand in order to hold the camera out over what he thought was the blow-hole, and click away. "Okay," the ex-SEAL said, as he thumped back onto his seat and took hold of the oars. "Let's get the hell out of here."

"Works for me," Stanton agreed, and took a long satisfying pull from his thermos as Dexter pushed the boat stern-first toward the beach beacon. "So," the older man continued conversationally. "What have you got planned for tomorrow?"

"Well," Dexter replied, "I need to get this film developed and deliver it to the right people."

*"And?"*

The businessman frowned. "'And' what?"

"Tomorrow is Christmas," Stanton said patiently.

"I'm Jewish," Dexter replied. "We don't do Christmas."

"You're full of shit," the ex-trucker replied. "My daughter lives in Renton. She makes one helluva Christmas dinner and you're coming."

"I think you should check with her before you invite additional guests," Dexter suggested. "Besides, I've had some legal problems of late, and all things considered, I'm not the sort of guy you should bring home to your daughter."

"You mean that voyeur stuff?"

"You knew about that?"

"Yeah, but what the hell. I had a subscription to *Playboy* back in the seventies."

"So you understand why the Christmas thing is a bad idea."

"I spoke with Linda earlier today," Stanton replied stubbornly. "She said any friend of mine is a friend of hers! Oh, and she wants you to bring a bottle of white wine."

Metal grated on gravel as the stern hit the bottom. The boat shuddered as a wave split itself against the bow and the mission was complete. Both men got out and waded ashore. Dexter checked his watch. It read 12:17. "Merry Christmas, Hank."

Stanton smiled. "Merry Christmas, Jack."

It took the better part of an hour to get the boat back on its trailer, reorganize the gear in the back of his SUV, and crawl into his sleeping bag. It took a while to fall asleep, but once he did, Dexter began to dream. They were bad dreams, but none of them were new, and that was all he could hope for.

In marked contrast to the long string of rainy holidays that Rossi considered to be typical, December 25 dawned bright, clear, and cold. It would have been nice to sleep in but that was impossible since she had a lot of presents to wrap before going to her ex-husband's home later that day. Still, it was pleasant to light a fire, listen to Christmas music, and sip hot chocolate while wrestling with paper, scotch tape, and stick-on bows, a process that Snowball found to be a lot more interesting than she did. The FBI agent noticed that while the first presents came out looking pretty good, the quality of her efforts began to deteriorate after a while, which meant that the last objects wrapped looked like hell, something that would become even more obvious once they were viewed side-by-side with those that Vanessa had been working on since September.

But there was no way to compete with perfection, and no reason to, since Vanessa had already taken possession of that dubious prize. Or was that sour grapes as Ed was everything that a lot of women wanted. Hell, he was what *she* wanted until he said goodbye and the custody battle began.

Later, once the presents had been loaded into shopping bags, Rossi ate some rewarmed pizza, half an apple, and one of the Christmas cookies that she had purchased for Missy. And, as with most days since the shoot-out in her home, there was a miserable moment when she was reminded of Dexter, the rotten bastard who had parachuted into her life, made it momentarily worth living, and trashed it on the way out.

As she prepared to leave Rossi wondered what *he* was doing for Christmas, came to the conclusion that it didn't matter, and opened a can of stinky food for Snowball. "At least I can count on *you*," the FBI agent said, and could do little more than hope that the feeling was reciprocal as the cat went nose-down in her bowl.

Though somewhat lighter than normal there was still plenty of traffic as Rossi followed 45th east toward Laurelhurst. And, because FedEx trucks are so ubiquitous, the FBI agent didn't notice the one that followed behind her.

The house, which had originally been a rather undistinguished rambler on a larger-than-average lot, had painstakingly been transformed into something twice as big. It managed to be sleek and modern without seeming stark, still another example of Vanessa's endless talents. As for Ed, his taste had blossomed under his new wife's tutelage, miraculously transforming himself from a man who knew nothing about interior design into an expert on Charles and Ray Eames, Mies van der Rohe, and Frank Alvah Parsons, a transformation that Rossi found to be both amusing and absurd.

The heavily loaded FBI agent was only halfway up the stairs that led to the front door when it swung open and Missy burst out. "Mom! What took you so long?" the ten-year-old demanded excitedly, and rushed down the steps. She was dressed in a bright green dress and was clearly delighted to see her mother, a fact that countered at least some of the misgivings that Rossi had regarding the rest of the afternoon and evening.

Meanwhile, Vanessa, who looked serenely elegant, emerged to watch the first scene in what promised to be a well-choreographed play. She was pleased to see that Rossi had not only taken the time and effort required to dress for the occasion, but had found time to wrap her gifts. A Christmas miracle if there ever was one. None of them noticed the FedEx truck as it passed by.

Once inside the house Rossi realized that it was a red year. She knew from previous experience that Vanessa owned two sets of Christmas decorations. And, since the green and gold decorations had been on display the previous year, it was time for the red and silver. All of the home's furnishings had been placed with care, went with each other, and combined to create a sense of well-integrated comfort. Ed rose from his highly prized Eames chair to greet Rossi and came forward to plant a formal kiss on her cheek. It was hard to believe that this slightly balding, somewhat fussy male was the same man who once made love to her in the bed of an old pick-up truck.

Rossi returned the kiss, put the rest of her gifts under the tree, and surrendered herself to the carefully scripted afternoon and evening that Vanessa had planned for them. There were drinks to accompany the carefully managed conversation, genuine laughter as Ed lost at Monopoly, and some delicious moments with Missy.

Later, over dinner, the FBI agent found herself surreptitiously eyeing her hostess. Vanessa had perfect skin, green eyes, and full lips. A carefully coiffed fall of strawberry blonde hair served to frame her face and emphasize her beauty. And it was then, as Ed told one of his long, boring stories and Missy experimented with her new MP3 player, that their eyes met and Vanessa winked. It was a small thing, but a precious thing, because it spoke to everything they had in common: Ed, Missy, and a female perspective. The gesture brought a smile to Rossi's lips and warmed her heart at the same time. Somehow, without really deserving to do so, Ed had spun life's roulette wheel and won. An hour and a half later, Rossi left with a shopping bag full of things that Vanessa thought that she should have. A man on a motorcycle followed her home.

The first hint that something unusual was about to happen took place when a HH-65A Dolphin helicopter with Coast Guard markings circled the sleepy little town of Coupeville, hovered over the field above the Ebey's Landing, and sent fifteen seagulls flapping into the air as it touched down. Lt. Tom Olman was aboard the chopper, as was Hawkins, Rossi, and Inez. The SNAKE EYE team members were barely on the ground, and still making their way over to the bluff when the Coast Guard cutter *Cuttyhunk* emerged from the off-shore mist and took up station a half mile out. And she wasn't alone. White water broke around their blunt bows as two black-over-orange Foyle Class rigid inflatables roared in from the west. Both carried light machine guns and boarding crews.

The occupants of the C-Dory that had harassed Dexter on Christmas Eve took one look at the incoming boats and tried to flee. But the Coasties were ready for that and moved to cut the snakeheads off. After warnings from the radio and bullhorn were ignored, a single burst of machine gun fire across the bow brought the suspicious boat to a stop. Two men were taken into custody. Once the area was secured a tubby forty-one-foot utility boat chugged in and positioned herself over the wreck. She was carrying a force of SCUBA divers who would be central to the raid.

It all made for quite a display—but the invasion had only begun. Even as the SNAKE EYE team followed a narrow track along the edge of the bluff a procession of police vehicles came down Ebey Road from Coupeville. There were ten sedans and SUVs and their lights were flashing as they appeared at the top of the hill. Those in the lead belonged to the Island County sheriff's department. They were followed by a parade of marked and unmarked Crown Victorias loaded with State Troopers and more representatives from the FBI, ICE, and the DEA—the latter being latecomers who had joined the task force subsequent to the Mo Pong ambush. A bus-sized mobile command post brought up the rear.

The SNAKE EYE team paused at the top of the trail that led down to the beach. "Damn," Rossi said. "Look at all those people. Don't they have anything else to do?"

The cowboy hat made Hawkins look a little out of place. He smiled philosophically. "Every single agency represented here today will claim credit for busting the snakeheads and request a larger budget. And that includes mine. I sure hope Mr. Dexter is correct about that underwater habitat, however—because we're going to look *real* stupid if the float he ran into was attached to a crab pot. Come on, let's get down to the beach."

As Rossi followed Hawkins down the muddy trail she felt a variety of emotions. Anger about the way in which Dexter had betrayed the man he could have been, guilt about her handling of the confrontation in the restaurant, and a touch of wonder as well. Because loony though it was—the FBI agent knew he was doing it for *her*.

Even so, Rossi wasn't ready for the fact that Dexter was already on the beach when she arrived, having been brought in by one of the sedans that were parked up on the road. Uniformed personnel were all over the place, and the ex-naval officer had just finished describing what he and Hank Stanton had seen on the evening of December 24 to a state trooper when he spotted the FBI agent. Their eyes met, and even though Rossi was determined not to, she felt the now-familiar flutter in the pit of her stomach. Dexter's expression was bleak. "Hello, Christina."

"Hello, Dex."

"How was Christmas?"

"Pretty good, all things considered. And yours?"

Dexter shrugged. "I spent most of it with Agent Hawkins over there—followed by dinner with friends." There might have been more had it not been for the deputy who arrived to take Dexter down to the water where some Coasties were waiting to speak with him. After the initial flurry of activity, everything slowed to a crawl. More than an hour passed before a team of armed divers went down to place lights, and cameras, and survey the wreck. Mission completed, they returned to the surface where they briefed a *second* set of divers.

Then, just as the second team of divers was about to enter the water, a lawyer representing the insurance company that owned the wreck demanded to see a search warrant. He was in New Jersey, which made communication all the more difficult, and the better part of two additional hours passed while the government's attorneys consulted with each other. Unable to find any case law to support the insurance company's request, they gave the task force permission to proceed.

It was raining by that time, which forced groups of officials and reporters to huddle together under a few multicolored umbrellas as the SCUBA divers splashed into the cold gray water. Thanks to the cameras placed earlier that day, officials were able to watch as the divers entered the lock and vanished from sight.

A full forty-five minutes elapsed before the first of what turned out to be a total of two SCUBA-equipped illegals were escorted to the surface. Then, even as they were being taken ashore, two snakeheads were brought to the surface as well. Neither one of them was Joe Chow, or would even admit to knowing him, although that was likely to change once the plea-bargaining process began.

Still, the raid had been a tremendous success, and Demont was in an expansive mood when he ducked under Rossi's umbrella. "You see?" the SAC demanded rhetorically. "The transfer from ECODOOM to SNAKE EYE was good for both you *and* the Bureau. You've had your critics but there's nothing like success to put the weasels in their place."

If not a weasel himself, Demont was certainly related to the slippery breed, and if anyone deserved credit for locating the habitat, it was Dexter. Rossi was about to say as much when Haxton intervened. "All's well that ends well," the ASAC said sweetly, as she pulled the agent away. "Come on, Christina. There's coffee at the command post. Let's get some while we can."

The two women were only halfway to the command post when what sounded like a distant swarm of angry bees was heard. One of the approaching choppers belonged to the federal government—but the rest were loaded with reporters. Someone must have been in charge because the helicopters dropped onto the field above one at a time. Rossi frowned. "Who invited the press?"

"Demont did," Haxton answered, as she shaded her eyes. "This raid is going to play pretty well back in DC."

Everyone was looking up into the rain. Rossi scanned the crowd, but the face she was searching for was nowhere to be seen. The raid was a success and Rossi knew she should be happy, but something was missing, something important, and there was no way to get it back.

Night had fallen and it was cold on the streets of what had once been called Chinatown. Traffic lights, neon lights, and Christmas lights glowed everywhere that Lena Ling looked but none offered the possibility of sanctuary. Not only was she an illegal, but a person of interest in a high-profile murder case, and even more sought after as a result. And that wasn't the worst of it, because Ling was being pursued by something far worse than the police. She was on the run from Joe Chow.

Ling knew that even though Little Chow had been born in the United States, he had been raised in his father's version of Chinese culture, and could be expected to behave accordingly. By running she had not only been disrespectful but defiant—and such behavior could not go unpunished lest Little Chow lose face.

That was why Ling felt sure that the snakehead and his men were looking for her and was careful to keep to the shadows as she walked the mostly empty streets. The International District was a bad place to spend time, Ling knew that, but it was hard to resist because she knew her way around it and some of the locals spoke Mandarin. A black limo turned the corner ahead and the young woman ducked into a doorway and stayed there until the vehicle had passed. A hot bath: That's what

Lena Ling wanted more than food or a safe place to sleep. But, with only $12.62 left from her hoard, there was scant chance of getting that.

Ling shivered in her thin leather coat, stepped out of the doorway, and continued to look for some temporary warmth. Buses were one of her favorite places to spend time. It was her experience that they were inexpensive, safe, and warm. Earlier that day she had enjoyed a truly magnificent ride from downtown to West Seattle and back, a journey that consumed the better part of three hours.

Other favorite haunts included 7-11 convenience stores, shopping malls, and the downtown branch of the Seattle Public Library. Not only did the modernistic building provide the illegal with an opportunity to use the ladies room, it stocked some Chinese books. Her favorite thus far was *Meiguo sheng huo shi yong hui hua,* or *Encounters in America.* The other book she liked to curl up with was *Xiao shi sheng huo Mei yu,* or, *Say it in American English.* Something she was getting better at all the time.

"Hey, come here for a minute. I want to ask you a question." The voice was male and originated from a Monte Carlo that had been seized in a drug raid three months earlier. It wasn't the first time Ling had been propositioned during the last few days, and the illegal knew that prostitution was an option. Perhaps a reasonable option given her circumstances, but the illegal had promised herself that she would never submit to sexual slavery again, even if that meant death. She refused to make eye contact with the man and hurried away.

The plainclothes cop in the Monte Carlo shrugged, rolled the window up, and passed a five-dollar bill to his partner. "You were right, Rita. She wasn't a whore. I guess I'm slipping."

Rita kissed the fiver, stuck it into her bra, and turned a corner. "You got that right, Pat. But what else is new?" The cops laughed as a Volvo with stolen plates passed headed in the opposite direction, turned a corner, and disappeared.

Having spent a good portion of the day watching the government take possession of his underwater way station, not to mention illegals worth sixty thousand each, Joe Chow was in a bad mood. And, making matters worse, was the fact that Ling was missing. And not just *missing,* as in arrested by the police, but missing as in run off. The snakehead knew that because he knew the police and their tendency to brag. If they had arrested Ling at the Prospector's Palace, they would have called a press conference to trumpet their accomplishment the next morning.

That being the case, Chow had put the word out for people to keep their eyes peeled for Ling, and sent his men to visit some of her favorite places, all without success—until twenty minutes earlier when a cell phone registered to Paco's dead aunt chirped and a tip came in. Ling, or a woman who looked very much like her, had entered a convenience store and purchased a cup of green tea. The proprietor attempted to stall her, or that's what he claimed, but the illegal grew suspicious and left. Now, in spite of the fact that every cop in the state of Washington was on the lookout for him, Chow was determined to find his mistress. "Slow down," he told Paco. "And pay attention. I want that bitch—and I want her *now*."

Ling had just crossed a street and was eyeing a well-lit apothecary shop when she heard the screech of tires. A quick glance over her shoulder was sufficient to confirm that a car was cruising up the street. It might have meant nothing, but that was a chance the illegal couldn't afford to take. She ran, saw the cleaners up ahead, and turned in. The Chinese proprietress looked up from her sewing machine as the door opened and was just starting to formulate a protest when Ling bolted past the counter. Plastic garment bags swayed back and forth as the illegal pushed her way through. They were still in motion when Skinner burst into the shop.

Ling heard a man shout as she emerged from the forest of clothes, passed through a cloud of warm steam, and found herself in a large kitchen. The fluorescent ceiling fixture gave the scene a bluish cast. A woman with a heavily seamed face looked up from a bowl of soup as the illegal rushed in and circled the table in order to reach the back door.

And that's where Ling was, fiddling with the lock, when the snakehead entered the room behind her. "Hold it right there!" Skinner ordered, and was halfway around the table when the crone extended her aluminum cane. The gang member tripped and went down hard.

The old woman yelled, *"Pao!"* (run) and hit the gang member with her stick. There was very little strength behind the blow and the snakehead barely felt the impact. It took time to rise though, exchange angry words with the old lady's son, and break free.

Ling felt a surge of hope as the bolt turned, she opened the door, and was grateful for the cold air. Once in the alley she ran and ran hard. She caught glimpses of the Volvo from time to time, but managed to elude it long enough to spot a bus and hop on board. The illegal didn't know where it was going nor did she care. The bus was warm and safe. That was all she could hope for.

Meanwhile, back at the cleaners, Mrs. Tianyi Jiang went back to eating her soup. Even though the old woman's opinion of her daughter-in-law was not especially high, there was no denying that the little hussy could cook, and that was something to be grateful for.

Though not as fancy as Bellevue Square, which was located on the east side of Lake Washington, Northgate Mall was easier to access from the Wallingford District where Rossi lived. It was a big sprawling affair surrounded by parking lots, box stores, and strip malls. As the FBI agent guided the Maxima into a row of empty parking spots, she noticed that a crew was hard at work removing the fake Christmas wreaths that had been attached to the light standards.

It was relatively early in the morning, but the combination of much-hyped post-Christmas sales, plus the need to exchange gifts, meant that a lot of people were likely to show up. "Okay," Rossi said, as she prepared to exit the car. "Have you got the outfit? Good. Let's get this over before the mall turns into a zoo."

Missy said, "Oh, mom," and rolled her eyes as she got out of the car. It was an expression Rossi had seen more and more of lately—and was probably a harbinger of things to come. A short walk took them through big glass doors and into Nordstrom's. It was warm inside, and judging from all the signs, just about everything was on sale. After a short detour into the shoe department, and a side trip to look at jackets, the twosome made their way to the Juniors section where the sweater-skirt combination could be exchanged—not because the clothes were too large or too small, but because they were "yesterday," and almost guaranteed to destroy Missy's social life were she foolish enough to wear them. That's what the pre-teen claimed at any rate, and since she had been young once, Rossi was willing to go along. Or that's what the agent believed until she heard Missy say, "Hey, Mom! Look at this!" and emerged from the racks holding what looked like half a skirt. She swallowed and forced a smile. "That's a nice color. Where's the rest of it?"

"Short is *in*," Missy announced airily. "Here, hold my bag, while I try it on."

"Not so fast," Rossi insisted. "Let me take a look at that thing."

The pre-teen's face registered an expression of pained exasperation as she was forced to surrender the garment to her mother. The FBI agent held the piece of clothing up and turned it around. That was when she saw that the word "Juicy" had been emblazoned across the back of the skirt. Rossi gave it back. "No way, hon. I don't approve of the 'junior hooker' look. Let's see what else they have to offer."

Missy slapped the skirt onto the top of a carousel. "It isn't fair!"

The FBI agent sighed. "Why not?"

"You go to bed with men you aren't even married to—and expect me to dress like a nun!"

The remark was so clear, and so well timed, that Rossi wondered whether it had been rehearsed. She felt a sudden stab of anger, followed by a tremendous sadness, and turned away. The cash register was only a few steps away. A salesperson accepted the return, made an adjustment to Rossi's account, and produced a much-practiced smile. "Thank you for shopping at Nordstrom's. Have a nice day."

It was too late for that, but the FBI agent nodded anyway and turned to leave. Missy's face registered concern—but defiance as well. There was an icy silence between mother and daughter as they left the store and entered the parking lot. Rossi looked for the Nissan but a van blocked her view. Then, as they began to get close to the car, the agent saw that her sedan was sandwiched between two *identical* vans. That struck her as unusual, but not especially worrisome, so long as their owners hadn't contributed to the collection of dings she already had. Lights flashed as she thumbed the remote.

Missy went down the right side of the Maxima and Rossi went down the left. Her hand was on the door handle, and the FBI agent was just about to pull on it, when she heard the door open behind her. That was when Rossi registered the fact that she hadn't seen so much as a blob through the darkened glass and went for the collapsible baton in her right hand jacket pocket. The handle came out smoothly and six inches of steel was transformed into sixteen as Rossi turned.

But Joe Chow had the advantage. Because unlike the FBI agent, who had to confirm a threat before she could counter it, the snakehead was free to hit anyone he chose to. The blow started low, came up fast, and connected with her jaw. The lights went out, the agent started to fall, and Chow was there to catch her.

Missy attempted to scream, just like she'd been taught to do, but never got the chance. A hand went over her mouth and one of her arms was bent up behind her back as she was hustled around the Nissan and into Chow's van. Her mother lay on the floor where the second row of seats would normally be. The pre-teen paused as if to help but another man was there to stop her. "Sit down," he instructed, "and keep your mouth shut." The ten-year-old had little choice but to obey.

Joe Chow took a look around, saw no signs of alarm, and spent the time necessary to toss a manila envelope into the Nissan. Once that was accomplished he locked the doors and pocketed the key. Then, having bent to retrieve Rossi's purse, the snakehead reentered the van. Skinner was in the back, next to the girl, and Paco had the wheel. The rest of the gang were in the second van. "We got what we came for," Little Chow said smugly. "Let's get out of here."

Both vans left the parking lot slowly, made their way onto an arterial, and followed it west toward old 99. Rossi, still unconscious, lay on the floor as Chow went through her handbag. "Well, well, look what we have here. A Glock, an extra magazine, and some lipstick! Wait.... There's more. Hey, Paco! I have a badge! Don't speed or I'll give you a ticket."

Paco laughed obediently as Chow twirled the Glock, cowboy-style, and pretended to shoot people through the windshield.

Rossi returned to the world of the living gradually. Her jaw hurt, the arm that was trapped under her torso had gone to sleep, and she needed to pee. That fact that she could hear an occasional sob was a relief. At least Missy was alive! But for how long? Relief surrendered to fear—and grim determination. If there was a way out of the situation Rossi would find it.

Rather than look around, and thereby signal the fact that she was conscious, the agent chose to remain as she was for the moment. They were in one of the vans. A *new* van judging from the smell and the clean carpeting that lay only inches from her nose. That much was painfully obvious. But bound for where? There was no way to tell from her position on the floor. One thing was for sure, however. Judging from what she could feel the vehicle was not being pursued. That was depressing because no one was likely to report the two of them missing until sometime late that evening, when the agent failed to bring Missy home and Vanessa began to fuss. Would the hyper-efficient house executive let the matter go? *Oh, she'll call,* Rossi thought to herself, *and go over to my house when there isn't any answer. But will Vanessa contact the cops? Or the FBI? Because, if she decides to call the cops, they might conclude that the whole thing is part of a custody battle, and sit on it for a day or two. Not Theel though… He would know better.*

There was no way to know what Vanessa would do, and her arm hurt like hell, so Rossi issued a theatrical groan. Skinner bought the act, kicked her in the ribs, and said, "Stay where you are, bitch."

The FBI agent did as she was told, but was able to shift weight off of her arm and restore some circulation. That hurt, too, and continued to bother Rossi as she managed to place two full sets of prints on the back of the vinyl driver's seat. Assuming the van was stolen, and would soon be abandoned, the prints would let the forensics people know that she had been in the vehicle and transported on the floor. Chow looked back over his shoulder. He smiled smugly. "So, Special Agent Rossi, it seems that congratulations are in order. You wanted to find me and here I am! Maybe you should call a press conference." That triggered laughter from Paco and Skinner.

Conscious of the fact that Missy was present, and extremely vulnerable, the FBI agent chose her words with care. "That would be terrific. You could turn yourself in on live television."

Chow didn't laugh, but he smiled, if somewhat tightly. "You've got balls, Agent Rossi, and balls are a good thing. Except on a woman." It was a laugh line and produced the predictable response from his subordinates.

"Thanks," the agent replied. "I think…. So, what's the plan? Are you going to send them a message? Like 'let me go or I'll cap the cop?'"

"Yeah," Chow replied evenly. "Something like that."

"Sounds good," Rossi lied. "I guess I'll find out who likes me."

"I guess you will," Little Chow replied. "*If* I decide to let you live."

The FBI agent didn't have a good comeback for that one—nor would it have been appropriate to use one. It didn't take a degree in psychology to know that it was a good idea to let Chow win the verbal sparring match. Especially with two of his men looking on. So Rossi chose to remain silent as Paco selected a hip-hop station on the radio and added his own sound effects to Eminem's "Bonnie and Clyde".

Rossi still had her watch, so she knew that about forty-minutes had passed by the time the van finally came to a halt. And, judging from the fact that there had been plenty of stops, the FBI surmised that they were still within the Seattle city limits. But where? The answer, or part of the answer, soon became apparent. "Back in as close as you can," Chow instructed. "And once we get into position, grab the wheelbarrow that Tian Lei and his men were using. Plus some sort of tarp. We'll take them across one at a time."

Rossi felt the van go into reverse and stop. Skinner made his way over to the side door, and the FBI agent wondered if that was her chance. She decided that it wasn't when Chow peered into the back. "Go ahead," he suggested, as the door slid open. "Make a run for it…. But the girl is mine."

Hearing that Missy said, "Mommy? Are you okay?" The pre-teen's voice was shaky—and she was clearly on the verge of tears.

Rossi attempted to sound confident. "I'm fine, honey. Hang in there. Everything will be okay."

The side door slammed closed just as the rear door opened and Paco stuck his head into the cargo compartment. "Take the girl first," Little Chow instructed. "And don't forget to tape her."

Rossi started to object, but thought better of it when the snakehead waggled the Glock at her and she was forced to lie on the floor and wait while Paco and Skinner hogtied her daughter, dumped the little girl into a wheelbarrow, and threw a tarp over the load.

The FBI agent's turn came ten minutes later, and rather than struggle against the inevitable, Rossi put all of her energy into intelligence gathering. The snakeheads forced their captive into a ball and secured her with three or four yards worth of tape before loading the helpless woman into the wheelbarrow. The conveyance had been used to mix concrete at some point and the inside surface felt like coarse sandpaper. Though not sure that they would take, Rossi did her best to register a good set of prints on the inside surface of the barrow, and tore out some of her hair as Paco took control of the one-wheeled vehicle. If found, the hair sample would provide the forensics people with yet another clue.

There was a small tear in the blue tarp, and moving by her head, Rossi discovered that she could see out. That was when she saw a wooden cabin cruiser sitting up on blocks and realized that she was near the water. But *which* water? Lake Washington? Lake Union? Puget Sound? There was no way to know.

There was a painful bump as the wheelbarrow was pushed up onto a gangplank, and another bump at the far end, followed by a relatively smooth trip along a central walkway. The FBI agent couldn't see what lay immediately around her, but caught a glimpse of calm, green water and a building before being wheeled through an open door and into a dark enclosure. That was when the wheelbarrow tilted forward, and Rossi was dumped onto rough wood decking. Skinner had entered by then and watched while Paco ripped the tape off the captive's mouth, flicked his knife open, and cut her free. Once that was accomplished Paco jerked the agent up onto her feet. "Put your hands on top of your head," the gang member ordered. "I'm going to search your ass. And when I say 'your ass'—that's what I mean."

Rossi had no choice but to stand there and grit her teeth as Paco squeezed her breasts, ran a hand down between her legs, and fondled her butt. Then it was Skinner's turn, and being a tit man, that was where the second snakehead invested all of his energy. But Paco got bored after a few minutes and chose to intervene. "All right," he said. "Save some for later. Now listen, bitch, here's the deal. You're going to hear voices from time to time. Don't try to communicate. If you do, I will come in here and kick your ass. Then, when that's over, I'll give the girl to Skinner. Understand?"

Rossi lowered her hands and jerked her blouse closed. "Yes," she replied grimly. "But if either one of you touches Missy, I'll kill you."

"And I'm *real* scared," Paco sneered dismissively. "There's a case of bottled water back in the corner, a big bag of Fritos, and a five-gallon bucket to pee in. Have a good time."

Both men laughed. The door slammed, and the cabin was suddenly dark. Rossi heard a loud *rattle*, followed by a *click*, and surmised that the door had been secured with a padlock. Missy, whose mouth was still secured with tape, made a noise. It was dark within the bunk house but daylight found its way in through holes and gaps. Rossi's eyes had adjusted by then, and she made her way over to where her daughter lay. It took the better part of five minutes plus a broken fingernail to remove the tape.

Finally, once Missy was free, she threw her arms around her mother's neck. The words came in between sobs. "I-saw-what-they-did-to-you.... Are-they-going-to-rape-and-kill-us?"

"No, honey, of course not," Rossi replied. "Mr. Chow wants to use us as hostages. We wouldn't be any good to him dead."

The pre-teen was silent for a moment. "I'm sorry, Mom."

"So, am I," Rossi replied. "But the FBI will find us and everything will be fine."

"No," Missy replied. "I'm sorry about what I said back at the store. It was a mean thing to say."

"Yes," Rossi agreed soberly. "It was. It's true that I went to bed with Dex, but I thought I was in love with him, and that we were going to have a lasting relationship. But Dex isn't the man I thought he was— and I made what turned out to be a very public mistake. I'm sorry if the other kids teased you about it."

"That's okay," Missy replied staunchly. "Vanessa says that I should be proud of you. And I am."

The FBI agent was surprised. "She does? You are? That's nice to hear."

The conversation might have continued except for the fact that they heard the rumble of powerful engines, followed by a distant shout and a distinct jerk as the barge went into motion. Rossi went from crack to crack before finding one that looked down the length of the barge. She could see a central walkway flanked by wooden racks, dozens of vertical tubes, and other paraphernalia the agent wasn't sure of. And beyond them Rossi could see a taut cable and the back end of a tug. The name on the stern read *Chow Endeavor.*

Then, as the barge followed the tug out into an unidentified waterway, Rossi began to put all the pieces of the puzzle together. She had never been on one before, but the barge was clearly set up to serve as a launching platform for fireworks, and Samuel Chow had sponsored the New Year's Eve fireworks display for the last three years. Would the authorities think to search a barge out in the middle of Lake Union? It didn't seem very likely.

Missy threw her arms around her mother's waist, and the FBI agent gave the pre-teen a hug as the temperature started to drop. It was going to be a long, cold afternoon—and the night would be even worse. *But there's always reason to hope,* Rossi thought to herself, *even if it's hard to see why.* The tug gave a mournful toot, the barge followed it out into the ship canal, and the sky began to darken as a cold rain fell. It formed a curtain around the barge—and everything within was lost.

# Chapter Ten

The FBI's command post, which was normally set aside for major emergencies, had been activated and was crammed with representatives from half a dozen law-enforcement agencies. And all of them were scared, worried, and angry. Special Agent Christina Rossi and her daughter Missy had been missing for more than twelve hours by then, and every person in the room knew that the odds of finding them dwindled with each passing hour. Demont was there, as were Haxton, Theel, Hawkins, the entire SNAKE EYE team, plus personnel from the SPD, the King County sheriff's department, and the DEA.

The murmur of conversation ended as Demont closed his flip-phone and made his way up to the front of the room. He had flown in from Washington D.C. in the wee hours of the morning and looked uncharacteristically rumpled. A box-shaped lectern and microphone rested on a folding table. The SAC lifted the mike, got a nod from a technician, and opened the meeting. "Good morning. For the benefit of those I haven't met, my name is Harley Demont. Thank you for coming. The purpose of this meeting is to provide you and the agencies you represent with the latest information regarding the abduction of Special Agent Christina Rossi and her daughter Missy and enlist your help. Each of you should have received a packet of information including a synopsis of what we know to date, photos of Agent Rossi and her daughter, and a contact list. If you don't have a packet please raise your hand."

There was a brief pause while two additional packets were distributed. "Okay," the SAC said, "let's begin. At 6:46 P.M. yesterday evening, Mrs. Vanessa Garrett contacted Supervisory Special Agent Theel to inform him that Agent Rossi and her daughter had failed to return home at the agreed-upon time. It should be mentioned that Mrs. Garrett is married to Rossi's ex-husband, which makes her Missy's stepmother.

"During the subsequent conversation, SSA Theel learned that when Rossi failed to show up, and Mrs. Garrett was unable to contact her by phone, she took it upon herself to visit the shopping mall where mother and daughter were headed. While checking the parking lot, Mrs. Garrett was able to locate Rossi's car. The vehicle was locked, but while peering through the window, Mrs. Garrett noticed an envelope. The words, 'For The FBI,' were visible on the front of it."

At that point Demon turned to make eye contact with his audience. "I'll come back to the envelope later. Both the SPD, the FBI, and members of the SNAKE EYE team under the leadership of ASAC Hawkins responded to the scene where the vehicle was opened and the envelope was recovered. While that was being evaluated agents worked with mall security to obtain surveillance video of the parking lot. Please direct your attention to the video screens as we roll that tape."

Inez, who was seated with the rest of the SNAKE EYE team, bit her lower lip as the footage appeared on the previously dark screens and a Maxima that the ICE agent recognized as being identical to Rossi's pulled into a vacant slot. "Rossi and her daughter exited the car at 10:26," Demont continued dispassionately. "And went directly into Nordstrom's. Now, watch what happens next."

Inez and the rest of the law enforcement personnel watched as two identical vans pulled into the slots adjacent to the Nissan. A man got out of the van on the left. He scanned the immediate area before going over to examine the front end of Rossi's sedan. "We think he was checking her license plate," the SAC explained, "to ensure that they had the right vehicle. If so, that suggests someone else followed Rossi to the mall before summoning the vans. Watch what the suspect does next."

The audience watched intently as the man straightened up from inspecting the plate, turned toward the nearest surveillance camera, and raised his right arm. "We had that enhanced," Demont commented. "Here it is."

Another video segment appeared, but this one had been magnified, and there was no doubt about the suspect's identity. The man in the parking lot was Joe Chow—and the middle finger of his right hand was in an upright position. No one laughed.

"That's right," the SAC confirmed grimly. "Many of you will recognize the man on the video as Joe Chow, a slimeball who is wanted for murder, human trafficking, and numerous other crimes. We believe that the fact that he made no attempt to hide his face, and even went so far as to give us the finger, is highly significant. More on that in a few minutes.

"At exactly 11:14, Agent Rossi returned two items of clothing to Nordstrom's and money was credited to her account. Then, at 11:29, Rossi and her daughter reentered the parking lot and returned to the Maxima. They say a picture is worth a thousand words—so here it is."

Inez felt cold lead trickle into the pit of her stomach as her friend made her way across the parking lot and approached the Nissan. Mother and daughter were just about to enter their car when a man emerged from the van on the right and took control of Missy. Meanwhile the passenger side door of the van directly behind Rossi opened. The FBI agent had already begun to turn when Chow stepped out. The snakehead hit Rossi and caught her as she fell. An angry mutter ran through the audience as the unconscious woman was loaded into the van. The girl followed. None of the other people in the parking lot saw what took place, or if they did, chose to get involved.

"By the way," Demont added soberly, "Rossi knew something was up. Later, when Mrs. Garrett arrived on the scene, she found a collapsible baton laying halfway under the Maxima. SSA Theel confirms that Rossi was in the habit of carrying one just like it. Okay, where does that leave us? Well, both of the vans used in the abduction were stolen from a car lot on Aurora. They were found parked in front of this building at 7:05 A.M. this morning. They were about to be towed when ASAC Haxton arrived for work, recognized the vans for what they were, and had them impounded. Some quick work by the forensics people turned up two sets of prints on the rear surface of driver's seat. All of the prints were Rossi's, and judging from the way they were positioned, it appears that she put them there on purpose. So, in spite of whatever injuries she may have sustained during the abduction, there is every reason to believe that she was alive immediately after being kidnapped."

Inez heard murmurs of approval, a chuckle or two, and a "Go Rossi!" from Detective Tolley.

"And that brings us back to the envelope I mentioned earlier," the SAC said, as his eyes swept the room. "Once they got it open the forensics people found a single sheet of paper inside. Here's what it looks like."

The law-enforcement officials shifted their attention back to the screen where the PowerPoint presentation had been. What they saw was a fingerprint, or a thumbprint, centered at the top of the page. The words immediately below had been written in what Inez thought was a childish scrawl. "If you want Agent Rossi to remain alive stop looking for me."

Demont gave his audience a moment to read the message before stabbing the print with a red dot from his laser pointer. "By now I doubt that any of you will be surprised to learn that this thumbprint belongs to Joe Chow. So," the SAC concluded, "here's how we see it…. Chow *knows* his apartment was wired, *knows* we heard him commit murder, and *knows* that bullets from his gun were recovered from Mr. Pasco's body. Rather than play defense, Chow went to offense, and abducted Rossi. Because her daughter was present he took her, too. And, having scored points, Chow rubs our noses in it. The question is why? Is this guy flailing about? Or does he have a plan? We can't eliminate the first possibility, but ASAC Hawkins and his team know this perp, and they have a theory. Dale?"

Hawkins rose and made his way up to the front of the room where Demont surrendered the microphone. The ICE agent had been up all night and looked tired. But there was fire in his eyes. "First, please allow me to join Special Agent in Charge Demont in thanking you for all of the extra hours that both you and your people have put in looking for Rossi. I know she gets more than her share of press, but I'm here to tell you that Agent Rossi is one hell of an agent, and we need to bring her back."

The words brought a scattering of applause along with a "Right on!" "You can say that again!" and a, "Well, said."

"Now," Hawkins continued, "this may be a situation in which a borderline psychotic is running amok and that's all there is to it. The fact that he's taking chances, flaunting his identity, and making non-specific demands seems to support that theory. But we don't think so. We believe he's waiting for something—a way out of the country because that's the only chance he has. And, given a recent meeting with an agent of the Chinese Military Intelligence Directorate, we figure China's where the scumbag plans to go. How is anybody's guess... You saw what the Chow family had going off Whidbey Island. These people are professional smugglers—which means anything is possible.

"So, assuming we're right, this bastard took Rossi as a way to waste our time, burn our resources, and generally piss us off. Then, when the magic moment arrives, he's going to vanish into thin air. Will he release Rossi and her daughter at that point? I hope so, but this guy is a cold-blooded killer, so don't count on it."

Hawkins paused to let his words sink in. "The SAC and his people have the lead on this, but my team will continue to watch Samuel Chow twenty-four-seven. Because, if somebody is trying to arrange for transportation, then it's probably him. Who knows? Maybe we'll get lucky. Other than that, and our ongoing efforts to find Joe Chow's mistress, I'm sorry to say that we don't have any actionable leads."

With that the ICE agent returned the mike to Demont, who reestablished eye contact with the audience. "Okay.... Individual team briefings and assignments will follow. Any questions?"

"Yes," a uniformed sheriff's deputy said. "What about the media?"

"Good question," the SAC replied. "While it's going to get messy, especially given Agent Rossi's high profile, we plan to hold a press conference tomorrow. Who knows? Maybe we'll get some decent tips. It's worth a try. Please refer media inquires to Agent Kissler."

The meeting broke up shortly after that, and Inez was on her way out when Hawkins waved her over. "Olivia, I have a job for you."

The ICE agent nodded. "Sure, boss. What's up?"

"You remember Dexter? The guy who owns the apartment house where Chow lived?"

"The pervert? Who could forget? Poor Christina. She deserves better than that."

"He's bent," Hawkins admitted, "but don't forget the wreck of the *Zhou Spring*. He was straight up with that one."

"True," Inez agreed thoughtfully. "So, what do you have in mind?"

"Talk to him," the ASAC instructed. "He was in contact with Chow so it's worth a shot."

Inez raised an eyebrow. "Should I tell him about Rossi?"

Hawkins paused for a moment then nodded. "Yeah, go ahead. Maybe I'm wrong, but it's my guess that he cares more about Rossi than we do, and that's a lot."

Inez eyed her supervisor with a new-found sense of respect. "You know, there are times when I think you're fairly smart."

Hawkins winced and shook his head. "Not smart enough to take Chow off the street when I could have."

Inez couldn't think of anything to say—and could do little more than stand and watch as the team leader walked away.

The wind came in from the southwest to chase white caps across Lake Union. The tug that was anchored off Gas Works Park rolled slightly in response, and jerked at its anchor as if eager to depart. Chow and his men preferred to spend their free time on the work boat rather than on the barge that wallowed a hundred feet away. The sixty-five-foot tug had a galley, four bunks, and a head, all of which made it a heck of a lot more comfortable than standing on the wind-swept barge while the Chinese pyrotechs wired things together.

But, comfortable or not, Little Chow insisted that one man stand guard in front of the stern cabin at all times lest Special Agent Rossi attempt to escape. To make that duty more palatable, and thereby reduce the bitching he would otherwise have to endure, Chow had authorized two-hour watches. Meanwhile most of *his* time was spent up in the tug's roomy pilot house watching DVDs and sleeping.

Now, as 3:00 P.M. approached, it was time for Kwong to leave the fuggy warmth of the smoke-filled wardroom for the open barge. "Here," Paco said, as the smaller man made for the door. "Take this. I hope the ladies like peanut butter and jelly sandwiches 'cause that's what they're getting. Bring the thermos back when Skinner relieves you. And don't fall in—that gold jewelry will take you straight to the bottom."

There was general laughter as Kwong gave Paco a one-fingered salute, accepted the sack, and opened the door. The truth was that Kwong didn't know how to swim, but the other snakeheads didn't know that, and he wasn't about to tell them. A ladder led down to the waterline where an inflatable boat rose and fell with the waves. Kwong descended the ladder, dropped the sack into the boat, and waited for a wave to lift the inflatable before making the transfer. Once both feet were planted in the Zodiac he sat down. An inch of water was sloshing around the bottom of the boat, which meant the sack was wet. Kwong took a peek inside and was pleased to discover that the sandwiches were protected by Ziplock bags. It wasn't because he cared about the prisoners—but because he didn't want to make the sort of mistake that would give the other guys an opportunity to pull his chain.

Kwong placed the food on his lap and pushed the oars into position before releasing the painter. Then, having checked to ensure that no one was looking, Kwong began to row, something he did rather poorly since it was only the second time in his life that he had touched a pair of oars. Meanwhile, from his vantage point on the deck of the fireworks barge, Tian Lei (Sweet Thunder) watched with amusement as the snakehead thrashed his way across the intervening stretch of water. Tian Lei wasn't his *real* name of course, but one that the Premier had given him after a particularly impressive display in Bejing a quarter century earlier. But a great many things had changed since then. Industries that had formerly been supported by the state had been forced to make it on their own or fold. Pyrotechnics was no exception. Which was why Samuel Chow had been able to hire Lei and his team and bring them to Seattle. It wasn't the sort of assignment that the fireworks master *wanted*, not at his age, but one does what one must.

Having moored the rubber boat Kwong made his way up a short metal ladder and climbed up onto the barge. "You don't know how to row, and you look like a fool," Lei said in Mandarin.

But the younger man didn't know any Chinese and was clearly confused. "What?"

"I said you row extremely well, and look very intelligent," Tian Lei lied.

"Oh," Kwong said brightly. "Thank you." And made his way back towards the stern. Two of Lei's technicians had overheard the interchange and found it difficult to contain their laughter as the snakehead passed by.

Rossi watched the interchange between the two men through what had become her favorite crack, an open space that was about a quarter-inch wide and four inches long. Thanks to it, and a few others, the FBI agent had been able to spy on both the snakeheads and the pyrotechs. It was obvious that they weren't on friendly terms. That was important because if Rossi wanted to escape, which she very definitely did, it would be necessary to disable or kill one of the guards—a difficult task at best, and most likely impossible, were one or more of the technicians to get involved.

Now, as Kwong made his way toward the stern, Rossi eyed the man she had chosen as her opponent. He was the smallest of the bunch, which would help even the odds, and based on what she'd been able to observe, the newest. That made Kwong less confident than the others and prone to mistakes. "Okay," the FBI agent whispered to her daughter. "Here he comes! It's time to take your position. And remember, no matter what happens next, stay in the corner."

Missy, her eyes big, said, "Yes, Mommy," and scampered over to the bunk beds that occupied one wall of the cabin. The plan was for her to take refuge on the top bunk while her mother ambushed the guard. "We could wait," Rossi had explained, "and odds are that help will come for us. But independent women like ourselves don't sit around waiting to be rescued."

That was what her mother *said*, but Missy didn't think it was true, especially the part about someone coming for them. It seemed obvious that nobody knew where they were—which was why it was necessary to handle the situation themselves.

Rossi heard a double thump as Tom-Tom's boots hit the deck. He was a gangly kid who spent most of his time sitting on a stool, and rarely removed the earphones that were clamped over the top of his knit cap. It had earflaps, which made him look more like a beagle than a hardcore gang banger, but there wasn't anything comical about his cold empty eyes—one more reason why the FBI agent had chosen to go one-on-one with Kwong instead.

But would she get to? The answer to that depended on what happened next. Kwong was carrying a sack, which if past experience was any guide, would almost certainly contain two peanut butter and jelly sandwiches and a thermos of hot chocolate, a small mercy that the prisoners had come to look forward to.

If Tom-Tom stayed, while Kwong opened the door, then the prison break was off. But if Tom-Tom left, and Kwong was stupid enough to enter alone, then his ass was hers. Surprise, plus the three-foot long piece of two-by-two that the agent had pried loose from the lower bunk, would make up for the difference in size. Then, armed with Kwong's .357 magnum, the rest would be relatively easy.

Words were exchanged outside as Rossi glanced over toward the bunks and saw the pale blur that was Missy's face. *Okay, asshole*, the FBI agent thought to herself. *Come to momma.*

Tom-Tom nodded as Kwong approached. "Hey, K-man. How's it hanging?"

Kwong made a face. "It's so cold I don't think I could find it."

Tom-Tom issued a sound that might have been a laugh or a hacking cough. Then, with earphones firmly in place, he walked away.

Certain that this was her chance Rossi took up a position next to the door. The lock rattled as Kwong inserted the key. Hinges squealed and the door opened. It was stupid to enter the cabin without checking first, but that's what the guard did, and paid the price. The FBI agent swung the two-by-two with all of her strength, felt it connect with Kwong's unprotected mid-section, and heard a whoosh of expelled air as the snakehead doubled over in pain.

Rossi brought the stick back and was just about to take a cut at the gang member's head when Tom-Tom appeared in the doorway. "Hey, dude, don't forget to…" The agent never got to hear what Kwong was supposed to remember because that was the moment when Tom-Tom saw Rossi standing over the guard and realized what had just taken place. The agent tried to shift her attack, but she was poorly positioned to deal with someone in the doorway, and was still making the necessary adjustment when Tom-Tom struck. He had big bony fists and one of them struck her head like a sledgehammer. Rossi took a second blow, lost her balance, and fell. That was Tom-Tom's cue to kick her with his lace-up combat boots. The agent felt a rib break and heard Missy shout. "Mommy!" Rossi was trying to summon the air necessary to yell *No!* when the youngster launched herself off the top bunk.

Tom-Tom was thrown forward as Missy landed on his back. Then, with her arms wrapped around the gang member's scrawny neck, the pre-teen held on. The snakehead stumbled, and was about to topple forward, when Kwong came to his rescue. Embarrassed by the manner in which he'd been suckered, and desperate to redeem himself, the smaller man jerked Missy off Tom-Tom's back and threw the ten-yea-old across the cabin.

Rossi swore, and tried to rise, but was felled by another blow. At that point all the FBI agent could do was assume the fetal position and bring her arms up to protect her head. But Tom-Tom had tired of the exercise by then. He drew his handgun, aimed it at Rossi's skull, was just about to pull the trigger when Kwong intervened. "Don't do it, man. Joe will be pissed. He wants the bitch alive."

Rossi closed her eyes and wondered if she would hear the explosion when the gun went off. Seconds seemed to stretch into an eternity. Finally there was an exhalation of breath followed by an almost imperceptible click as Tom-Tom let the hammer down without firing the .44. "You're right, K-man. We taught the bitch good! She won't try that shit again." Rossi battled the tidal wave of darkness that threatened to overwhelm her as the door swung closed, felt her consciousness start to slip, and was forced to succumb.

Missy tried to pull herself up off the floor, realized that something was wrong with her right arm, and felt a stab of pain. Was the limb broken? Yes, the pre-teen believed it was. She wanted to cry but bit her lower lip instead. "Mom? Can you hear me?"

Not receiving any answer Missy made use of her good arm to capture and control the injured limb. The pre-teen winced as she struggled to her feet and stumbled across the cabin to where her mother lay. She felt dizzy and there was a thump as her knees hit the floor. "Mommy. It's me, Missy."

There was a vast emptiness in the pit of the youngster's stomach as she fumbled for a pulse. Mrs. Ebbers, her health teacher, had taught all of her students how to do that never imagining that one of her charges might employ the skill under such harrowing circumstances. After three attempts the ten-year-old eventually found a thready pulse. Her mother was alive! That made the youngster feel better, for a moment at least, before the dull ache began to assert itself. Then, with her good arm wrapped around her mother, Missy fought to keep the darkness at bay.

It was the morning of December 31, and thanks to the fact that most of Seattle's office workers had the day off, the Bell Town area was nearly deserted. The absence of external activity, combined with the fact that Jack Dexter had already finished what little work there was to do, left the businessman feeling lethargic. And that was why he was seated at his desk, tossing paper clips into an empty Starbucks cup, when a nicely dressed woman entered the lobby.

The ex-naval officer couldn't make out her features at first, not through the etched glass that separated them, and something about the way the woman carried herself caused his heart to jump. Had Rossi been sent to speak with him? Or better yet, come of her own volition? The possibility brought Dexter to his feet.

But it wasn't to be. When the door opened it was another woman who entered his office. She was pretty and had dark hair, but the similarity ended there. "Good morning," the ICE agent said gravely. "My name is Olivia Inez—and I'm with Immigration and Customs Enforcement."

Inez showed Dexter her credentials but the businessman barely took notice. He forced a smile. "I'm Jack Dexter—but I suppose you know that. Please, have a seat. What can I do for you?"

Inez had seen video of the man and caught a glimpse of him on Whidbey Island, but had never been up close to him. Now, as she looked into the ex-naval officer's eyes, she could see what Rossi saw. If Dexter was a pervert, he was a *complicated* pervert, and might have redeeming qualities.

But Inez had her game face on, which meant that none of her inner feelings were visible as she sat down and looked across the mostly empty desk. Their eyes met and the ICE agent noticed that Dexter's expression was uncertain. Was the visit about Chow or him? He wasn't sure. Inez cleared her throat. "I'm sorry to inform you that Special Agent Rossi is missing."

There was no mistaking the look of alarm on Dexter's face. "Missing? How? When?"

"The day before yesterday," the ICE agent replied. "Joe Chow and his men abducted both Christina and her daughter in broad daylight at the Northgate Shopping Mall. They left a note threatening to kill them if we continue the search for Chow. That won't stop us of course. We don't cut deals with hostage takers."

Dexter felt an almost overwhelming sense of guilt. He was the one who constructed the room that led to Pasco's death and Rossi's abduction. "That's horrible," the ex-SEAL said hoarsely. "How can I help?"

"We believe that Rossi is being held somewhere in Seattle," Inez answered. "The question is where? Together with the SPD, the FBI, and other law enforcement agents, we are turning the city upside in an attempt to find her, and we're interviewing all of Chow's known associates, which includes you. Perhaps he told you something that would provide us with a lead. Places he liked to go, things he liked to do, that sort of thing."

Dexter shook his head. "Nothing comes to mind. Not at the moment. He wasn't very talkative. Not with me anyway."

Inez nodded. "I understand. "Here's my card. If you remember something please call me day or night. If I don't answer leave a detailed message and I'll get back to you as quickly as I can."

The woman stood so the ex-naval officer did likewise. "Agent Inez…"

"Yes?"

"If it wouldn't be too much trouble—would you call me when you find her?"

Inez nodded and plucked one of the cards out of the holder on his desk. "Yes, I will. And oh, by the way, we would appreciate it if you kept this interview to yourself."

"I will," Dexter promised. "And thank you." Dexter opened the door for his visitor and watched as she crossed the lobby and exited through the front door. A cold breeze found its way in, chased a leaf across the tiled floor, and suddenly ceased to exist.

After Agent Inez left, Dexter moped around his apartment for a few hours before opening the refrigerator and noticing it was nearly empty. So, partly out of necessity, and partly because he had nothing better to do, he decided to go shopping. Like all the denizens of the downtown area, the ex-naval officer had two choices. He could get in his SUV and drive to a supermarket up on Queen Anne, or over on Capital Hill, or he could make his way down First Avenue to Seattle's world famous Pike Place Market. After a moment's reflection the second option got the nod. Perhaps the friendly hustle-bustle of the place would help take his mind off Rossi and Missy.

Having bundled up against the cold, and with two sturdy canvas bags in which to carry his groceries, the businessman ventured out into the unwelcoming arms of the year's final day. There wasn't much traffic as he hiked more than a mile down to the corner of First and Pike and turned right. From there it was a short walk down to the slightly funky and always colorful marketplace. The crowd was thin, and many of the stands were empty, but a few were open for business. Further back, he could see display cases packed with seafood and windows full of baked goods.

And that's where the ex-SEAL was, preparing to buy a loaf of fresh-baked bread, when he saw the flash of a familiar face. He couldn't believe it at first—but a second look confirmed the first. Lena Ling, the very woman he had watched Joe Chow abuse, was standing not fifty feet away!

Ling was hungry and had been for more than twelve hours. So now, with only thirty-six cents left to her name, the illegal was about to steal an apple. There were bananas, and oranges too, but it was an apple that she wanted. The first step was to select a piece of fruit and examine it for soft spots, while the man who ran the fruit stand made change for a customer. Then, when he looked down, it was a simple task to drop the apple into the plastic bag that dangled from Ling's left wrist.

But the fruit vendor had been working at the market for more than twenty years—and during that time he had witnessed every possible type of thievery. So, when a pretty but unkempt girl paused to examine his produce, he immediately put her down as a drug addict, street whore, or both. And, while watching from the corner of his eye, he saw the theft take place. "Hey, *you*," the vendor said angrily. "Put the apple back!"

Ling turned and started to run. But the next vendor down the line was waiting. He grabbed the illegal's collar and brought her to a stop. He was a big, burly man in a black watch cap and a red-plaid jacket. "Oh, no you don't," he said gruffly. "We're tired of your kind. It's back to jail for you!"

Ling was about to plead for mercy when another voice was heard.

"Excuse me," Dexter said, as he appeared out of the crowd. "Perhaps I can be of assistance here. My name is Dexter, *Father* Dexter, and Lena is enrolled in our "Off the Streets" program."

He turned to the first vendor. "What did she take? An apple? Here's a five, and I'm sorry about the inconvenience."

Then, moving with the surety of someone who deals with recalcitrant street people every day, the businessman led Ling away. Though thankful for the manner in which the man had rescued her from what could have been a disastrous situation, Ling didn't want to surrender her freedom and tried to pull away. But the ex-SEAL was prepared for that and had a good grip on her arm. "Think about it Lena," he said. "You met me before. I own the apartment house where you and Joe Chow used to live."

Ling had never been allowed to speak in his presence, so Dexter didn't know if Ling could speak English, and if so how much. But he saw the look of understanding that appeared on her face and hurried to take advantage of it. "Look, I know Chow is on the run, and judging from appearances so are you. I promise I won't turn you in if you'll answer a few questions. Do you understand?"

The twosome had come to a stop by that time. Ling had no reason to trust men, especially *this* man, since he had a relationship with Joe Chow. But she saw no lust in his eyes. Only a look of deep concern. Finally, after what felt like an eternity for Dexter, Ling said, "Yes, I understand."

"Good," the businessman said gratefully. "Promise you won't run and I'll release your arm."

Ling nodded solemnly. "I promise."

Dexter could run on the prosthetic leg, but knew Ling could probably run faster, and prayed that he wouldn't regret letting go. But he knew it was important to build trust if he wanted to obtain accurate information. Slowly, one finger at a time, the ex-naval officer released his grip. Ling, true to her word, remained where she was. "Look." Dexter said. "I suggest that we go to my apartment where you can take a bath, have a hot meal, and answer a few questions. Then, assuming you agree, I will give you five hundred dollars in cash."

There was another pause while Ling thought about it. "No sex."

"No," the businessman agreed gravely. "No sex."

"You let me leave?"

"Yes," Dexter assured her. "I will let you leave."

"Okay," Ling said solemnly, imitating the way she had heard Chow do business. "But you give two-fifty up front."

The businessman grinned. "You came to the right country, Lena. It's a deal. I will give you two hundred and fifty dollars as soon as we enter my apartment. But, before we go there, you must answer a very important question. Joe Chow took a woman and her ten-year-old daughter. They are in great danger. Can you tell me where they are?"

Ling shook her head. "I leave Joe four-five days ago. No woman-girl then."

Unfortunately everything about Ling's tone and expression suggested that she was telling the truth. Dexter, who had been hoping for a miraculous breakthrough, felt an almost overwhelming sense of disappointment. Still, it was possible that Ling could provide him some sort of lead, so a little hope remained.

The businessman knew he should call Inez, and turn the illegal over to the proper authorities, but he couldn't bring himself to do it, partly because he felt sorry for Ling, and knew what would happen to the illegal if he called ICE, but also because of a quixotic desire to somehow put things right all by himself.

It was a short taxi ride back to the apartment house where Dexter showed Ling into the bathroom, demonstrated the way that the lock worked, and invited her to take a shower or bath. Then, once the water began to run, the ex-naval officer went out into the sixth-floor lobby. He broke the seal that the police had placed on Joe Chow's front door, entered the apartment beyond, and headed for the master bedroom. In their hurry to leave Chow and his mistress had been forced to leave a lot of clothing in the big walk-in closet. Dexter grabbed an armful of female garments, carried them back into his apartment, and heaped them in front of the bathroom door.

Then, satisfied that Ling would have something clean to wear, and having removed some cash from his safe, the ex-SEAL returned to the kitchen where he made tea. The pot of hot water and a selection of tea bags were waiting for the freshly scrubbed young woman when she reappeared. Her hair was damp, but her clothes were clean, and there was a shy smile on her face. "Thank you."

Dexter handed her a cup. "You're welcome. I'll give you a duffle bag so you can take the rest of the clothes with you. Here's half the money I promised you—and there's soup on the stove. It will be ready in about five minutes. Now, given how urgent the situation is, may I ask you some questions?"

Ling took her first sip of tea. It warmed the pit of her stomach. No one had been polite to her in a long time. It felt good. "Yes," she replied. "You ask."

The ex-SEAL had been taught how to interrogate prisoners and put that knowledge to work with a series of gentle but carefully framed questions. It wasn't long before he had a chronology for the hours and days immediately after the shooting. Someone like Inez, or Rossi for that matter, might have been interested in the particulars of who Chow spent time with, and the nature of such relationships, but Dexter was listening for something else. What he wanted was some clue as to where Rossi was being held. And eventually, just as Ling finished her second cup of soup, he heard one. "Chow took you aboard a barge?" the ex-naval officer inquired. "Whatever for?"

"He not tell me," Ling answered simply. "But it have fireworks. For New Year."

Dexter felt a rising sense of excitement. Fireworks! Of course! Everyone knew that Samuel Chow sponsored the annual New Year's Eve fireworks display over Lake Union. He looked at his watch. It was 7:32 P.M. and already dark. The barge would already be in position as people from all over the city streamed into the Gas Works park. Would the authorities think to check it? No, that didn't seem likely. Which made it the perfect place to hide. "Okay," the ex-SEAL said. "Tell me about the barge. Every detail that you can remember."

So Ling told him. And while Dexter was interested in everything the young woman said, he took particular note of the fact that what the illegal described as a "house" occupied one end of the barge. Ten minutes later the businessman had everything he was likely to get. "Alright," Dexter said. "Eat the rest of the soup if you want it and I'll go get the second half of your money."

The ex-naval officer returned to his safe, removed both of the handguns he kept there, along with all of what he thought of as his emergency fund. He slipped a couple of hundred dollars into his pocket. Leaving weapons behind, Dexter returned to the kitchen. "Here," he said, as he handed Ling a thick stack of currency. "There's a couple thousand dollars. Enough to get you out of Seattle. It's a big country. Make a life for yourself."

Ling frowned. "Five hundred. We agree. Why more?"

Dexter looked away. The memory of how Chow had removed the illegal's clothing and raped her was still fresh in his mind. "I don't have time to explain—but I owe you more than five-hundred dollars. More than two thousand, but that's all I have on hand."

Ling didn't understand, but the man was obviously sincere, and she needed the money. "I take it," the illegal said decisively. "For my sister."

The businessman wasn't aware of a sister, but nodded politely and glanced at his watch. "Look, I'm sorry to run, but that's what I have to do. I'd invite you to stay, but that would be a mistake. I'm going to be in big trouble by nine o'clock this evening and the police will come here. I won't tell them about you, but they will figure it out, so get on the next Greyhound bus. You don't need any I.D. for that—and it's cheap."

Ling had happened across the bus depot during her wanderings and considered making a trip to California, but lacked the necessary fare. Now, with plenty of money, she could buy a ticket. "Thank you. I go."

Five minutes later, duffle bag in hand, the illegal was gone. Dexter returned to his closet, opened one of the built-in drawers, and found what he was looking for. There were two boxes of ammo for the Heckler & Koch P7 that he had purchased for himself after being discharged from the service, and one box of .45 ACP for his father's Colt M1911.

So, with two extra magazines for the P7, and one for the .45, the ex-SEAL figured he would be able to put out a pretty good rate of fire. A shotgun like Rossi's would have been nice, but he didn't own one, and something like that would show.

It took fifteen minutes to charge all the clips, load both weapons, and change into black clothing. Then, just as he was about to leave, Dexter put in a call to Agent Inez. However the ICE agent was at a New Year's

Eve party. The cell phone was in her purse and Inez was about twenty feet away when it rang. Dexter waited for voicemail, left a message outlining what he believed to be the situation, and felt a sense of relief as he put the receiver down. It was stupid, the ex-lieutenant knew that, but he didn't want any help.

Having locked the apartment Dexter rode one of the elevators down to his truck. It felt like a thousand butterflies were flying in formation in the pit of his stomach and his nerves were on edge, but there was a welcome sense of anticipation too. It stemmed from a need to do what he had been trained for—to find the enemy, and if necessary, kill him.

With only thirty-seven minutes left until midnight and the beginning of the new year, Joe Chow eyed the scene around him. Having blown away the clouds, and exhausted itself in the process, the southwesterly wind left the surface of Lake Union looking like black glass. The fireworks barge was surrounded by a flotilla of pleasure craft. Their running lights sparkled like red, green, and white jewels. Further out, all along the lake's gently curving shores, thousands of people were preparing to watch the display from rooftops, balconies, and parks, with half a million more getting ready to watch the extravaganza on television. All the while the snakehead and his men hid in plain sight! The thought pleased Little Chow and caused him to smile. The voice came from behind him. "Hey, boss. I think we have a problem."

Chow turned to face Paco. "Yeah? What's up?"

"Skinner opened the cabin to give the law bitch some food. She looks pretty bad."

Chow swore. Rossi was his ace in the hole, his last bargaining chip if the authorities managed to track him down, but only if she was alive. So what did dumbass Kwong and shit-for-brains Tom-Tom go and do? They damned near beat the agent to death! It was an act so stupid, it nearly left him speechless. "Okay," Chow responded. "Let's take a look."

Paco led the way, and as the two men started down the central walkway, Tian Lei and his pyrotechs could be seen tending to what the fireworks master sometimes referred to as his "children," all under the watchful eye of an officious but not especially bright fire inspector. He assumed that since most of the men on the barge were Asian, all of them reported to Lei. So far no one had seen fit to put him straight.

Plywood boxes had been installed on either side of the elevated walkway. Each box contained multiple racks, and each rack contained a cluster of mortars, all of which were grouped by caliber and packed in sand. The shells had been loaded into polyethylene mortars by that time and covered with tinfoil, which was held in place with duct tape. The purpose of the tinfoil was to protect the unexploded shells from the flaming debris that would rain down on the barge once the mortars began to fire.

And, making the entire endeavor that much more complex, was the fact that each shell or bomb was wired to a laptop computer located in the booth that Lei and his men had constructed in the bow. Once launched, the computer program would control the entire show. The fire inspector, who was down on his knees next to one of the plywood boxes, didn't even look up as the snakeheads passed by.

Skinner, Tom-Tom, and Kwong were waiting next to the cabin when the snakehead arrived. The last two looked worried—not for Rossi or Missy, but for themselves. Chow was pissed. They knew that and feared his wrath. "Okay, let's have a look at her," the snakehead said irritably. "And keep an eye on Mr. Fireman. Head the bozo off if he starts to come this way."

Metal rattled as Kwong unlocked the door, and a beam of light stabbed the darkness as Tom-Tom began to probe the cabin's interior. The blob of white light caressed the wooden walls before wobbling onto the bunks where two pale faces could be seen. Rossi blinked as the light speared her eyes and wondered how many men were standing behind it. Not that it mattered much, because although she could move, the pain from the broken rib would prevent her from taking on one snakehead, much less two or three. That didn't mean the FBI agent couldn't *shoot* the bastards though, which was why she had resisted her daughter's attempts to clean up her bloodied face and sat huddled beside her. Maybe, if she could convince the snakeheads that she was harmless, she would be able to lure one of them in close. Then, if she could get hold of his weapon, a whole lot of people were going to die. It was a long shot, Rossi knew that, but a long shot was better than no shot. A man spoke and the agent recognized the voice as belonging to Chow. "Damn, woman. You look like forty miles of bad road."

Consistent with the part she was playing, the FBI agent ran her tongue over dry lips. "Water…. Thirsty…."

Chow took the flashlight away from Tom-Tom and moved in closer. Rossi's left eye was little more than a reddened slit. Her left cheek was a dark shade of blue and badly swollen. At some point, her upper lip had been cut and dried blood was caked on her chin. The little girl looked frightened. Tears made tracks down her dirty face. Two pieces of wood, both pried loose from the lower bunk, had been used to fashion a splint for her arm. The supports had been tied in place with pantyhose. Missy cradled the injured arm the way a mother would cradle a baby.

"C-c-cold," Rossi said pitifully, and it was true. The two of them had been hugging each other for hours using their combined body heat to stay warm.

"Give them your coats," Chow ordered, looking from Kwong to Tom-Tom.

"But it's cold!" Tom-Tom complained. "We'll freeze."

"You should have thought of that earlier," the snakehead replied angrily. "Now take off your fucking coats or I'll blow your god-damned heads off!"

Right then, for one split second, Tom-Tom considered pulling his weapon and shooting Chow in the face. But Paco already had a hand on his semi-auto, as did Skinner, and Tom-Tom knew Kwong was too scared to back his play. "Okay," he said, reluctantly, and surrendered his coat.

Kwong did likewise and Chow threw both garments up onto the top bunk. Then, just as the snakehead was about to order Kwong to fetch a bottle of water, the entire barge shivered. The first shells had been launched and a series of overlapping Chrysanthemums lit up the sky. A new year had begun.

# Chapter Eleven

Dexter heard a series of *whumps*, followed by a reedy cheer, as three successive explosions lit the sky. These were followed by the crackle of firecrackers as local citizens got into the act, and a gigantic brocade bomb went off high above. But, rather than the exuberance the people on the surrounding docks clearly felt, the businessman was frustrated. After crossing the Aurora bridge, and making his way to the north shore of Lake Union, Dexter quickly discovered that some streets had been blocked off by the police. In addition to that, hordes of incoming spectators had already claimed what on-street parking there was, forcing latecomers such as himself to leave lower Wallingford, and park their vehicles elsewhere.

The process of finding a place to park then hiking back took more than an hour. That was bad enough, but what proved to be the most frustrating was Dexter's subsequent inability to cross the half-mile stretch of black water that separated him from the barge. The original plan had been to hire a boat, or, failing that, to "borrow" one, but neither approach had proved feasible. It seemed that the type of people who had boats were not interested in renting them out to strangers on a night when they wanted to venture out themselves. And, what with so many people about, it was hard to steal one.

So, as the fireworks display began, the ex-naval officer had little choice but to turn pirate. Having spotted a likely looking couple, he followed them up to the gate that fronted one of the marinas and offered to help with their coolers. Both had been drinking—and they assumed the neatly dressed man had a boat of his own. A serious error indeed.

Once out on a pier, with rows of sleek cabin cruisers to either side, Dexter helped the couple load their supplies onto a twenty-foot cuddy cabin cruiser. Then, just as the unsuspecting mariners were about to thank the nice man, he produced an ugly looking pistol and demanded the ignition key. The couple were forced to step back onto the dock as the 5.OL MerCruiser noisily came to life. Water boiled around the Bayliner's stern as the businessman backed the boat out of its slip. "I'm sorry!" he shouted, as he cranked the wheel to starboard. "It's an emergency!"

The downcast couple weren't able to take much comfort from the statement and were already fumbling for a cell phone as the cabin cruiser nosed out into the lake's dark waters. The ex-SEAL knew they would call 911—but what the hell? Having already taken it upon himself to interfere with a federal investigation, why not add armed robbery to the list? *Because they'll send you away for a long time,* the more logical part of his mind replied, *especially if you board that barge and discover Rossi isn't there.*

But it was too late to be sensible. What was done was done. The ex-naval officer had a deck under his feet and gloried in the way the cold air pressed against his face. As the Bayliner continued to pick up speed Dexter heard a series of loud *crumps.* A glorious red poinsettia blossomed over his head and the ex-SEAL was reminded of nights when illumination rounds burst high in the sky and incandescent flares drifted slowly to the ground.

But there was no more time for reflection as the boat neared the barge. A restricted zone had been established around it, but the Harbor Patrol was busy dealing with a ski boat full of drunk teenagers when the Bayliner entered the area. Dexter cut power by seventy-five percent. The runabout slowed dramatically and pitched forward and back as its own wake caught up with it. It rumbled throatily as it slid along next to the barge's slab-sided hull. Being only lightly loaded, the boxy cargo vessel sat high in the water, and that made it necessary to find a ladder in order to get aboard. The businessman saw metal gleam up ahead, knew he was moving too fast, and shifted the engine into reverse. The cabin cruiser slowed, then came to a full stop, as it nosed its way in between an aluminum boat with the words "Fire Department" emblazoned on its side and a rubber raft.

Dexter killed the engine, winced as the bow nudged the barge, and went forward. Then, having made the bow line fast to the ladder, the ex-SEAL climbed upwards. It was the right leg, or what he thought of as his "good" leg, that provided most of the power, a habit Dexter was trying to break.

The show was well underway by that time, which meant that the air stank of sulfur and the atmosphere was filled with the sounds of mock battle. Each time a mortar fired there was a loud *boom*! That was followed by a high-pitched reverberation and an explosion up in the sky. Except that it wasn't just one mortar going off, but dozens, which created a multilayered *boom-scream-boom* sound. When combined with the persistent rattle of fireworks, it was like a bad night in Baghdad.

As Dexter continued to climb he could see a faint ring of smoke and a trail of sparks as each round climbed up into the night sky. Then, as the most recent shells exploded, a magnificent golden dahlia appeared. That was followed by a red palm and a silver peony. But beautiful though the display was the businessman knew he had to ignore the fireworks and focus on his mission. Assuming he was correct, and the snakeheads were using the barge as a hideout, they weren't likely to welcome uninvited guests. So the ex-SEAL was hyper-alert as he swung a leg in over the rail.

The control booth was about fifteen feet away. None of the goggled men huddled around the laptop computer resembled Chow or the bodyguards that Dexter had seen at the apartment house. In fact, judging from the uniform one of them had on, he worked for the Seattle Fire Department, a fact that served to dampen the ex-naval officer's spirits since it seemed to suggest that none of the snakeheads were present. A technician spotted Dexter and came over to speak with him. "I'm looking for Joe Chow!" the ex-naval officer shouted, as the man in the overalls removed his protective earmuffs. "I have a message for him."

It seemed like a silly thing to say in a way, but having been unable to come up with anything better, it would have to do. Much to the businessman's surprise the pyrotech nodded and pointed towards the stern. "He back there!"

Dexter said, "Thanks!" and felt a rising sense of excitement as he turned away. His guess had been correct—and knowing that made him feel good. The next part wouldn't be so easy, he knew, but he was determined to keep moving. Could the techs communicate with

Chow via walkie-talkie? He couldn't be sure so speed was of the essence. Fountains of fire rose on both sides of him as Dexter stepped onto the central walkway and headed for the stern. They roared and hissed as they shot thirty feet up into the air. The ex-SEAL coughed as a thick layer of smoke spread out to half-conceal the deck. If he had been able to, the ex-naval officer would have sought cover rather than allow himself to be channeled into what might be an ambush. But the continuous mortar fire made that impossible. Thankfully, from Dexter's perspective at least, visibility had dropped to near zero. So, in spite of the fact that Chow might be aware that *someone* was on the way, the snakehead had no way of knowing who the visitor was.

Meanwhile, not thirty feet ahead, Chow stood on the plywood platform that fronted the stern-cabin and stared into the swirling smoke. One of the pyrotechs had contacted him via handheld radio, but the man spoke Cantonese rather than Mandarin, and the noise generated by the fireworks made it difficult to hear. Still, assuming that he understood correctly, someone was on the way to see him. A single visitor didn't sound very threatening, so the snakehead wasn't especially alarmed when the figure of a man materialized out of the fire and smoke. Then, as the apparition drew close enough to recognize, Chow could hardly believe his eyes. Incredibly, the man in front of him was none other than his ex-landlord!

Paco, Skinner, Tom-Tom, and Kwong were all equally surprised, and stood in a rough semicircle as Dexter stopped about fifteen feet away. Chow spoke first. "What the hell are *you* doing here?"

The ex-SEAL felt his stomach muscles tighten. His hands hung at his sides. Each held a pistol. The weight was reassuring. There was a momentary pause between mortar rounds and his voice was loud enough for everyone to hear. "You left without paying your rent."

"Look boss!" Paco said shrilly. "The bastard has heat!"

"He's here for the woman," Chow said. "Kill him."

No one had seen fit to close the cabin door, and that was a mistake, because although Rossi was in pain, the FBI agent wasn't as helpless as she appeared to be. By the time Dexter emerged from the smoke she was peering through the door. A strobe shell went off and a quick succession of explosions lit up the ex-SEAL's face. The sight was so amazing, so completely unexpected, that it took Rossi's breath away. Somehow, impossible though it seemed, Dexter had come for her!

But there were *five* snakeheads, all heavily armed, and the crazy bastard was just standing there waiting for one of them to make a move. Then Paco shouted his warning. The spell was broken, and everything went into motion. As Paco struggled to free the Beretta from the waistband of his pants, Dexter brought the .45 up and squeezed the trigger. The Colt bucked. Paco was thrown backwards and there was a muted *thump* as he hit the cabin before sliding to the deck.

Confident that one opponent was down for good Dexter swung the P7 left, and was in the process of bringing the pistol to bear on Tom-Tom when Rossi side-kicked the snakehead from behind. Tom-Tom stumbled, felt himself start to fall, and threw out his hands. It didn't do much good as the snakehead landed face-down on a cluster of ten-inch mortars. His body was literally torn apart as they went off in sequence. The headphones that the gang banger habitually wore flew high into the sky, fell back onto the barge, and punctured the tinfoil covering a twelve-inch round.

Meanwhile, even as Tom-Tom died, Chow fired his Browning. But having seen Paco go down, the snakehead was too scared to take the time necessary to aim. A fountain of brass squirted through the air as he unloaded the semi-auto's thirteen-round magazine in Dexter's general direction. But, as luck would have it, only one of the .9mm slugs made contact with its target.

The ex-SEAL staggered as the bullet smashed into the lower part of his prosthesis but managed to remain upright nonetheless. Though not especially logical the attack on his artificial limb struck the ex-naval officer as especially offensive. "Wrong leg, you bastard!" Dexter shouted angrily. "Now, let's see how *you* like it!"

Chow pulled the trigger once more and was rewarded with a *click*, as his opponent's Heckler & Koch went off and twin sledgehammer blows struck his knees. That was followed by an explosion of pain more intense than anything the snakehead had ever experienced before. As if to illustrate how it felt a red, gold, and white Crossette exploded directly overhead. It seemed to wheel as he fell.

Having knee-capped Chow, Dexter was about to turn his attention to the surviving gang members when Rossi blew Skinner's brains out. The FBI agent didn't like wheel guns, especially big iron like Tom-Tom's .44, since they were heavy and the recoil was hellacious. But there was no denying how effective the humongous revolvers could be and she was happy to have it.

Once Skinner went down that left Kwong. He was backing away and giving serious consideration to a timely surrender when Dexter shot him once in the head and once in the chest, the traditional double-tap that makes body armor irrelevant. The little man staggered and fell.

All of the threats were down. Dexter looked at Rossi, saw what he had always hoped for in her eyes, and felt a sudden sense of warmth. Here, within his grasp, was everything he desired. Then Chow pulled the trigger on the FBI agent's Glock. A .9mm bullet sped through the air and smashed into the ex-SEAL's chest. He went down hard.

Rossi shouted, "No!" and Missy watched from the doorway as her mother emptied the big revolver into Joe Chow's head and torso. The first shot shattered his skull. The second blew a fist-sized hole through his chest and the third took his balls off.

Stars wheeled and constellations were born as Dexter stared up into the night sky. Then a much-abused face appeared to hover above him as Rossi knelt to hold the ex-SEAL in her arms. There was a lot of blood, more than she could possibly stop, and both of them knew his life was leaking away. Tears fell and Dexter blinked as one of them landed on his eyelid. "Oh, Dex," the agent said softly, "what have you done?"

Dexter coughed and blood trickled down his chin. "I'm sorry, Christina. I'm sorry about everything."

"And so am I," Rossi answered tenderly.

Dexter smiled. "You want to know something funny?"

The FBI agent bit her lower lip. "Yes, I do."

"The leg? The one they blew off? It hurts like hell."

As the fireworks display entered the final stage, there was a loud *BOOM,* followed by a series of overlapping explosions as violet, blue, and pink rings strobed across the huge black canvas. The star shells lit up the entire city, but when Rossi looked down at Dexter, the light in his eyes was gone.

The FBI agent wanted to stay there and cry until she ran out of tears, but there was Missy to consider. Slowly, tenderly, Rossi lay the ex-SEAL down on the blood-stained deck. Then, having appropriated Dexter's P7, the FBI agent went back to retrieve Missy and her Glock. With pistols at the ready, Rossi led her daughter down the central aisle towards the bow.

Both the Chinese pyrotechs and the fire marshal had evacuated the barge soon after the firefight began, but Tian Lei was still at his post, eyes agleam as his creation approached its final climax. He bowed as Rossi and Missy passed and was still staring upwards when the FBI agent boarded the stolen cabin cruiser, saw that the key was in the ignition, and brought the big MerCruiser engine to life. Missy managed to cast off in spite of her arm. She made her way back to the cockpit and stood by her mother's side as Rossi took the power boat out into the lake.

In spite of the millions of eyes that were focused on the scene, none of them saw the single spark that fell past Tom-Tom's blood-spattered earphones and into the mouth of the unfired mortar. When the bomb went off, and detonated the shells all around it, the onlookers assumed the explosion was part of the show—until the barge flew apart in front of their eyes, a powerful ring-shaped shock wave rocked the surrounding boats, and a resonant *BOOM*! rattled windows all around the lake.

Rossi wrapped an arm around her daughter's shoulders and remembered the old man in the control booth. Was that how he would have chosen to go? There was no way to know. Missy looked up into her mother's face. She had to shout in order to be heard. "What are you going to do now?"

The Bayliner was planing by that time and Rossi put the wheel over to avoid a slow-moving sailboat. "Do you remember the Hartleys? The people who took you water skiing last summer? I thought we'd call Vanessa from there."

"She'll make me go to the hospital."

"Yes, she will. And I'm grateful."

"But you aren't coming."

"No, honey," Rossi said glancing into her daughter's eyes. "Can you forgive me? A good mother would take you to the hospital herself, and stay until you were safely in bed. But, I have something important to do."

"You're going to finish your job."

"Something like that. Yes."

Missy looked up at her mother. Her eyes were big and bright. "It's okay, Mom. I understand."

Rossi gave her a quick hug. "Do you really? If so, I'm grateful for that. By the way, it took a lot of courage to jump onto that man's back, but don't do anything that foolish again."

Missy grinned mischievously. "I won't if you don't."

The FBI agent might have replied, but the dock was coming up fast and quick work was required to shift into reverse before scraping the side of pier. Then, having secured the boat to the dock, mother and daughter climbed a flight of gently curving concrete stairs. A well-lit house loomed above, and judging from the subdued *thud, thud, thud* of bass, a New Year's eve party was well underway. The doors out onto a balcony were open and the sounds of excited conversation could be heard as the distressed party goers discussed what they had witnessed on television only fifteen minutes earlier.

When the bell rang it was Marianne Hartley who went to open the front door. The society matron barely recognized the ragged looking couple who stood on her porch. Rossi's hair was tangled, one eye was half-swollen shut, and her face was badly bruised. Missy's face was dirty, one arm had been splinted, and her clothes were filthy. "Christina? Missy? What happened?"

"Sorry to barge in on you like this," Rossi said apologetically, "but I need to use your phone."

"It was," as a prominent businessman told a society reporter the next morning, "a night to remember."

It was almost two in the morning by the time Rossi drove her ex-husband's BMW 745i across the University bridge and headed downtown. It was what Vanessa had described as "a Christmas present from Ed to Ed," and there were only 412 miles on the odometer. Although the Hartleys had agreed to transport both Vanessa and Missy to Children's Hospital in their SUV, Rossi could tell they took issue with her decision to leave her daughter, and would probably remove her name from their Christmas card list.

She wound her way through the mostly empty downtown streets and pulled up in front of Samuel Chow's apartment building. That put the Beemer in a tow-away zone but the agent didn't think there were likely to be any SPD meter maids out and about at that hour of the morning.

Then, conscious of the fact that a little bit of preparation was in order, Rossi got out of the car, made her way over to the curb, and laid out her arsenal on the BMW's flawlessly shiny hood. She had her Glock, plus Dexter's Heckler & Koch, but what about ammo? Both weapons had been fired so it was important to check.

Meanwhile, directly across the street, there was consternation inside the SNAKE EYE surveillance van. Agents Moller and Hagger had the duty, but Inez had decided to bring her teammates some coffee on her way home from a party and was just about to check her voicemail when a brand new Beemer stopped in front of Chow's high-rise and a woman emerged. Hagger shifted his chocolate-covered doughnut to his left hand, which allowed him to zoom in. It was too dark to make out the woman's features at first, but once she rounded the front end of the car, the glare from a street-light illuminated her badly ravaged face. "My God!" Inez said as she peered at the monitor mounted over Hagger's head. "It's Rossi!"

"It can't be," Moller said incredulously. "Joe Chow has her."

"Not anymore," Inez said grimly, and reached for the side door handle. "She looks like hell—but that's our girl. Call Hawk. Tell him that Rossi not only managed to escape, but judging from the hardware on the hood of that car, she's getting ready to visit Samuel Chow."

When the van door opened Rossi looked up. The FBI agent wasn't surprised to see an agent get out, but the fact that the agent was Inez brought a smile to her face, and that hurt. "Hi, Olivia. I need some nine-millimeter. Have you got some loose rounds?"

"Damn, girl," Inez said, as she drew closer. "I'll get you a rocket launcher if you need one. But not until you come clean. Where the hell have you been? And how did you escape? Every cop in Washington State is out looking for you!"

Meanwhile, as the two agents spoke, the security cameras mounted on the front of the apartment building swiveled around to focus on them. Inez listened in astonishment as Rossi provided a brief synopsis of her capture, imprisonment, and the recent shoot-out. "So Dexter came for you?" the ICE agent demanded incredulously. "How the hell did he know where to look? And why didn't he call me?"

Rossi shrugged. "It beats me. There were a lot of things I would have liked to ask him but it's too late now. Once Missy and I were clear, the barge blew up."

"Yeah," Inez said in wonderment. "I saw that on TV. They're still searching for possible survivors. You were damned lucky."

"Yeah," Rossi said, remembering the way Dexter had stood there waiting for the snakeheads to make their move. "*Real* lucky. So back to the nine-millimeter…. You carry a Glock—can I borrow a clip?"

"That depends," Inez answered cautiously. "What are you going to do with it?"

"I'm going to arrest Samuel Chow," Rossi answered evenly. "He has a lot to answer for."

"Arrest him for *what*?" the ICE agent demanded. "You need probable cause."

"I have it," the FBI agent lied. "Joe Chow spilled his guts."

"But he's *dead*," Inez objected. "That won't work."

"Why not?" Rossi asked reasonably.

But Inez never got the opportunity to answer the other woman's question because that was the moment when both of them heard the roar of an aircraft engine and looked up to see that a helicopter was circling Chow's building. "You see?" Rossi demanded mildly. "My guess is that Mr. Chow is leaving for parts unknown…. Do I get my ammo? Or, do I go upstairs with what I have?"

"You'll get it," Inez replied. "Wait here!" The ICE agent ran across the street, entered the van, and was back a few moments later. "Here," Inez said, as she handed over a box of .9mm rounds. Moller and Hagger arrived a minute later. They wore protective vests and Hagger had armed himself with a Heckler & Koch UMP .40 caliber sub-machine gun. After weeks of sitting around in cramped vehicles he looked happy. "I put in a call to the SPD… The SWAT team is on the way. How do we get in?"

"I have a key," Rossi said confidently as she inserted a fully recharged clip into the Glock. "Follow me."

Both security cameras tilted in and downwards as the sound of the helicopter echoed back and forth between the surrounding buildings and the agents approached the front door. Rossi had a pistol in each hand, and the safety glass shattered into a million pieces as she fired both weapons at once. "All right!" Hagger exclaimed approvingly. "That's what I call a *key*!"

A security alarm began to bleat as the agents stepped through the empty door frame and entered the lobby. There was a reception desk with a "Closed" sign sitting on top of it, a nicely furnished waiting area, and two banks of opposing elevators. Rossi touched the "Up" button. Stainless steel doors parted and the foursome entered. Inez was armed with a 12-gauge shotgun and it made a distinctive clacking sound as the ICE agent racked the action and pumped a round into the weapon's chamber. Rossi raised an eyebrow. "What's with the cannon?"

"Don't tell anyone," Inez replied with a wink. "But I forgot my contacts. But it's hard to miss with a scatter gun—so don't worry."

"*Now* she tells us," Moller said, her Glock at the ready.

Hagger was going to make a comment as well, but Rossi interrupted as double-digit numbers started to appear on the floor indicator and the elevator began to slow. "Get down!" the FBI agent ordered. "All the way down!" and dropped to the floor.

The other agents followed Rossi's example so that when the car came to a stop all four of them were in the prone position, weapons at the ready. The doors had just started to part company when Hippo pulled the trigger on a fully automatic AK-47. The big man was firing from the hip. The military-style rounds punched their way through the metal facing, whipped over the agents' heads, and dug divets in the paneling behind them.

Hagger fired two bursts from the Heckler & Koch. The bullets hit Hippo's lower legs, shattered bone, and brought him crashing down. Bullets from the AK-47 stitched holes up the wall and across the ceiling as the snakehead fell. Seconds later Hagger was kneeling on Hippo's chest with the SMG pointed at the gang member's face as Moller patted him down. She removed a 9mm pistol from the big man's waistband as Hagger used a handheld radio to call for an aid car.

Rossi didn't know how long it would take Chow to board the

helicopter but the FBI agent knew time was of the essence as she tried the door that led from the lobby into the penthouse and discovered that it was locked. "Here," Inez said cheerfully, "allow me."

The *Boom*! sounded especially loud within the enclosed space. The handle, the lock, and a sizeable chunk of wood simply vanished. Rossi, who was standing next to the door, reached around to give it a push.

There was no gunfire as the door swung open, so Rossi shouted "FBI!" before entering what appeared to be a small antechamber. The walls were covered in red, black, and gold wallpaper, and an empty aquarium rested on a sturdy stand. A couch sat in front of that.

With no opposition present to slow her down, Rossi positioned herself beside the next door, even as Inez and Moller prepared themselves to provide covering fire. But, before the FBI agent could try the handle, the barrier opened inwards and an immaculately clad houseboy appeared. He bowed. "Good morning," he said politely. "Mr. Chow see you now."

Though surprised, Rossi was far from amazed, since a man with Samuel Chow's resources might fare better by facing the legal system rather than running from it. But it pays to be careful, so the agents followed one at a time, each ready to respond should a snakehead open fire. As Rossi followed the manservant into the great room, she couldn't help but notice the rich décor. Judging from the well-lit sculptures and carefully placed paintings, the apartment had been professionally decorated *before* all of the wood, metal, and ceramic serpents had been added.

Samuel Chow sat with his back to the room as the agents entered. His chair made a *whirring* noise as he turned. Although Rossi had never met Samuel Chow face-to-face, she had seen countless pictures of him, and was struck by how ill he looked. For some reason his eyes seemed to bulge slightly, his skin looked gray, and a sheen of sweat covered his forehead. "Please," the man said, "help me!"

Rossi frowned. "Help you? In what way?"

"I'm not Samuel Chow," the elderly man explained urgently. "I work as his body double. He left me here to delay you."

"I'd know that face anywhere," Moller insisted. "He's lying."

"No!" the body double replied. "Look at my wrists!" A blanket had been wrapped around the old man's shoulders. It was folded shawl-style and held in place with a single bejeweled clip. But his hands were visible, as were his wrists, and Rossi saw that the man in front of her had been secured to the chair with plastic ties.

"Watch out!" Inez cautioned. "There's something under that blanket!"

The old man uttered what could only be described as a pathetic whimper as the blanket rippled and a Black-Headed python stuck its head up next to the body double's. It sampled the air with its tongue and hissed menacingly.

Rossi fired the P7 twice. The python's head flew off, which left its long, sinuous body to thrash around under the blanket. The body double started to scream, but the sound was cut off as the coils around his torso spasmed, and the air was expelled from his lungs. Fortunately, what remained of the snake released the old man after that, leaving him to gasp for air as Moller disconnected the chair's power supply. "There," she said. "That should hold him."

Rossi turned to look for the majordomo, only to find that the man had disappeared. "Chow's up on the roof by now," she announced. "There must be a freight elevator! Let's find it."

The body double was rocking from side-to-side, still trying to extricate himself from the remains of the snake, as the agents went looking for the service elevator. Moller located the shaft back behind the kitchen. But pushing on the "Up" button didn't produce the desired response—so Rossi tried the door marked "Exit." It was locked so the FBI motioned for Inez to join her. "Open sesame."

There was another loud *boom* as the 12-gauge went off and the locking mechanism was destroyed. "Your wish is my command," the ICE agent said, as she slipped a replacement shell up into the receiver.

"You're very kind," Rossi replied politely as she eased the door open, confirmed that the way was clear, and started up the concrete stairs. The roar of the helicopter's engine could be heard by then, which suggested that while the aircraft was still on top of the building, it wouldn't be for long. It was a relatively short climb up to the door that opened onto the roof. It had been propped open and that seemed to be a bit *too* convenient, so Rossi belly-crawled up to the raised sill.

Maybe it was all the cigarettes he had smoked in the past, or a general lack of exercise, but whatever the reason, Weed was bushed. He and Kango had been hard pressed to lift Chow *and* his motorized wheelchair up into the helicopter. But now, just as the snakehead was about to board the chopper, he saw movement by the door. He drew his semi-auto, brought it up, and fired.

The 9mm slug passed through the open door, *spanged* off the rear wall, and whined away. Moller climbed the next two steps, raised her Glock, and fired over Rossi's head. Weed looked surprised. He staggered and went down.

Rossi came to her feet, stepped out onto the roof, and found herself completely exposed as the chopper took to the air. Kango stood with both feet on the port skid as the aircraft began to rise. His machine pistol burped fire as the agents spilled out onto the roof. Rossi stood her ground as bullets pinged the ductwork around her. She was frightened, *very* frightened, as both pistols made the long journey up to the proper position. And it was then, while waiting to find out if she would live or die, that the FBI agent caught a momentary glimpse of Samuel Chow through the open door. He was seated behind his bodyguard, looking straight at her, and there was no denying the hatred on his face. Had he seen the barge explode on TV? Yes, probably, which meant he knew that his son was dead.

Finally, after what seemed like an eternity, both barrels were lined up on her target and Rossi opened fire. Two slugs hit Kango in the chest. He released the machine pistol in an effort to plug the bullet holes with his fingers, lost his balance as the chopper turned, and the gangster pitched face-down onto the roof.

Meanwhile the helicopter completed its turn and came her way. The skids were only about two feet off the surface of the roof, which meant that the aircraft's undercarriage was almost certain to hit her. The FBI agent opened fire on the canopy, ran out of ammo a few seconds later, and was preparing to drop when Moller and Inez brought their weapons into play. The sharp, percussive sound of the Glock blended with the shotgun's deep basso to generate a rolling *boom-crack, boom-crack, boom-crack* that echoed between the surrounding buildings.

Perhaps the pilot took a hit, or something important had been damaged, but whatever the reason the helicopter pulled up. And not just *up*, but so far up that the agents got a momentary view of the chopper's belly before it completed a full loop and disappeared into the canyon that separated Chow's building from the high-rise on the other side of First Avenue. That was followed by a horrible *crash*, an audible *whump* as the wreckage caught fire, and the approaching *bleat* of sirens.

Rossi, Inez, and Moller all ran to the east side of the roof to peer over the side. It was like looking into the bowels of hell. The helicopter was a ball of twisted metal at the center of a raging fire. Half a dozen SPD patrol cars were on the scene by then, as were two fire engines, both of which were busy pumping foam onto the wreckage. There wouldn't be any survivors, *couldn't* be any survivors, and Rossi wasn't sure how she felt about that. Chow deserved to die—but what about the pilot? Had he or she been aware of who their passenger was? Or taken the job in good faith? If so, she was sorry. There had been lots of innocent victims, thousands of them, some of whom were still working to pay off their *bao*. But like a child who knows she shouldn't giggle during the church service, but can't help herself, Rossi began to laugh.

Inez frowned. "What's so funny?"

"The helicopter!" Rossi replied, barely able to get the words out in between bouts of laughter. "It landed right on top of my ex-husband's brand new BMW!"

Inez looked mystified for a moment. Then she smiled, giggled, and started to laugh. The reaction was part humor, part relief, and part hysteria. And that's where they were, both laughing uproariously, when the SPD SWAT team arrived on the roof. All were male and looked suitably grim. Moller grinned and held her credentials up for them to see. "Hi guys. Don't worry about my friends. It's a girl thing."

The twelve hours that followed made all of the other scrapes that Rossi had been through look like child's play. Hawk tried to protect her, as did both Theel and Haxton. But, given the FBI agent's recent past, her much-publicized abduction, the escape from the barge, and the dramatic shoot-out at Chow's apartment building, there was no escaping the aftermath. Even as the media glorified the agent a battalion of pencil pushers from the FBI, ICE, and even the FAA put Rossi's every action under the microscope in an attempt to figure out whether she should be congratulated or sacrificed to the bureaucratic gods.

But finally, once the smoke cleared, it was Demont who delivered the preliminary finding to the press. "All indications are that Agent Rossi's actions were in keeping with the bureau's policies and procedures, but a final decision regarding her status will be made once the investigation has been completed. In the meantime Agents Rossi, Inez, Moller, and Hagger have all been placed on administrative leave."

And for once in her career the agent *wanted* some time off. Except that she couldn't go home, not with the media types swarming all over her house, so the agent decided to go someplace else instead, somewhere outside of the city, where she could think about everything that had taken place, and try to come to terms with it.

The trip to Coupeville on Whidbey Island took the better part of two hours. It was mid-afternoon by the time she arrived. Rather than risk not having a place to stay Rossi checked into a bed and breakfast. If the pleasant-looking matron who ran the establishment recognized the woman with the badly bruised face, she gave no hint of it, something for which Rossi was grateful.

Having secured a place to stay, the agent drove down to Ebey's landing, partly because it was an easy way to access the beach before the sun went down, but mostly because it represented one of the intersections between her life and Dexter's. As luck would have it, an old pick-up camper combo was sitting in the parking lot when she arrived. And even though Rossi had never met Hank Stanton, the retired trucker recognized the FBI agent, and came over to introduce himself.

It wasn't long thereafter that Stanton went to retrieve the bottle of whiskey from his camper. Then, sitting side-by-side on a weather worn log, the only two people who cared about Jack Dexter drank a series of toasts to him. And, as if summoned by their thoughts, it wasn't long before an especially strong wave surged up onto the beach. Finally, having come within inches of their feet, the water became one with the sand.

-The End-

For sales, editorial information, subsidiary rights information
or a catalog, please write or phone or e-mail
Brick Tower Press
1230 Park Avenue
New York, NY 10128, US
Sales: 1-800-68-BRICK
Tel: 212-427-7139 Fax: 212-860-8852
www.BrickTowerPress.com
email: bricktower@aol.com.

For sales in the United States, please contact
National Book Network
nbnbooks.com
Orders: 800-462-6420
Fax: 800-338-4550
custserv@nbnbooks.com

For sales in the UK and Europe please contact our distributor,
Gazelle Book Services
Falcon House, Queens Square
Lancaster, LA1 1RN, UK
Tel: (01524) 68765 Fax: (01524) 63232
email: gazelle4go@aol.com.

For Australian and New Zealand sales please contact
Bookwise International
174 Cormack Road, Wingfield, 5013, South Australia
Tel: 61 (0) 419 340056 Fax: 61 (0)8 8268 1010
email: karen.emmerson@bookwise.com.au